UNFINISHED PORTRAIT

Celia is alone, bereft of the three people she has held most dear — her mother, her daughter, and her husband. At only thirty-nine, she feels unable to face the decades of existence stretching out ahead of her. She travels to a picturesque island, determined to end her life with the minimum of inconvenience to others. But an artist named Larraby encounters her, divines her purpose — and persuades her to pause. A long night of talk reveals how she is afraid to commit herself to a chance of happiness with another person, yet not brave enough to face life alone . . .

Agatha Christie

UNFINISHED PORTRAIT

A MARY WESTMACOTT NOVEL

Complete and Unabridged

PS...

PUBLISHER SELECTION
Leicester

First published in Great Britain in 1934 by
Collins
Glasgow

This Ulverscroft Edition
published 2020
by arrangement with
HarperCollins*Publishers*
London

A catalogue record for this book is available
from the British Library.

ISBN 978–1–4448–4566–2

Published by
Ulverscroft Limited
Anstey, Leicestershire

Set by Words & Graphics Ltd.
Anstey, Leicestershire
Printed and bound in Great Britain by
T. J. International Ltd., Padstow, Cornwall

This book is printed on acid-free paper

Contents

Book Three: The Island

Foreword

My Dear Mary: I send you this because I don't know what to do with it. I suppose, really, I want it to see the light of day. One does. I suppose the complete genius keeps his pictures stacked in the studio and never shows them to anybody. I was never like that, but then I was never a genius — just Mr Larraby, the promising young portrait painter.

Well, my dear, *you* know what it is, none better — to be cut off from the thing you loved doing and did well because you loved doing it. That's why we were friends, you and I. And you know about this writing business — I don't.

If you read this manuscript, you'll see that I've taken Barge's advice. You remember? He said, 'Try a new medium.' This is a portrait — and probably a damned bad one because I don't know my medium. If you say it's no good, I'll take your word for it, but if you think it has, in the smallest degree, that significant form we both believe to be the fundamental basis of art — well, then, I don't see why it shouldn't be published. I've put the real names, but you can change them. And who is to mind? Not Michael. And as for Dermot he would never recognize himself! He isn't made that way. Anyway, as Celia herself said, her story is a very ordinary story. It might happen to anybody. In fact, it frequently does. It isn't her story I've been

1

interested in. All along it's been Celia herself. Yes, Celia herself . . .

You see I wanted to nail her in paint to a canvas, and that being out of the question, I've tried to get her in another way. But I'm working in an unfamiliar medium — these words and sentences and commas and full stops — they're not my craft. You'll remark, I dare say, *que ça se voit*!

I've seen her, you know, from two angles. First, from my own. And secondly, owing to the peculiar circumstances of twenty-four hours, I've been able — at moments — to get inside her skin and see her from her own. And the two don't always agree. That's what's so tantalizing and fascinating to me! I should like to be God and know the truth.

But a novelist can be God to the creatures he creates. He has them in his power to do what he likes with — or so he thinks. But they do give him surprises. I wonder if the real God finds that too . . . Yes, I wonder . . .

Well, my dear, I won't wander on any more. Do what you can for me.

Yours ever,

J.L.

Book One

The Island

There is a lonely isle
Set apart
In the midst of the sea
Where the birds rest awhile
On their long flight
To the South
They rest a night
Then take wing and depart

To the Southern seas . . .
I am an island set apart
In the midst of the sea
And a bird from the mainland
Rested on me . . .

1

The Woman in the Garden

Do you know the feeling you have when you know something quite well and yet for the life of you can't recollect it?

I had that feeling all the way down the winding white road to the town. It was with me when I started from the plateau overhanging the sea in the Villa gardens. And with every step I took, it grew stronger and — somehow — more urgent. And at last, just when the avenue of palm trees runs down to the beach, I stopped. Because, you see, I knew it was now or never. This shadowy thing that was lurking at the back of my brain had got to be pulled out into the open, had got to be probed and examined and nailed down, so that I knew what it was. I'd got to pin the thing down — otherwise it would be too late.

I did what one always does do when trying to remember things. I went over the facts.

The walk up from the town — with the dust and the sun on the back of my neck. Nothing there.

The grounds of the Villa — cool and refreshing with the great cypresses standing dark against the skyline. The green grass path that led to the plateau where the seat was placed overlooking the sea. The surprise and slight

5

annoyance at finding a woman occupying the seat.

For a moment I had felt awkward. She had turned her head and looked at me. An English-woman. I felt the need of saying something — some phrase to cover my retirement.

'Lovely view from up here.'

That was what I had said — just the ordinary silly conventional thing. And she answered in exactly the words and tone that an ordinary well-bred woman would use.

'Delightful,' she had said. 'And such a beautiful day.'

'But rather a long pull up from the town.'

She agreed and said it *was* a long dusty walk.

And that was all. Just that interchange of polite commonplaces between two English people abroad who have not met before and who do not expect to meet again. I retraced my steps, walked once or twice round the Villa admiring the orange berberis (if that's what the thing is called) and then started back to the town.

That was absolutely all there was to it — and yet, somehow, it wasn't. There was this feeling of knowing something quite well and not being able to remember it.

Had it been something in her manner? No, her manner had been perfectly normal and pleasant. She'd behaved and looked just as ninety-nine women out of a hundred women would have behaved.

Except — no, it was true — she hadn't looked at my hands.

There! What an odd thing to have written

down. It amazes me when I look at it. An Irish bull if there ever was one. And yet to put it down correctly wouldn't express my meaning.

She hadn't looked at my hands. And you see, I'm used to women looking at my hands. Women are so quick. And they're so soft-hearted I'm used to the expression that comes over their faces — bless them and damn them. Sympathy, and discretion, and determination not to show they've noticed. And the immediate change in their manner — the gentleness.

But this woman hadn't seen or noticed.

I began thinking about her more closely. A queer thing — I couldn't have described her in the least at the moment I turned my back on her. I would have said she was fairish and about thirty-odd — that's all. But all the way down the hill, the picture of her had been growing — growing — it was for all the world like a photographic plate that you develop in a dark cellar. (That's one of my earliest memories — developing negatives with my father in our cellar.)

I've never forgotten the thrill of it. The blank white expanse with the developer washing over it. And then, suddenly, the tiny speck that appears, darkening and widening rapidly. The thrill of it — the uncertainty. The plate darkens rapidly — but still you can't see exactly. It's just a jumble of dark and light. And then recognition — you know what it is — you see that this is the branch of the tree, or somebody's face, or the back of the chair, and you know whether the negative is upside down or not — and you reverse it if it is — and then you watch the whole picture emerging from nothingness till it begins to darken and you lose it again.

Well, that's the best description I can give of what happened to me. All the way down to the town, I saw that woman's face more and more clearly. I saw her small ears, set very close against her head, and the long lapis-lazuli earrings that hung from them, and the curved wave of intensely blonde flaxen hair that lay across the top of the ear. I saw the contour of her face, and the width between the eyes — eyes of a very faint clear blue. I saw the short, very thick dark brown lashes and the faint pencilled line of the brows with their slight hint of surprise. I saw the small square face and the rather hard line of the mouth.

The features came to me — not suddenly — but little by little — exactly, as I have said, like a photographic plate developing.

I can't explain what happened next. The surface development, you see, was over. I'd arrived at the point where the image begins to darken.

But, you see, this wasn't a photographic plate, but a human being. And so the development went on. From the surface, it went *behind* — or *within*, whichever way you like to put it. At least, that's as near as I can get to it in the way of explanation.

I'd known the truth, I suppose, all along, from the very moment I'd first seen her. The development was taking place in *me*. The picture was coming from my subconscious into my conscious mind . . .

I *knew* — but I didn't know what it was I knew until suddenly it came! Bang up out of the black whiteness! A speck — and then an image.

I turned and fairly ran up that dusty road. I was in pretty good condition, but it seemed to me that I wasn't going nearly fast enough. Through the Villa gates and past the cypresses and along the grass path.

The woman was sitting exactly where I had left her.

I was out of breath. Gasping, I flung myself down on the seat beside her.

'Look here,' I said. 'I don't know who you are or anything about you. But you mustn't do it. Do you hear? You mustn't do it.'

2

Call to Action

I suppose the queerest thing (but only on thinking it over afterwards) was the way she didn't try to put up any conventional defence. She might have said: 'What on earth do you mean?' or 'You don't know what you're talking about.' Or she might have just *looked* it. Frozen me with a glance.

But of course the truth of it was that she had gone past that. She was down to fundamentals. At that moment, nothing that anyone said or did could possibly have been surprising to her.

She was quite calm and reasonable about it — and that was just what was so frightening. You can deal with a mood — a mood is bound to pass, and the more violent it is, the more complete the reaction to it will be. But a calm and reasonable determination is very different, because it's been arrived at slowly and isn't likely to be laid aside.

She looked at me thoughtfully, but she didn't say anything.

'At any rate,' I said, 'you'll tell me why?'

She bent her head, as though allowing the justice of that.

'It's simply,' she said, 'that it really does seem best.'

'That's where you're wrong,' I said. 'Completely and utterly wrong.'

10

Violent words didn't ruffle her. She was too calm and far away for that.

'I've thought about it a good deal,' she said. 'And it really *is* best. It's simple and easy and — quick. And it won't be — inconvenient to anybody.'

I realized by that last phrase that she had been what is called 'well brought up'. 'Consideration for others' had been impressed upon her as a desirable thing.

'And what about — afterwards?' I asked.

'One has to risk that.'

'Do you believe in an afterwards?' I asked curiously.

'I'm afraid,' she said slowly, 'I do. Just nothing — would be almost too good to be true. Just going to sleep — peacefully — and just — not waking up. That *would* be so lovely.'

Her eyes half closed dreamily.

'What colour was your nursery wallpaper?' I asked suddenly.

'Mauve irises — twisting round a pillar — ' She started. 'How did you know I was thinking about them just then?'

'I just thought you were. That's all,' I went on. 'What was your idea of Heaven as a child?'

'Green pastures — a green valley — with sheep and the shepherd. The hymn, you know.'

'Who read it to you — your mother or your nurse?'

'My nurse . . . ' She smiled a little. 'The Good Shepherd. Do you know, I don't think I'd ever seen a shepherd. But there were two lambs in a field quite near us.' She paused and then added:

11

'It's built over now.'

And I thought: 'Odd. If that field weren't built over, well, perhaps *she* wouldn't be here now.' And I said: 'You were happy as a child?'

'Oh, *yes*!' There was no doubting the eager certainty of her assent. She went on: 'Too happy.'

'Is that possible?'

'I think so. You see, you're not prepared — for the things that happen. You never conceive that — they might happen.'

'You've had a tragic experience,' I suggested.

But she shook her head.

'No — I don't think so — not really. What happened to me isn't out of the ordinary. It's the stupid, commonplace thing that happens to lots of women. I wasn't particularly unfortunate. I was — stupid. Yes, just stupid. And there isn't really room in the world for stupid people.'

'My dear,' I said, 'listen to me. I know what I'm talking about. I've stood where you are now — I've felt as you feel that life isn't worth living. I've known that blinding despair that can only see one way out — and I tell you, child — *that it passes*. Grief doesn't last forever. Nothing lasts. There is only one true consoler and healer — time. Give time its chance.'

I had spoken earnestly, but I saw at once that I had made a mistake.

'You don't understand,' she said. 'I know what you mean. I *have* felt that. In fact, I had one try — that didn't come off. And afterwards I was glad that it hadn't. This is different.'

'Tell me,' I said.

'This has come quite slowly. You see — it's

12

rather hard to put it clearly. I'm thirty-nine — and I'm very strong and healthy. It's quite on the cards that I shall live to at least seventy — perhaps longer. And I simply can't face it, that's all. Another thirty-five long empty years.'

'But they won't be empty, my dear. That's where you're wrong. Something will bloom again to fill them.'

She looked at me.

'*That* is what I'm most afraid of,' she said below her breath. 'It's the thought of that that I simply can't face.'

'In fact, you're a coward,' I said.

'Yes.' She acquiesced at once. 'I've always been a coward. I've thought it funny sometimes that other people haven't seen it as clearly as I have. Yes, I'm afraid — afraid — afraid.'

There was silence.

'After all,' she said, 'it's natural. If a cinder jumps out of a fire and burns a dog, he's frightened of the fire in future. He never knows when another cinder might come. It's a form of intelligence, really. The complete fool thinks a fire is just something kind and warm — he doesn't know about burning or cinders.'

'So that really,' I said, 'it's the possibility of — happiness you won't face.'

It sounded queer as I said it, and yet I knew that it wasn't really as strange as it sounded. I know something about nerves and mind. Three of my best friends were shell-shocked in the war. I know myself what it is for a man to be physically maimed — I know just what it can do to him. I know, too, that one can be mentally

13

maimed. The damage can't be seen when the wound is healed — but it's there. There's a weak spot — a flaw — you're crippled and not whole.

I said to her: 'All that will pass with time.' But I said it with assurance I did not feel. Because superficial healing wasn't going to be any good. The scar had gone deep.

'You won't take one risk,' I went on. 'But you will take another — a simply colossal one.'

She said less calmly, with a touch of eagerness:

'But that's entirely different — entirely. It's when you know what a thing's like that you won't risk it. An unknown risk — there's something rather alluring about that — something adventurous. After all, death might be anything — '

It was the first time the actual word had been spoken between us. Death . . .

And then, as though for the first time a natural curiosity stirred in her, she turned her head slightly and asked:

'How did you know?'

'I don't quite profess to be able to tell,' I confessed. 'I've been through — well, something, myself. And I suppose I knew that way.'

She said:

'I see.'

She displayed no interest in what my experience might have been, and I think it was at that moment that I vowed myself to her service. I'd had so much, you see, of the other thing. Womanly sympathy and tenderness. My need — though I didn't know it — was not to be given — but to give.

14

There wasn't any tenderness in Celia — any sympathy. She'd squandered all that — and wasted it. She had been, as she saw herself, stupid about it. She'd been too unhappy herself to have any pity left for others. That new hard line about her mouth was a tribute to the amount of suffering she had endured. Her understanding was quick — she realized in a moment that to me, too, 'things had happened'. We were on a par. She had no pity for herself, and she wasted no pity on me. My misfortune was, to her, simply the reason of my guessing something which on the face of it was seemingly unguessable.

She was, I saw in that moment, a child. Her real world was the world that surrounded herself. She had gone back deliberately to a childish world, finding there refuge from the world's cruelty.

And that attitude of hers was tremendously stimulating to me. It was what for the last ten years I had been needing. It was, you see, a call to action.

Well, I acted. My one fear was leaving her to herself. I didn't leave her to herself. I stuck to her like the proverbial leech. She walked down with me to the town amiably enough. She had plenty of common sense. She realized that her purpose was, for the moment, frustrated. She didn't abandon it — she merely postponed it. I knew that without her saying a word.

I'm not going into details — this isn't a chronicle of such things. There's no need to describe the quaint little Spanish town, or the meal we had together at her hotel, or the way I had my luggage secretly conveyed from my hotel to the one she was staying at.

No, I'm dealing only with the essentials. I knew that I'd got to stick to her till something happened — till in some way she broke down and surrendered.

As I say, I stayed with her, close by her side. When she went to her room I said:

'I'll give you ten minutes — then I'm coming in.'

I didn't dare give her longer. You see, her room was on the fourth floor, and she might override that 'consideration for others' that was part of her upbringing and embarrass the hotel manager by jumping from one of his windows instead of jumping from the cliff.

Well, I went back. She was in bed, sitting up, her pale gold hair combed back from her face. I don't think she saw anything odd in what we were doing. I'm sure I didn't. What the hotel thought, I don't know. If they knew that I entered her room at ten o'clock that night and left it at seven the next morning, they would have jumped, I suppose, to the one and only conclusion. But I couldn't bother about that.

I was out to save a life, and I couldn't bother about a mere reputation.

Well, I sat there, on her bed, and we talked.

We talked all night.

A strange night — I've never known a night like it.

I didn't talk to her about her trouble, whatever it was. Instead we started at the beginning — the mauve irises on the wallpaper, and the lambs in the field, and the valley down by the station where the primroses were . . .

After a while, it was she who talked, not I. I had ceased to exist for her save as a kind of human recording machine that was there to be talked to.

She talked as you might talk to yourself — or to God. Not, you understand, with any heat or passion. Just sheer remembrance, passing from one unrelated incident to another. The building up of a life — a kind of bridge of significant incidents.

It's an odd question, when you come to think of it, the things we choose to remember. For choice there must be, make it as unconscious as you like. Think back yourself — take any year of your childhood. You will remember perhaps five — six incidents. They weren't important, probably; why have you remembered them out of those three hundred and sixty-five days? Some of them didn't even mean much to you at the time. And yet, somehow, they've persisted. They've gone with you into these later years . . .

It is from that night that I say I got my inside vision of Celia. I can write about her from the standpoint, as I said, of God . . . I'm going to endeavour to do so.

She told me, you see, all the things that mattered and that didn't matter. She wasn't trying to make a story of it.

No — but I wanted to! I seemed to catch glimpses of a pattern that *she* couldn't see.

It was seven o'clock when I left her. She had

17

turned over on her side at last and gone to sleep like a child . . . The danger was over.

It was as though the burden had been taken from her shoulders and laid on mine. She was safe . . .

Later in the morning I took her down to the boat and saw her off.

And that's when it happened. The thing, I mean, that seems to me to embody the whole thing . . .

Perhaps I'm wrong . . . Perhaps it was only an ordinary trivial incident . . .

Anyway I won't write it down now . . .

Not until I've had my shot at being God and either failed or succeeded.

Tried getting her on canvas in this new unfamiliar medium . . . Words . . .

Strung together words . . .

No brushes, no tubes of colour — none of the dear old familiar stuff.

Portrait in four dimensions, because, in your craft, Mary, there's time as well as space . . .

Book Two

Canvas

'*Set up the canvas. Here's a subject to hand.*'

1

Home

1

Celia lay in her cot and looked at the mauve irises on the nursery wall. She felt happy and sleepy.

There was a screen round the foot of her cot. This was to shut off the light of Nannie's lamp. Invisible to Celia, behind that screen, sat Nannie reading the Bible. Nannie's lamp was a special lamp — a portly brass lamp with a pink china shade. It never smelt because Susan, the housemaid, was very particular. Susan was a good girl, Celia knew, although sometimes guilty of the sin of 'flouncing about'. When she flounced about she nearly always knocked off some small ornament in the immediate neighbourhood. She was a great big girl with elbows the colour of raw beef. Celia associated them vaguely with the mysterious words 'elbow grease'.

There was a faint whispering sound: Nannie murmuring over the words to herself as she read. It was soothing to Celia. Her eyelids drooped . . .

The door opened, and Susan entered with a tray. She endeavoured to move noiselessly, but her loud and squeaking shoes prevented her.

She said in a low voice:

'Sorry I'm so late with your supper, Nurse.'

Nurse merely said, 'Hush. She's asleep.'

'Oh, I wouldn't wake her for the world, I'm sure.' Susan peeped round the corner of the screen, breathing heavily.

'Little duck, ain't she? My little niece isn't half so knowing.'

Turning back from the screen, Susan ran into the table. A spoon fell to the floor.

Nurse said mildly:

'You must try and not flounce about so, Susan, my girl.'

Susan said dolefully:

'I'm sure I don't mean to.'

She left the room tiptoeing, which made her shoes squeak more than ever.

'Nannie,' called Celia cautiously.

'Yes, my dear, what is it?'

'I'm not asleep, Nannie.'

Nannie refused to take the hint. She just said:

'No, dear.'

There was a pause.

'Nannie?'

'Yes, dear.'

'Is your supper nice, Nannie?'

'Very nice, dear.'

'What is it?'

'Boiled fish and treacle tart.'

'Oh!' sighed Celia ecstatically.

There was a pause. Then Nannie appeared round the screen. A little old grey-haired woman with a lawn cap tied under her chin. In her hand she carried a fork. On the tip of the fork was a minute piece of treacle tart.

'Now you're to be a good girl and go to sleep at once,' said Nannie warningly.

'Oh! Yes,' said Celia fervently.

Elysium! Heaven! The morsel of treacle tart was between her lips. Unbelievable deliciousness.

Nannie disappeared round the screen again. Celia cuddled down on her side. The mauve irises danced in the firelight. Agreeable sensation of treacle tart within. Soothing rustling noises of Somebody in the Room. Utter contentment.

Celia slept . . .

2

It was Celia's third birthday. They were having tea in the garden. There were eclairs. She had been allowed only one eclair. Cyril had had three. Cyril was her brother. He was a big boy — eleven years old. He wanted another, but her mother said, 'That's enough, Cyril.'

The usual kind of conversation then happened. Cyril saying 'Why?' interminably.

A little red spider, a microscopic thing, ran across the white tablecloth.

'Look,' said his mother, 'that's a lucky spider. He's going to Celia because it's her birthday. That means great good luck.'

Celia felt excited and important. Cyril brought his questioning mind to another point.

'Why are spiders lucky, Mum?'

Then at last Cyril went away, and Celia was left with her mother. She had her mother all to herself. Her mother was smiling at her across the table — a nice smile — not the smile that thought you were a funny little girl.

'Mummy,' said Celia, 'tell me a story.'

She adored her mother's stories — they weren't like other people's stories. Other people, when asked, told you about Cinderella, and Jack and the Beanstalk, and Red Riding Hood. Nannie told you about Joseph and his brothers, and Moses in the bulrushes. (Bulrushes were always visualized by Celia as wooden sheds containing massed bulls.) Occasionally she told you about Captain Stretton's little children in India. But Mummy!

To begin with, you never knew, not in the least, what the story was going to be about. It might be about mice — or about children — or about princesses. It might be anything . . . The only drawbacks about Mummy's stories were that she never told them a second time. She said (most incomprehensible to Celia) that she couldn't remember.

'Very well,' said Mummy. 'What shall it be?'

Celia held her breath.

'About Bright Eyes,' she suggested. 'And Long Tail and the cheese.'

'Oh! I've forgotten all about them. No — we'll have a new story.' She gazed across the table, unseeing for the moment, her bright hazel eyes dancing, the long delicate oval of her face very serious, her small arched nose held high. All of her tense in the effort of concentration.

'I know — ' She came back from afar suddenly. 'The story is called the Curious Candle . . . '

'Oh!' Celia drew an enraptured breath. Already she was intrigued — spellbound . . . The Curious Candle!

3

Celia was a serious little girl. She thought a great deal about God and being good and holy. When she pulled a wishbone, she always wished to be good. She was, alas! undoubtedly a prig, but at least she kept her priggishness to herself.

At times she had a horrible fear that she was 'worldly' (perturbing mysterious word!). This especially when she was all dressed in her starched muslin and big golden-yellow sash to go down to dessert. But on the whole she was complacently satisfied with herself. She was of the elect. She was *saved*.

But her family caused her horrible qualms. It was terrible — but she was not quite sure about her mother. Supposing Mummy should not go to Heaven? Agonizing, tormenting thought.

The laws were so very clearly laid down. To play croquet on Sunday was wicked. So was playing the piano (unless it was hymns). Celia would have died, a willing martyr, sooner than have touched a croquet mallet on the 'Lord's Day', though to be allowed to hit balls at random about the lawn on other days was her chief delight.

But her mother played croquet on Sunday and so did her father. And her father played the piano and sang songs about 'He called on Mrs C and took a cup of tea when Mr C had gone to town.' Clearly *not* a holy song!

It worried Celia terribly. She questioned Nannie anxiously. Nannie, good earnest woman, was in something of a quandary.

'Your father and mother are your father and mother,' said Nannie. 'And everything they do is right and proper, and you mustn't think otherwise.'

'But playing croquet on Sunday is wrong,' said Celia.

'Yes, dear. It's not keeping the Sabbath holy.'

'But then — but then — '

'It's not for you to worry about these things, my dear. You just go on doing your duty.'

So Celia went on shaking her head when offered a mallet 'as a treat'.

'Why on earth — ?' said her father.

And her mother murmured:

'It's Nurse. She's told her it's wrong.'

And then to Celia:

'It's all right, darling, don't play if you don't want to.'

But sometimes she would say gently:

'You know, darling. God has made us a lovely world, and He wants us to be happy. His own day is a very special day — a day we can have special treats on — only we mustn't make work for other people — the servants, for instance. But it's quite all right to enjoy yourself.'

But, strangely enough, deeply as she loved her mother, Celia's opinions were not swayed by her. A thing was so because Nannie knew it was.

Still, she ceased to worry about her mother.

26

Her mother had a picture of St Francis on her wall, and a little book called *The Imitation of Christ* by her bedside. God, Celia felt, might conceivably overlook croquet playing on a Sunday.

But her father caused her grave misgivings. He frequently joked about sacred matters. At lunch one day he told a funny story about a curate and a bishop. It was not funny to Celia — it was merely terrible.

At last, one day, she burst out crying and sobbed her horrible fears into her mother's ear.

'But, darling, your father is a very good man. And a very religious man. He kneels down and says his prayers every night just like a child. He's one of the best men in the world.'

'He laughs at clergymen,' said Celia. 'And he plays games on Sundays, and he sings songs — worldly songs. And I'm so afraid he'll go to Hell Fire.'

'What do you know about a thing like Hell Fire?' said her mother, and her voice sounded angry.

'It's where you go if you're wicked,' said Celia.

'Who has been frightening you with things like that?'

'I'm not frightened,' said Celia, surprised. 'I'm not going there. I'm going to be always good and go to Heaven. But' — her lips trembled — 'I want Daddy to be in Heaven too.'

And then her mother talked a great deal — about God's love and goodness, and how He would never be so unkind as to burn people eternally.

27

But Celia was not in the least convinced. There was Hell and there was Heaven, and there were sheep and goats. If only — if only she were *quite* sure Daddy was not a goat!

Of course there was Hell as well as Heaven. It was one of the immovable facts of life, as real as rice pudding or washing behind the ears or saying, Yes, please, and No, thank you.

4

Celia dreamt a good deal. Some of her dreams were just funny and queer — things that had happened all mixed up. But some dreams were specially nice. Those dreams were about places she knew which were, in the dreams, different.

Strange to explain why this should be so thrilling, but somehow (in the dream) it was.

There was the valley down by the station. In real life the railway line ran along it, but in the good dreams there was a river there, and primroses all up the banks and into the wood. And each time she would say in delighted surprise: 'Why, I never knew — I always thought it was a railway here.' And instead there was the lovely green valley and the shining stream.

Then there were the dream fields at the bottom of the garden where in real life there was the ugly red-brick house. And, almost most thrilling of all, the secret rooms inside her own home. Sometimes you got to them through the pantry — sometimes, in the most unexpected way, they led out of Daddy's study. But there they were all the time — although you had forgotten them for so long. Each time you had a delighted thrill of recognition. And yet, really, each time they were quite different. But there was always that curious secret joy about finding them . . .

Then there was the one terrible dream — the Gun Man with his powdered hair and his blue and red uniform and his gun. And, most horrible of all, where his hands came out of his sleeves — there were *no* hands — only *stumps*. Whenever he came into a dream, you woke up screaming. It was the safest thing to do. And there you were, safe in your bed, and Nannie in her bed next to you and everything All Right.

There was no special reason why the Gun Man should be so frightening. It wasn't that he might shoot you. His gun was a symbol, not a direct menace. No, it was something about his face, his hard, intensely blue eyes, the sheer malignity of the look he gave you. It turned you sick with fright.

Then there were the things you thought about in the daytime. Nobody knew that as Celia walked sedately along the road she was in reality mounted upon a white palfrey. (Her ideas of a palfrey were rather dim. She imagined a super horse of the dimensions of an elephant.) When she walked along the narrow brick wall of the cucumber frames she was going along a precipice with a bottomless chasm at one side. She was on different occasions a duchess, a princess, a goose girl, and a beggar maid. All this made life very interesting to Celia, and so she was what is called 'a good child', meaning she kept very quiet, was happy playing by herself, and did not importune her elders to amuse her.

The dolls she was given were never real to her. She played with them dutifully when Nannie suggested it, but without any real enthusiasm.

'She's a good little girl,' said Nannie. 'No imagination, but you can't have everything. Master Tommy — Captain Stretton's eldest, he never stopped teasing me with his questions.'

Celia seldom asked questions. Most of her world was inside her head. The outside world did not excite her curiosity.

5

Something that happened one April was to make her afraid of the outside world.

She and Nannie went primrosing. It was an April day, clear and sunny with little clouds scudding across the blue sky. They went down by the railway line (where the river was in Celia's dreams) and up the hill beyond it into a copse where the primroses grew like a yellow carpet. They picked and they picked. It was a lovely day, and the primroses had a delicious, faint lemony smell that Celia loved.

And then (it was rather like the Gun Man dream) a great harsh voice roared at them suddenly.

'Here,' it said. 'What are you a-doing of here?'

It was a man, a big man with a red face, dressed in corduroys. He scowled.

'This is private here. Trespassers will be prosecuted.'

Nurse said: 'I'm sorry, I'm sure. I didn't know.'

'Well, you get on out of it. Quick, now.' As they turned to go his voice called after them: 'I'll boil you alive. Yes. I will. Boil you alive if you're not out of the wood in three minutes.'

Celia stumbled forward tugging desperately at Nannie. Why wouldn't Nannie go faster? The man would come after them. He'd catch them. They'd be boiled alive in a great pot. She felt sick with fright . . . She stumbled desperately on, her whole quivering little body alive with terror. He was coming — coming up behind them — they'd be boiled . . . She felt horribly sick. Quick — oh, quick!

They were out on the road again. A great gasping sigh burst from Celia.

'He — he can't get us now,' she murmured.

Nurse looked at her, startled by the dead white of her face.

'Why, what's the matter, dear?' A thought struck her. 'Surely you weren't frightened by what he said about boiling — that was only a joke — you knew that.'

And obedient to the spirit of acquiescent falsehood that every child possesses, Celia murmured:

'Oh, of course, Nannie. I knew it was a joke.'

But it was a long time before she got over the terror of that moment. All her life she never quite forgot it.

The terror had been so horribly *real*.

31

6

On her fourth birthday Celia was given a canary. He was given the unoriginal name of Goldie. He soon became very tame and would perch on Celia's finger. She loved him. He was her bird whom she fed with hemp seeds, but he was also her companion in adventure. There was Dick's Mistress who was a queen, and the Prince Dicky, her son, and the two of them roamed the world and had adventures. Prince Dicky was very handsome and wore garments of golden velvet with black velvet sleeves.

Later in the year Goldie was given a wife called Daphne. Daphne was a big bird with a lot of brown about her. She was awkward and ungainly. She spilled her water and upset things that she perched on. She never became as tame as Goldie. Celia's father called her Susan because she 'flounced'.

Susan used to poke at the birds with a match 'to see what they would do,' as she said. The birds were afraid of her and would flutter against the bars when they saw her coming. Susan thought all sorts of curious things funny. She laughed a great deal when a mouse's tail was found in the mousetrap.

Susan was very fond of Celia. She played games with her such as hiding behind curtains and jumping out to say Bo! Celia was not really very fond of Susan — she was so big and so bouncy. She was much fonder of Mrs Rouncewell, the cook. Rouncy, as Celia called her, was an enormous, monumental woman, and she was the embodiment of calm. She never hurried. She moved about her kitchen in dignified slow motion, going through the ritual of her cooking. She was never harried, never flustered. She served meals always on the exact stroke of the hour. Rouncy had no imagination. When Celia's mother would ask her: 'Well, what do you suggest for lunch today?' she always made the same reply. 'Well, ma'am, we could have a nice chicken and a ginger pudding.' Mrs Rouncewell could cook soufflés, vol-au-vents, creams, salmis, every kind of pastry, and the most elaborate French dishes, but she never suggested anything but a chicken and a ginger pudding.

Celia loved going into the kitchen — it was rather like Rouncy herself, very big, very vast, very clean, and very peaceful. In the midst of the cleanliness and space was Rouncy, her jaws moving suggestively. She was always eating. Little bits of this, that, and the other.

She would say:

'Now, Miss Celia, what do you want?'

And then with a slow smile that stretched right across her wide face she would go across to a cupboard, open a tin, and pour a handful of raisins or currants into Celia's cupped hands. Sometimes it would be a slice of bread and treacle that she was given, or a corner of jam tart, but there was always *something*.

And Celia would carry off her prize into the garden and up into the secret place by the garden wall, and there, nestled tightly into the bushes, she would be the Princess in hiding from her enemies to whom her devoted followers had brought provisions in the dead of night . . .

Upstairs in the nursery Nannie sat sewing. It was nice for Miss Celia to have such a good safe garden to play in — no nasty ponds or dangerous places. Nannie herself was getting old, she liked to sit and sew — and think over things — the little Strettons — all grown-up men and women now — and little Miss Lilian — getting married she was — and Master Roderick and Master Phil — both at Winchester . . . Her mind ran gently backwards over the years . . .

7

Something terrible happened. Goldie was lost. He had become so tame that his cage door was left open. He used to flutter about the nursery. He would sit on the top of Nannie's head and tweak with his beak at her cap and Nannie would say mildly: 'Now, now, Master Goldie, I can't have that.' He would sit on Celia's shoulder and take a hemp seed from between her lips. He was like a spoilt child. If you did not pay attention to him, he got cross and squawked at you.

And on this terrible day Goldie was lost. The nursery window was open. Goldie must have flown away.

Celia cried and cried. Both Nannie and her mother tried to console her.

'He'll come back, perhaps, my pet.'

'He's just gone to fly round. We'll put his cage outside the window.'

But Celia cried inconsolably. Birds pecked canaries to death — she had heard someone say

34

so. Goldie was dead — dead somewhere under the trees. She would never feel his little beak again. She cried on and off all day. She would not eat either her dinner or her tea. Goldie's cage outside the window remained empty.

At last bedtime came. Celia lay in her little white bed. She still sobbed automatically. She held her mother's hand very tight. She wanted Mummy more than Nannie. Nannie had suggested that Celia's father would perhaps give her another bird. Mother knew better than that. It wasn't just a *bird* she wanted — after all, she still had Daphne — it was *Goldie*. Oh! Goldie — Goldie — Goldie . . . She *loved* Goldie — and he was gone — pecked to death. She squeezed her mother's hand frenziedly. Her mother squeezed back.

And then, in the silence broken only by Celia's heavy breathing, there came a little sound — the tweet of a bird.

Master Goldie flew down from the top of the curtain pole where he had been roosting quietly all day.

All her life Celia never forgot the incredulous wonderful joy of that moment . . .

It became a saying in the family when you began to worry over anything:

'Now, then, *remember Goldie and the curtain pole!*'

8

The Gun Man dream changed. It got, somehow, more frightening.

35

The dream would start well. It would be a happy dream — a picnic or a party. And suddenly, just when you were having lots of fun, a queer feeling crept over you. Something was wrong somewhere . . . What was it? Why, of course, the Gun Man was there. But he wasn't himself. One of the guests was the Gun Man . . .

And the awful part of it was, he might be anybody. You looked at them. Everyone was gay, laughing and talking. And then suddenly you knew. It might be Mummy or Daddy or Nannie — someone you were just talking to: You looked up in Mummy's face — of course it was Mummy — and then you saw the light steely-blue eyes — and from the sleeve of Mummy's dress — oh, horror! — that horrible stump. It wasn't Mummy — it was the Gun Man . . . And you woke screaming . . .

And you couldn't explain to anyone — to Mummy or to Nannie — it didn't sound frightening just told. Someone said: 'There, there, you've had a bad dream, my dearie,' and patted you. And presently you went to sleep again — but you didn't like going to sleep because *the dream might come again*.

Celia would say desperately to herself in the dark night: 'Mummy *isn't* the Gun Man. She isn't. She isn't. I *know* she isn't. She's Mummy.'

But in the night, with the shadows and the dream still clinging round you, it was difficult to be sure of anything. Perhaps *nothing* was what it seemed and you had always known it really.

'Miss Celia had another bad dream last night, ma'am.'

'What was it, Nurse?'

'Something about a man with a gun, ma'am.'

Celia would say:

'No, Mummy, not a man with a gun. The Gun Man. My Gun Man.'

'Were you afraid he'd shoot you, darling? Was it that?'

Celia shook her head — shivered.

She couldn't explain.

Her mother didn't try to make her. She said very gently:

'You're quite safe, darling, here with us. No one can hurt you.'

That was comforting.

9

'Nannie, what's that word there — on that poster — the big one?'

' 'Comforting', dear. 'Make yourself a comforting cup of tea.' '

This went on every day. Celia displayed an insatiable curiosity about words. She knew her letters, but her mother had a prejudice against children being taught to read too early.

'I shan't begin teaching Celia to read till she is six.'

But theories of education do not always turn out as planned. By the time she was five and a half Celia could read all the story books in the nursery shelves, and practically all the words on the posters. It was true that at times she became confused between words. She would come to

37

Nannie and say, 'Please, Nannie, is this word 'greedy' or 'selfish'? I can't remember.' Since she read by sight and not by spelling out the words, spelling was to be a difficulty to her all her life.

Celia found reading enchanting. It opened a new world to her, a world of fairies, witches, hobgoblins, trolls. Fairy stories were her passion. Stories of real-life children did not much interest her.

She had few children of her own age to play with. Her home was in a remote spot and motors were as yet few and far between. There was one little girl a year older than herself — Margaret McCrae. Occasionally Margaret would be asked to tea, or Celia would be asked to tea with her. But on these occasions Celia would beg frenziedly not to go.

'Why, darling, don't you like Margaret?'

'Yes, I *do*.'

'Then why?'

Celia could only shake her head.

'She's shy,' said Cyril scornfully.

'It's absurd not to want to see other children,' said her father. 'It's unnatural.'

'Perhaps Margaret teases her?' said her mother.

'No,' cried Celia, and burst into tears.

She could not explain. She simply could not explain. And yet the facts were so simple. Margaret had lost all her front teeth. Her words came out very fast in a hissing manner — and Celia could never understand properly what she was saying. The climax had occurred when Margaret had accompanied her for a walk. She had said: 'I'll tell you a nice story, Celia,' and had straight away embarked upon it — hissing and lisping about a 'Printheth and poithoned thweth.' Celia listened in an agony. Occasionally Margaret would stop and demand: 'Ithn't it a nithe thtory?' Celia, concealing valiantly the fact that she had not the faintest idea what the story was about, would try to answer intelligently. And inwardly, as was her habit, she would have recourse to prayer.

'Oh, please, please, God, let me get home soon — don't let her know I don't know. Oh, let's get home soon — please, God.'

In some obscure way she felt that to let Margaret know that her speech was incomprehensible would be the height of cruelty. Margaret must never know.

But the strain was awful. She would reach home white and tearful. Everyone thought that she didn't like Margaret. And really it was the opposite. It was because she liked Margaret so much that she could not bear Margaret to know.

And nobody understood — nobody at all. It made Celia feel queer and panic stricken and horribly lonely.

10

On Thursdays there was dancing class. The first time Celia went she was very frightened. The room was full of children — big dazzling children in silken skirts.

In the middle of the room, fitting on a long pair of white gloves, was Miss Mackintosh, who was quite the most awe-inspiring but at the same time fascinating person that Celia had ever seen. Miss Mackintosh was very tall — quite the tallest person in the world, so Celia thought. (In later life it came as a shock to Celia to realize that Miss Mackintosh was only just over medium height. She had achieved her effect by billowing skirts, her terrific uprightness, and sheer personality.)

'Ah!' said Miss Mackintosh graciously. 'So this is Celia. Miss Tenderden?'

Miss Tenderden, an anxious-looking creature who danced exquisitely but had no personality, hurried up like an eager terrier.

Celia was handed over to her and was presently standing in a line of small children manipulating 'expanders' — a stretch of royal blue elastic with a handle at each end. After 'expanders' came the mysteries of the polka, and after that the small children sat down and watched the glittering beings in the silk skirts doing a fancy dance with tambourines.

After that, Lancers was announced. A small boy with dark mischievous eyes hurried up to Celia.

'I say — will you be my partner?'

'I can't,' said Celia regretfully. 'I don't know how.'

'Oh, what a shame.'

But presently Miss Tenderden swooped down upon her.

'Don't know how? No, of course not, dear, but

40

you're going to learn. Now, here is a partner for you.'

Celia was paired with a sandy-haired boy with freckles. Opposite them was the dark-eyed boy and his partner. He said reproachfully to Celia as they met in the middle:

'I say, you wouldn't dance with me. I think it's a shame.'

A pang she was to know well in after years swept through Celia. How explain? How say, 'But I want to dance with you. I'd much rather dance with you. This is all a mistake.'

It was her first experience of that tragedy of girlhood — the Wrong Partner!

But the exigencies of the Lancers swept them apart. They met once more in the grand chain, but the boy only gave her a look of deep reproach and squeezed her hand.

He never came to dancing class again, and Celia never learnt his name.

11

When Celia was seven years old Nannie left. Nannie had a sister even older than herself, and that sister was now broken down in health, and Nannie had to go and look after her.

Celia was inconsolable and wept bitterly. When Nannie departed, Celia wrote to her every day short, wildly written, impossibly spelt letters which caused an infinite of trouble to compose.

Her mother said gently:

'You know, darling, you needn't write every day to Nannie. She won't really expect it. Twice a week will be quite enough.'

But Celia shook her head determinedly.

'Nannie might think I'd forgotten her. I shan't forget — ever.'

Her mother said to her father:

'The child's very tenacious in her affections. It's a pity.'

Her father said, with a laugh:

'A contrast from Master Cyril.'

Cyril never wrote to his parents from school unless he was made to do so, or unless he wanted something. But his charm of manner was so great that all small misdemeanours were forgiven him.

Celia's obstinate fidelity to the memory of Nannie worried her mother.

'It isn't natural,' she said. 'At her age she ought to forget more easily.'

No new nurse came to replace Nannie. Susan looked after Celia to the extent of giving her her bath in the evening and getting up in the morning. When she was dressed Celia would go to her mother's room. Her mother always had her breakfast in bed. Celia would be given a small slice of toast and marmalade, and would then sail a small fat china duck in her mother's wash basin. Her father would be in his dressing-room next door. Sometimes he would call her in and give her a penny, and the penny would then be introduced into a small painted wooden money box. When the box was full the pennies would be put into the savings bank and when there was enough in the savings bank, Celia was to buy herself something really exciting with her own money. What that something was to be was one of the main preoccupations of Celia's life. The favourite objects varied from week to week. First, there was a high tortoiseshell comb covered with knobs for Celia's mother to wear in her black hair. Such a comb had been pointed out to Celia by Susan in a shop window. 'A titled lady might wear a comb like that,' said Susan in a reverent voice. Then there was an accordion-pleated dress in a white silk to go to dancing class in — that was another of Celia's dreams. Only the children who did skirt dancing wore accordion-pleated dresses. It would be many years before Celia would be old enough to learn skirt dancing, but, after all, the day would come. Then there was a pair of real gold slippers (Celia had no doubt of there being such things) and there was a summer house to put in the wood, and there was a pony. One of these delectable things was waiting for her on the day when she had got 'enough in the savings bank'.

In the daytime she played in the garden, bowling a hoop (which might be anything from a stagecoach to an express train), climbing trees in a gingerly and uncertain manner, and making secret places in the midst of dense bushes where she could lie hidden and weave romances. If it was wet she read books in the nursery or painted in numbers of the *Queen*. Between tea and dinner there were delightful plays with her mother. Sometimes they made houses with towels spread over chairs and crawled in and out of them — sometimes they blew bubbles. You never knew beforehand, but there was always some enchanting and delightful game — the kind of game that you couldn't think of for yourself, the kind of game that was only possible with Mummy.

In the morning now there were 'lessons', which made Celia feel very important. There was arithmetic, which Celia did with Daddy. She loved arithmetic, and she liked hearing Daddy say: 'This child's got a very good mathematical brain. She won't count on her fingers like you do, Miriam.' And her mother would laugh and say: 'I never did have any head for figures.' First Celia did addition and then subtraction, and then multiplication which was fun, and then division which seemed very grown up and difficult, and then there were pages called 'Problems'. Celia adored problems. They were about boys and apples, and sheep in fields, and cakes, and men working, and though they were really only addition, subtraction, multiplication, and division in disguise, yet the answers were in boys or apples or sheep, which made it ever so much more exciting. After arithmetic there was 'copy' done in an exercise book. Her mother would write a line across the top, and Celia would copy it down, down, down the page till she got to the bottom. Celia did not care for copy very much, but sometimes Mummy would write a very funny sentence such as 'Cross-eyed cats can't cough comfortably,' which made Celia laugh very much. Then there was a page of

44

spelling to be learnt — simple little words, but they cost Celia a good deal of trouble. In her anxiety to spell she always put so many unnecessary letters into words that they were quite unrecognizable.

In the evening, after Susan had given Celia her bath, Mummy would come into the nursery to give Celia a 'last tuck'. 'Mummy's tuck,' Celia would call it, and she would try to lie very still so that 'Mummy's tuck' should still be there in the morning. But somehow or other it never was.

'Would you like a light, my pet? Or the door left open?'

But Celia never wanted a light. She liked the nice warm comforting darkness that you sank down into. The darkness, she felt, was friendly.

'Well, you're not one to be frightened of the dark,' Susan used to say. 'My little niece now, she screams her life out if you leave her in the dark.'

Susan's little niece, Celia had for some time thought privately, must be a very unpleasant little girl — and also very silly. Why should one be frightened of the dark? The only thing that could frighten one was dreams. Dreams were frightening because they made real things go topsy-turvy. If she woke up with a scream after dreaming of the Gun Man, she would jump out of bed, knowing her way perfectly in the dark, and run along the passage to her mother's room. And her mother would come back with her and sit a while, saying, 'There's no Gun Man, darling. You're quite safe — you're quite safe.' And then Celia would fall asleep again, knowing that Mummy had indeed made everything safe, and in a few minutes she would be wandering in the valley by the river picking primroses and saying triumphantly to herself, 'I knew it wasn't a railway line, really. Of course, the river's always been here.'

2

Abroad

1

It was six months after Nannie had departed that Mummy told Celia a very exciting piece of news. They were going abroad — to France.

'Me too?'

'Yes, darling, you too.'

'And Cyril?'

'Yes.'

'And Susan and Rouncy?'

'No. Daddy and I and Cyril and you. Daddy hasn't been well, and the doctor wants him to go abroad for the winter to somewhere warm.'

'Is France warm?'

'The south is.'

'What is it like, Mummy?'

'Well, there are mountains there. Mountains with snow on them.'

'Why have they got snow on them?'

'Because they are so high.'

'How high?'

And her mother would try to explain just how high mountains were — but Celia found it very hard to imagine.

She knew Woodbury Beacon. It took you half an hour to walk to the top of that. But Woodbury Beacon hardly counted as a mountain at all.

It was all very exciting — particularly the travelling bag. A real travelling bag of her very own in dark green leather, and inside it had bottles, and a place for a brush and comb and clothes brush, and there was a little travelling clock and even a little travelling inkpot!

It was, Celia felt, the loveliest possession she had ever had.

The journey was very exciting. There was crossing the Channel, to begin with. Her mother went to lie down, and Celia stayed on deck with her father, which made her feel very grown up and important.

France, when they actually saw it, was a little disappointing. It looked like any other place. But the blue-uniformed porters talking French were rather thrilling, and so was the funny high train they got into. They were to sleep in it, which seemed to Celia another thrilling thing.

She and her mother were to have one compartment, and her father and Cyril the one next door.

Cyril was, of course, very lordly about it all. Cyril was sixteen, and he made it a point of honour not to be excited about anything. He asked questions in a would-be indolent fashion, but even he could hardly conceal his passion and curiosity for the great French engine.

Celia said to her mother:

'Will there *really* be mountains, Mummy?'

'Yes, darling.'

'Very, very, *very* high?'

'Yes.'

'Higher than Woodbury Beacon?'

48

'Much, much higher. So high that there's snow on top of them.'

Celia shut her eyes and tried to imagine. Mountains. Great hills going up, up, up — so high that perhaps you couldn't see the tops of them. Celia's neck went back, back — in imagination she was looking up the steep sides of the mountains.

'What is it, darling? Have you got a crick in your neck?' Celia shook her head emphatically.

'I'm thinking of big mountains,' she said.

'Silly little kid,' said Cyril with good-humoured scorn.

Presently there was the excitement of going to bed. In the morning, when they woke up, they would be in the South of France.

It was ten o'clock on the following morning when they arrived at Pau. There was a great fuss about collecting the luggage, of which there was a lot — no less than thirteen great round-topped trunks and innumerable leather valises.

At last, however, they were out of the station and driving to the hotel. Celia peered out in every direction.

'Where are the mountains, Mummy?'

'Over there, darling. Do you see that line of snow peaks?'

Those! Against the skyline was a zigzag of white, looking as though it were cut out of paper. A low line. Where were those great towering monuments rising up into the sky far, far up above Celia's head?

'Oh!' said Celia.

49

A bitter pang of disappointment swept through her. Mountains indeed!

2

After she had got over her disappointment about the mountains, Celia enjoyed her life in Pau very much. The meals were exciting. Called for some strange reason Tabbeldote, you had lunch at a long table of all sorts of strange and exciting dishes. There were two other children in the hotel, twin sisters a year older than Celia. She and Bar and Beatrice went about everywhere together. Celia discovered, for the first time in her eight solemn years, the joys of mischief. The three children would eat oranges on their balcony and throw over the pips on to passing soldiers gay in blue and red uniforms. When the soldiers looked up angrily, the children would have dived back and become invisible. They put little heaps of salt and pepper on all the plates laid for Tabbeldote and annoyed Victor, the old waiter, very much indeed. They concealed themselves in a niche under the stairs and tickled the legs of all the visitors descending to dinner with a long peacock's feather. Their final feat came on a day when they had worried the fierce chambermaid of the upper floor to the point of distraction. They had followed her into a little sanctum of mops and pails and scrubbing brushes. Turning on them angrily and pouring forth a torrent of that incomprehensible language — French — she swept out, banging the door on them and locking it. The three children were prisoners.

'She's done us,' said Bar bitterly.

'I wonder how long it'll be before she lets us out?'

They looked at each other sombrely. Bar's eyes flashed rebelliously.

'I can't bear to let her crow over us. We must do something.'

Bar was always the ringleader. Her eyes went to a microscopic slit of a window which was all the room possessed.

'I wonder if we could squeeze through that. We're none of us very fat. What's outside, Celia, anything at all?'

Celia reported that there was a gutter.

'It's big enough to walk along,' she said:

'Good, we'll do Suzanne yet. Won't she have a fit when we come jumping out on her?'

They got the window open with difficulty, and one by one they squeezed themselves through. The gutter was a ledge about a foot wide with an edge perhaps two inches high. Below it was a sheer drop of five storeys.

The Belgian lady in No. 33 sent a polite note to the English lady in No. 54. Was Madame aware of the fact that her little girl and the little girls of Madame Owen were walking round the parapet on the fifth storey?

The fuss that followed was to Celia quite extraordinary and rather unjust. She had never been told not to walk on parapets.

'You might have fallen and been killed.'

'Oh! No, Mummy, there was lots of room — even to put both feet together.'

The incident remained one of those inexplicable ones where grown-ups fuss about nothing at all.

3

Celia would, of course, have to learn French. Cyril had a young Frenchman who came every day. For Celia a young lady was engaged to take her for walks every day and talk French. The lady was actually English, the daughter of the proprietor of the English bookshop, but she had lived her whole life in Pau and spoke French as easily as English.

Miss Leadbetter was a young lady of extreme refinement. Her English was mincing and clipped. She spoke slowly, with condescending kindness.

'See, Celia, that is a shop where they bake bread. A *boulangerie*.'

'Yes, Miss Leadbetter.'

'Look, Celia, there is a little dog crossing the road. *Un chien qui traverse la rue. Qu'est-ce qu'il fait?* That means, what is he doing?'

Miss Leadbetter had not been happy in this last attempt. Dogs are indelicate creatures apt to bring a blush to the cheek of ultra-refined young women. This particular dog stopping crossing the road and engaged in other activities.

'I don't know how to say what he is doing in French,' said Celia.

'Look the other way, dear,' said Miss Leadbetter. 'It's not very nice. That is a church in front of us. *Voilà une église.*'

The walks were long, boring, and monotonous.

After a fortnight, Celia's mother got rid of Miss Leadbetter.

'An impossible young woman,' she said to her husband. 'She could make the most exciting thing in the world seem dull.'

Celia's father agreed. He said the child would never learn French except from a Frenchwoman. Celia did not much like the idea of a Frenchwoman. She had a good insular distrust of all foreigners. Still, if it was only for walks . . . Her mother said that she was sure she would like Mademoiselle Mauhourat very much. It struck Celia as an extraordinarily funny name.

Mademoiselle Mauhourat was tall and big. She always wore dresses made with a number of little capes which swung about and knocked things over on tables.

Celia was of opinion that Nannie would have said she 'flounced'.

Mademoiselle Mauhourat was very voluble and very affectionate.

'*Oh, la chère mignonne!*' cried Mademoiselle Mauhourat, '*la chère petite mignonne.*' She knelt down in front of Celia and laughed in an engaging manner into her face. Celia remained very British and stolid and disliked this very much. It made her feel embarrassed.

'*Nous allons nous amuser. Ah, comme nous*

allons nous amuser!'

Again there were walks. Mademoiselle Mauhourat talked without ceasing, and Celia endured politely the flow of meaningless words. Mademoiselle Mauhourat was very kind — the kinder she was the more Celia disliked her.

After ten days Celia got a cold. She was slightly feverish.

'I think you'd better not go out today,' said her mother. 'Mademoiselle can amuse you here.'

'No,' burst out Celia. 'No. Send her away. Send her away.'

Her mother looked at her attentively. It was a look Celia knew well — a queer, luminous, searching look. She said quietly:

'Very well, darling, I will.'

'Don't even let her come in here,' implored Celia.

But at that moment the door of the sitting room opened and Mademoiselle, very much becaped, entered.

Celia's mother spoke to her in French. Mademoiselle uttered exclamations of chagrin and sympathy.

'Ah, *la pauvre mignonne*,' she cried when Celia's mother had finished. She plopped down in front of Celia. '*La pauvre, pauvre mignonne.*'

Celia glanced appealingly at her mother. She made terrible faces at her. 'Send her away,' the faces said, 'send her away.'

Fortunately at that moment one of Mademoiselle Mauhourat's many capes knocked over a vase of flowers, and her whole attention was absorbed by apologies.

When she had finally left the room, Celia's mother said gently:

'Darling, you shouldn't have made those faces. Mademoiselle Mauhourat was only meaning to be kind. You would have hurt her feelings.'

Celia looked at her mother in surprise.

'But, Mummy,' she said, 'they were *English* faces.'

She didn't understand why her mother laughed so much.

That evening Miriam said to her husband:

'This woman's no good, either. Celia doesn't like her. I wonder — '

'What?'

'Nothing,' said Miriam. 'I was thinking of a girl in the dressmaker's today.'

The next time she went to be fitted she spoke to the girl. She was only one of the apprentices; her job was to stand by holding pins. She was about nineteen, with dark hair neatly piled up in a chignon, a snub nose, and a rosy, good-humoured face.

Jeanne was very astonished when the English lady spoke to her and asked her whether she would like to come to England. It depended, she said, on what Maman thought. Miriam asked for her mother's address. Jeanne's father and mother kept a small café — very neat and clean. Madame Beauge listened in great surprise to the English lady's proposal. To act as lady's-maid and look after a little girl? Jeanne had very little experience — she was rather awkward and clumsy. Berthe now, her elder daughter — but it was Jeanne the English lady wanted. M. Beauge was called in for consultation. He said they must not stand in Jeanne's way. The wages were good, much better than Jeanne got in the dressmaking establishment.

Three days later Jeanne, very nervous and elated, came to take up her duties. She was rather frightened of the little English girl she was to look after. She did not know any English. She learnt a phrase and said it hopefully. 'Good morning — mees.'

Alas, so peculiar was Jeanne's accent that Celia did not understand. The toilet proceeded in silence. Celia and Jeanne eyed each other like strange dogs. Jeanne brushed Celia's curls round her fingers. Celia never stopped staring at her.

'Mummy,' said Celia at breakfast, 'doesn't Jeanne talk any English at all?'

'No.'

'How funny.'

'Do you like Jeanne?'

'She's got a very funny face,' said Celia. She thought a minute. 'Tell her to brush my hair harder.'

At the end of three weeks Celia and Jeanne could understand each other. At the end of the fourth week they met a herd of cows when out on their walk.

'*Mon Dieu!*' cried Jeanne. '*Des vaches — des vaches! Maman, maman.*'

And catching Celia frenziedly by the hand, she rushed up a bank.

'What's the matter?' said Celia.

'*J'ai peur des vaches.*'

Celia looked at her kindly.

'If we meet any more cows,' she said, 'you get behind me.'

After that they were perfect friends. Celia found Jeanne a most entertaining companion. Jeanne dressed some small dolls that had been given to Celia and sustained dialogues would ensue. Jeanne was, in turn, the *femme de chambre* (a very impertinent one), the maman, the papa (who was very military and twirled his moustache), and the three naughty children. Once she enacted the part of M. le Curé and heard their confessions and imposed dreadful penances on them. This enchanted Celia, who was always begging for a repetition.

'*Non, non, mees, c'est très mal ce que j'ai fait là.*'

'*Pourquoi?*'

Jeanne explained.

'I have made a mock of M. le Curé. It is a sin, that!'

'Oh, Jeanne, couldn't you do it once more? It was so *funny.*'

The soft-hearted Jeanne imperilled her immortal soul and did it again even more amusingly.

Celia knew all about Jeanne's family. About Berthe who was *très sérieuse*, and Louis who was *si gentil*, and Edouard who was *spirituel*, and *la petite* Lise who had just made her first communion, and the cat who was so clever that he could curl himself up in the middle of the glasses in the café and never break one of them.

Celia, in her turn, told Jeanne about Goldie and Rouncy and Susan, and the garden, and all the things they would do when Jeanne came to

England. Jeanne had never seen the sea. The idea of going on a boat from France to England frightened her very much.

'*Je me figure,*' said Jeanne, '*que j'aurais horriblement peur. N'en parlons pas! Parlez-moi de votre petit oiseau.*'

4

One day, as Celia was walking with her father, a voice hailed them from a small table outside one of the hotels.

'John! I declare it's old John!'

'Bernard!'

A big jolly-looking man had jumped up and was wringing her father warmly by the hand.

This, it seemed, was a Mr Grant, who was one of her father's oldest friends. They had not seen each other for some years, and neither of them had had the least idea that the other was in Pau. The Grants were staying in a different hotel, but the two families used to foregather after *déjeuner* and drink coffee.

Mrs Grant was, Celia thought, the loveliest thing she had ever seen. She had silver-grey hair, exquisitely arranged, and wonderful dark-blue eyes, clear-cut features, and a very clear incisive voice. Celia immediately invented a new character, called Queen Marise. Queen Marise had all the personal attributes of Mrs Grant and was adored by her devoted subjects. She was three times the victim of attempted assassination, but was rescued by a devoted young man

58

called Colin, whom she at once knighted. Her coronation robes were of emerald green velvet and she had a silver crown set with diamonds.

Mr Grant was not made a king. Celia thought he was nice, but that his face was too fat and too red — not nearly so nice as her own father with his brown beard and his habit of throwing it up in the air when he laughed. Her own father, Celia thought, was just what a father should be — full of nice jokes that didn't make you feel silly like Mr Grant's sometimes did.

With the Grants was their son Jim, a pleasant freckle-faced schoolboy. He was always good-tempered and smiling, and had very round blue eyes that gave him rather a surprised look. He adored his mother.

He and Cyril eyed each other like strange dogs. Jim was very respectful to Cyril, because Cyril was two years older and at a public school. Neither of them took any notice of Celia because, of course, Celia was only a kid.

The Grants went home to England after about three weeks. Celia overheard Mr Grant say to her mother:

'It gave me a shock to see old John, but he tells me he is ever so much fitter since being here.'

Celia said to her mother afterwards:

'Mummy, is Daddy ill?'

Her mother looked a little queer as she answered:

'No. No, of course not. He's perfectly well now. It was just the damp and the rain in England.'

Celia was glad her father wasn't ill. Not, she

59

thought, that he could be — he never went to bed or sneezed or had a bilious attack. He coughed sometimes, but that was because he smoked so much. Celia knew that, because her father told her so.

But she wondered why her mother had looked — well, queer . . .

5

When May came they left Pau and went first to Argelès at the foot of the Pyrenees and after that to Cauterets up in the mountains.

At Argelès Celia fell in love. The object of her passion was the lift boy — Auguste. Not Henri, the little fair lift boy who played tricks sometimes with her and Bar and Beatrice (they also had come to Argelès), but Auguste. Auguste was eighteen, tall, dark, sallow, and very gloomy in appearance.

He took no interest in the passengers he propelled up and down. Celia never gathered courage to speak to him. No one, not even Jeanne, knew of her romantic passion. In bed at night Celia would envisage scenes in which she saved Auguste's life by catching the bridle of his furiously galloping horse — a shipwreck in which she and Auguste alone survived, she saving his life by swimming ashore and holding his head above water. Sometimes Auguste saved her life in a fire, but this was somehow not quite so satisfactory. The climax she preferred was when Auguste, with tears in his eyes, said:

60

'Mademoiselle, I owe you my life. How can I ever thank you?'

It was a brief but violent passion. A month later they went to Cauterets, and Celia fell in love with Janet Patterson instead.

Janet was fifteen. She was a nice pleasant girl with brown hair and kindly blue eyes. She was not beautiful or striking in any way. She was kind to younger children and not bored by playing with them.

To Celia the only joy in life was some day to grow up to be like her idol. Some day she too would wear a striped blouse and collar and tie, and would wear her hair in a plait tied with a black bow. She would have, too, that mysterious thing — a figure. Janet had a figure — a very apparent one sticking out each side of the striped blouse. Celia — a very thin child (described indeed by her brother Cyril when he wanted to annoy as a Scrawny Chicken — a term which never failed to reduce her to tears) — was passionately enamoured of plumpness. Some day, some glorious day, she would be grown up and sticking out and going in in all the proper places.

'Mummy,' she said one day, 'when shall I have a chest that sticks out?'

Her mother looked at her and said:

'Why, do you want one so badly?'

'Oh, yes,' breathed Celia anxiously.

'When you're about fourteen or fifteen — Janet's age.'

'Can I have a striped blouse then?'

'Perhaps, but I don't think they're very pretty.'

Celia looked at her reproachfully.

'I think they're lovely. Oh, Mummy, do say I can have one when I'm fifteen.'

'You can have one — if you still want it.'

Of course she would want it.

She went off to look for her idol. To her great annoyance Janet was walking with her French friend Yvonne Barbier. Celia hated Yvonne Barbier with a jealous hatred. Yvonne was very pretty, very elegant, very sophisticated. Although only fifteen, she looked more like eighteen. Her arm linked through Janet's, she was talking to her in a cooing voice.

'*Naturellement, je n'ai rien dit à Maman. Je lui ai répondu —* '

'Run away, darling,' said Janet kindly. 'Yvonne and I are busy just now.'

Celia withdrew sadly. How she hated that horrible Yvonne Barbier.

Alas, two weeks later, Janet and her parents left Cauterets. Her image faded quickly from Celia's mind, but her ecstatic anticipation of the day when she would have 'a figure' remained.

Cauterets was great fun. You were right under the mountains here. Not that even now they looked at all as Celia had pictured them. To the end of her life she could never really admire mountain scenery. A sense of being cheated remained at the back of her mind. The delights of Cauterets were varied. There was the hot walk in the morning to La Raillière where her mother and father drank glasses of nasty tasting water. After the water drinking there was the purchase of sticks of *sucre d'orge*. They were twirly sticks of different colours and flavours. Celia usually had *ananas* — her mother liked a green one — aniseed. Her father, strangely enough, liked none of them. He seemed buoyant and happier since he came to Cauterets.

'This place suits me, Miriam,' he said. 'I can feel myself getting a new man here.'

His wife answered:

'We'll stay here as long as we can.'

She too seemed gayer — she laughed more. The anxious pucker between her brows smoothed itself away. She saw very little of Celia. Satisfied with the child being in Jeanne's keeping, she devoted herself heart and soul to her husband.

After the morning excursion Celia would come home with Jeanne through the woods, going up and down zigzag paths, occasionally tobogganing down steep slopes with disastrous results to the seats of her drawers. Agonized wails would arise from Jeanne.

'Oh, mees — *ce n'est pas gentille ce que vous faites là. Et vos pantalons. Que dirait Madame votre mère?*'

'*Encore une fois, Jeanne. Une fois seulement.*'

'*Non, non.* Oh, mees!'

After lunch Jeanne would be busy sewing. Celia would go out into the Place and join some of the other children. A little girl called Mary Hayes had been specially designated as a suitable companion. 'Such a nice child,' said Celia's mother. 'Pretty manners and so sweet. A nice little friend for Celia.'

Celia played with Mary Hayes when she could not avoid it, but, alas, she found Mary woefully dull. She was sweet-tempered and amiable but, to Celia, extremely boring. The child whom Celia liked was a little American girl called Marguerite Priestman. She came from a Western state and had a terrific twang in her speech which fascinated the English child. She played games that were new to Celia. Accompanying her was her nurse, an amazing old woman in an enormous flopping black hat whose standard phrase was, 'Now you stay right by Fanny, do you hear?'

Occasionally Fanny came to the rescue when a dispute was in progress. One day she found both children almost in tears, arguing hotly.

'Now, just you tell Fanny what it's all about,' she commanded.

'I was just telling Celia a story, and she says what I say isn't so — and it is so.'

'You tell Fanny what the story was.'

'It was going to be just a lovely story. It was about a little girl who grew up in a wood kinder lonesome because the doctor had never fetched her in his black bag — '

Celia interrupted.

'That isn't true. Marguerite says babies are found by doctors in woods and brought to the mothers. That's not true. The angels bring them in the night and put them into the cradle.'

'It's doctors.'

'It's angels.'

'It isn't.'

Fanny raised a large hand.

'You listen to me.'

They listened. Fanny's little black eyes snapped intelligently as she considered and then dealt with the problem.

'You've neither of you call to get excited. Marguerite's right and so's Celia. One's the way they do with English babies and the other's the way they do with American babies.'

How simple after all! Celia and Marguerite beamed on each other and were friends again.

Fanny murmured, 'You stay right by Fanny,' and resumed her knitting.

'I'll go right on with the story, shall I?' asked Marguerite.

'Yes, do,' said Celia. 'And afterwards I'll tell you a story about an opal fairy who came out of a peach stone.'

Marguerite embarked on her narrative, later to be interrupted once more.

'What's a scarrapin?'

'A scarrapin? Why, Celia, don't you know what a scarrapin is?'

'No, what is it?'

That was more difficult. From the welter of Marguerite's explanation Celia only grasped the fact that a scarrapin was in point of fact a scarrapin! A scarrapin remained for her a fabulous beast connected with the continent of America.

Only one day when she was grown up did it suddenly flash into Celia's mind.

'Of course. Marguerite Priestman's scarrapin was a *scorpion*.'

And she felt quite a pang of loss.

65

6

Dinner was very early at Cauterets. It took place at half-past six. Celia was allowed to sit up. Afterwards they would all sit outside round little tables, and once or twice a week the conjurer would conjure.

Celia adored the conjurer. She liked his name. He was, so her father told her, a *prestidigitateur*.

Celia would repeat the syllables very slowly over to herself.

The conjurer was a tall man with a long black beard. He did the most entrancing things with coloured ribbons — yards and yards of them he would suddenly pull out of his mouth. At the end of his entertainment he would announce 'a little lottery'. First he would hand round a large wooden plate into which every one would put a contribution. Then the winning numbers would be announced and the prizes given — a paper fan — a little lantern — a pot of paper flowers. There seemed to be something very lucky for children in the lottery. It was nearly always children who won the prizes. Celia had a tremendous longing to win the paper fan. She never did, however, although she twice won a lantern.

One day Celia's father said to her, 'How would you like to go to the top of that fellow there?' He indicated one of the mountains behind the hotel.

'Me, Daddy? Right up to the top?'

'Yes. You shall ride there on a mule.'

'What's a mule, Daddy?'

He told her that a mule was rather like a donkey and rather like a horse. Celia was thrilled at the thought of the adventure. Her mother seemed a little doubtful. 'Are you sure it's quite safe, John?' she said.

Celia's father pooh-poohed her fears. Of course the child would be all right.

She, her father, and Cyril were to go. Cyril said in a lofty tone, 'Oh! is the kid coming? She'll be a rotten nuisance.' Yet he was quite fond of Celia, but her coming offended his manly pride. This was to have been a man's expedition — women and children left at home.

Early on the morning of the great expedition Celia was ready and standing on the balcony to see the mules arrive. They came at a trot round the corner — great big animals — more like horses than donkeys. Celia ran downstairs full of joyful expectation. A little man with a brown face in a beret was talking to her father. He was saying that the *petite demoiselle* would be quite all right. He would charge himself with looking after her. Her father and Cyril mounted; then the guide picked her up and swung her up to the saddle. How very high up it felt! But very, very exciting.

They moved off. From the balcony above, Celia's mother waved to them. Celia was thrilling with pride. She felt practically grown up. The guide ran beside her. He chatted to her, but she understood very little of what he said, owing to his strong Spanish accent.

It was a marvellous ride. They went up zigzag paths that grew gradually steeper and steeper.

Now they were well out on the mountain side, a wall of rock on one side of them and a sheer drop on the other. At the most dangerous looking places Celia's mule would stop reflectively on the precipice edge and kick out idly with one foot. It also liked walking on the extreme edge. It was, Celia thought, a very nice horse. Its name seemed to be Aniseed, which Celia thought a very queer name for a horse to have.

It was midday when they reached the summit. There was a tiny little hut there with a table in front of it, and they sat down, and presently the woman there brought them out lunch — a very good lunch too. Omelette, some fried trout, and cream cheese and bread. There was a big woolly dog with whom Celia played.

'*C'est presque un Anglais*,' said the woman. '*Il s'appelle Milor.*'

Milor was very amiable and allowed Celia to do anything she pleased with him.

Presently Celia's father looked at his watch and said it was time to start down again. He called to the guide.

The latter came smiling. He had something in his hands.

'See what I have just caught,' he said.

It was a beautiful big butterfly.

'*C'est pour Mademoiselle*,' he said.

And quickly, deftly, before she knew what he was going to do, he had produced a pin and skewered the butterfly to the crown of Celia's straw hat.

'*Voilà que Mademoiselle est chic,*' he said,

68

falling back to admire his handiwork.

Then the mules were brought round, the party was mounted, and the descent was begun.

Celia was miserable. She could feel the wings of the butterfly fluttering against her hat. It was alive — alive. Skewered on a pin! She felt sick and miserable. Large tears gathered in her eyes and rolled down her cheeks.

At last her father noticed.

'What's the matter, poppet?'

Celia shook her head. Her sobs increased.

'Have you got a pain? Are you very tired? Does your head ache?'

Celia merely shook her head more and more violently at each suggestion.

'She's frightened of the horse,' said Cyril.

'I'm not,' said Celia.

'Then what are you blubbing for?'

'*La petite demoiselle est fatiguée*,' suggested the guide.

Celia's tears flowed faster and faster. They were all looking at her, questioning her — and how could she say what was the matter? It would hurt the guide's feelings terribly. He had meant to be kind. He had caught the butterfly specially for her. He had been so proud of his idea in pinning it to her hat. How could she say out loud that she didn't like it? And now nobody would ever, *ever* understand! The wind made the butterfly's wings flap more than ever. Celia wept unrestrainedly. Never, she felt, had there been misery such as hers.

'We'd better push on as fast as we can,' said her father. He looked vexed. 'Get her back to her mother. She was right. It's been too much for the child.'

Celia longed to cry out: 'It hasn't, hasn't. It's not that at all.' But she didn't because she realized that then they would ask her again, 'But then what *is* it?' She only shook her head dumbly.

She wept all the way down. Her misery grew blacker and blacker. Still weeping she was lifted from her mule, and her father carried her up to the sitting-room where her mother was sitting waiting for them. 'You were right, Miriam,' said her father. 'It's been too much for the child. I don't know whether she's got a pain or whether she's overtired.'

'I'm not,' said Celia.

'She was frightened of coming down those steep places,' said Cyril.

'I wasn't,' said Celia.

'Then what is it?' demanded her father.

Celia stared dumbly at her mother. She knew now that she could never tell. The cause of her misery would remain locked in her own breast forever and ever. She wanted to tell — oh, how badly she wanted to tell — but somehow she couldn't. Some mysterious inhibition had been laid on her, sealing her lips. If only Mummy knew. Mummy would understand. But she couldn't tell Mummy. They were all looking at her — waiting for her to speak. A terrible agony welled up in her breast. She gazed dumbly, agonizingly, at her mother. 'Help me,' that gaze said. 'Oh, do help me.'

Miriam gazed back at her.

'I believe she doesn't like that butterfly in her hat,' she said, 'Who pinned it there?'

Oh, the relief — the wonderful, aching, agonizing relief.

'Nonsense,' her father was beginning, but Celia interrupted him. Words burst from her released like water at the bursting of a dam.

'I 'ate it. I 'ate it,' she cried. 'It flaps. It's alive. It's being hurt.'

'Why on earth didn't you say so, you silly kid?' said Cyril.

Celia's mother answered: 'I expect she didn't want to hurt the guide's feelings.'

'Oh, Mummy!' said Celia.

It was all there — in those two words. Her relief, her gratitude — and a great welling up of love.

Her mother had understood.

3

Grannie

1

The following winter Celia's father and mother went to Egypt. They did not think it practicable to take Celia with them, so she and Jeanne went to stay with Grannie.

Grannie lived at Wimbledon, and Celia liked staying with her very much. The features of Grannie's house were, first, the garden — a square pocket handkerchief of green, bordered with rose trees, every tree of which Celia knew intimately, remembering even in winter: 'That's the pink la France — Jeanne, you'd like that one,' but the crown and glory of the garden was a big ash tree trained over wire supports to make an arbour. There was nothing like the ash tree at home, and Celia regarded it as one of the most exciting wonders of the world. Then there was the WC seat of old-fashioned mahogany set very high. Retiring to this spot after breakfast, Celia would fancy herself a queen enthroned, and securely secluded behind a locked door she would bow regally, extend a hand to be kissed by imaginary courtiers and prolong the court scene as long as she dared. There was also Grannie's store cupboard situated by the door into the garden. Every morning, her large bunch of keys clanking, Grannie would visit her store cupboard, and with the punctuality of a child, a dog, or a lion at feeding time, Celia would be there too. Grannie would hand out packets of sugar, butter, eggs, or a pot of jam. She would hold long acrimonious discussions with old Sarah, the cook. Very different from Rouncy, old Sarah. As thin as Rouncy was fat. A little old woman with a nut-cracker wrinkled face. For fifty years of her life she had been in service with Grannie, and during all those fifty years the discussions had been the same. Too much sugar was being used: what happened to the last half pound of tea? It was, by now, a kind of ritual — it was Grannie going through her daily performance of the careful housewife. Servants were so wasteful! You had to look after them sharply. The ritual finished, Grannie would pretend to notice Celia for the first time.

'Dear, dear, what's a little girl doing here?'

And Grannie would pretend great surprise.

'Well, well,' she would say, 'you can't *want* anything?'

'I do, Grannie, I do.'

'Well, let me see now.' Grannie would burrow leisurely in the depths of the cupboard. Something would be extracted — a jar of French plums, a stick of angelica, a pot of quince preserve. There was always something for a little girl.

Grannie was a very handsome old lady. She had pink and white skin, two waves of white crimped hair each side of her forehead, and a big good-humoured mouth. In figure she was majestically stout with a pronounced bosom and stately hips. She wore dresses of velvet or brocade, ample as to skirts, and well pulled in round the waist.

'I always had a beautiful figure, my dear,' she used to tell Celia. 'Fanny — that was my sister — had the prettiest face of the family, but she'd no figure — no figure at all! As thin as two boards nailed together. No man looked at her for long when *I* was about. It's figure the men care for, not face.'

'The men' bulked largely in Grannie's conversation. She had been brought up in the days when men were considered to be the hub of the universe. Women merely existed to minister to those magnificent beings.

'You wouldn't have found a handsomer man anywhere than my father. Six foot tall, he was. All we children were afraid of him. He was very severe.'

'What was your mother like, Grannie?'

'Ah, poor soul. Only thirty-nine when she died. Ten of us children, there were. A lot of hungry mouths. After a baby was born, when she was staying in bed — '

'Why did she stay in bed, Grannie?'

'It's the custom, dearie.'

Celia accepted the mandate incuriously.

'She always took her month,' went on Grannie. 'It was the only rest she got, poor soul. She enjoyed her month. She used to have breakfast in bed and a boiled egg. Not that she got much of that. We children used to come and bother her. 'Can I have a taste of your egg,

Mother? Can I have the top of it?' There wouldn't be much left for her after each child had had a taste. She was too kind — too gentle. She died when I was fourteen. I was the eldest of the family. Poor father was heart-broken. They were a devoted couple. He followed her to the grave six months later.'

Celia nodded. That seemed right and fitting in her eyes. In most of the child's books in the nursery there was a deathbed scene — usually that of a child — a peculiarly holy and angelic child.

'What did he die of?'

'Galloping consumption,' replied Grannie.

'And your mother?'

'She went into a decline, my dear. Just went into decline. Always wrap your throat up well when you go out in an east wind. Remember that, Celia. It's the east wind that kills. Poor Miss Sankey — why, she had tea with me only a month ago. Went to those nasty swimming baths — came out afterwards with an east wind blowing and no boa round her neck — and she was dead in a week.'

Nearly all Grannie's stories and reminiscences ended like this. A most cheerful person herself, she delighted in tales of incurable illness, of sudden death, or of mysterious disease. Celia was so well accustomed to this that she would demand with eager and rapturous interest in the middle of one of Grannie's stories, 'And then did he die, Grannie?' And Grannie would reply, 'Ah, yes, he died, poor fellow.' Or girl or boy, or woman — as the case might be. None of

75

Grannie's stories ever ended happily. It was perhaps her natural reaction from her own healthy and vigorous personality.

Grannie was also full of mysterious warnings.

'If anybody you don't know offers you sweets, dearie, never take them. And when you're an older girl, remember never to get into a train with a single man.'

This last injunction rather distressed Celia. She was a shy child. If one was not to get into a train with a single man, one would have to ask him whether or not he was married. You couldn't tell if a man was married or not to look at him. The mere thought of having to do such a thing made her squirm uneasily.

She did not connect with herself a murmur from a lady visitor.

'Surely unwise — put things into her head.'

Grannie's answer rose robustly.

'Those that are warned in time won't come to grief. Young people ought to know these things. And there's a thing that perhaps you never heard of, my dear. My husband told me about it — my first husband.' (Grannie had had three husbands — so attractive had been her figure — and so well had she ministered to the male sex. She had buried them in turn — one with tears — one with resignation — and one with decorum.) 'He said women ought to know about such things.'

Her voice dropped. It hissed in sibilant whispers.

What she could hear seemed to Celia dull. She strayed away into the garden . . .

76

Jeanne was unhappy. She became increasingly homesick for France and her own people. The English servants, she told Celia, were not kind.

'The *cuisinière*, Sarah, she is *gentille*, though she calls me a papist. But the others, Mary and Kate — they laugh because I do not spend my wages on my clothes, and send it all home to Maman.'

Grannie attempted to cheer Jeanne.

'You go on behaving like a sensible girl,' she told Jeanne. 'Putting a lot of useless finery on your back never caught a decent man yet. You go on sending your wages home to your mother, and you'll have a nice little nest egg laid by for when you get married. That neat plain style of dressing is far more suitable to a domestic servant than a lot of fallals. You go on being a sensible girl.'

But Jeanne would occasionally give way to tears when Mary or Kate had been unusually spiteful or unkind. The English girls did not like foreigners, and Jeanne was a papist too, and everyone knew that Roman Catholics worshipped the Scarlet Woman.

Grannie's rough encouragements did not always heal the wound.

'Quite right to stick to your religion, my girl. Not that I hold with the Roman Catholic religion myself, because I don't. Most Romans I've known have been liars. I'd think more of them if their priests married. And these convents! *All those beautiful young girls shut up in convents and never being heard of again.* What happens to them, I should like to know? The priests could answer *that* question, I dare say.'

Fortunately Jeanne's English was not quite equal to this flow of remarks.

Madame was very kind, she said, she would try not to mind what the other girls said.

Grannie then had up Mary and Kate and denounced them in no measured terms for their unkindness to a poor girl in a strange country. Mary and Kate were very soft spoken, very polite, very surprised. Indeed, they had said nothing — nothing at all. Jeanne was such a one as never was for imagining things.

Grannie got a little satisfaction by refusing with horror Mary's plea to be allowed to keep a bicycle.

'I am surprised at you, Mary, for making such a suggestion. No servant of mine shall ever do such an unsuitable thing.'

Mary, looking sulky, muttered that her cousin at Richmond was allowed to have one.

'Let me hear nothing more about it,' said Grannie. 'Anyway, they're dangerous things for women. Many a woman has been prevented from having children for life by riding those nasty things. They're not good for a woman's inside.'

Mary and Kate retired sulkily. They would have given notice, but they knew that the place was a good one. The food was first class — no inferior tainted stuff bought for the kitchen as in some places — and the work was not heavy. The old lady was rather a tartar, but she was kind in her way. If there was any trouble at home, she'd often come to the rescue, and nobody could be more generous at Christmas. There was old Sarah's tongue, of course, but you had to put up with that. Her cooking was prime.

Like all children, Celia haunted the kitchen a good deal. Old Sarah was much fiercer than Rouncy, but then, of course, she was terribly old. If anyone had told Celia that Sarah was a hundred and fifty she would not have been in the least surprised. Nobody, Celia felt, had ever been quite so old as Sarah.

Sarah was most unaccountably touchy about the most extraordinary things. One day, for instance, Celia had gone into the kitchen and had asked Sarah what she was cooking.

'Giblet soup, Miss Celia.'

'What are giblets, Sarah?'

Sarah pursed her mouth.

'Things that it's not nice for a little lady to make inquiries about.'

'But what *are* they?' Celia's curiosity was pleasantly aroused.

'Now, that's enough, Miss Celia. It's not for a little lady like you to ask questions about such things.'

'Sarah.' Celia danced about the kitchen. Her flaxen hair bobbed. 'What are giblets? Sarah, what are giblets? Giblets — giblets — giblets?'

The infuriated Sarah made a rush at her with a frying pan, and Celia retreated, to poke her head in a few minutes later with the query, 'Sarah, what are giblets?'

She next repeated the question from the kitchen window.

Sarah, her face dark with annoyance, made no answer, merely mumbled to herself.

Finally, tiring suddenly of this sport, Celia sought out her grandmother.

Grannie always sat in the dining-room, which was situated looking out over the short drive in front of the house. It was a room that Celia could have described minutely twenty years later. The heavy Nottingham lace curtains, the dark red and gold wallpaper, the general air of gloom, and the faint smell of apples and a trace still of the midday joint. The broad Victorian dining table with its chenille cloth, the massive mahogany sideboard, the little table by the fire with the stacked-up newspapers, the heavy bronzes on the mantelpiece ('Your grandfather gave £70 for them at the Paris Exhibition'), the sofa upholstered in shiny red leather on which Celia sometimes had her 'rest', and which was so slippery that it was hard to remain in the centre of it, the crocheted woolwork that was hung over the back of it, the dumbwaiters in the windows crammed with small objects, the revolving bookcase on the round table, the red velvet rocking chair in which Celia had once rocked so violently that she had shot over backwards and developed an egg-like bump on her head, the row of leather upholstered chairs against the wall, and lastly the great high-backed leather chair in which Grannie sat pursuing this, that, and the other activity.

Grannie was never idle. She wrote letters — long letters in a spiky spidery handwriting, mostly on half sheets of paper because it used them up, and she couldn't bear waste. ('Waste not, want not, Celia.') Then she crocheted shawls — pretty shawls in purples and blues and mauves. They were usually for the servants' relations. Then she knitted with great balls of soft fleecy wool. That was usually for somebody's baby. And there was netting — a delicate foam of netting round a little circle of damask. At tea time all the cakes and biscuits reposed on these foamy doilies. Then there were waistcoats — for the old gentlemen of Grannie's acquaintance. You did them on strips of huckaback towelling, running through the stitches with lines of coloured embroidery cotton. This was, perhaps, Grannie's favourite work. Though eighty-one years of age, she still had an eye for 'the men'. She knitted them bed socks, too.

Under Grannie's guidance Celia was doing a set of washstand mats as a surprise for Mummy on her return. You took different-sized rounds of bath towelling, buttonholed them round first in wool, and then crocheted into the buttonholing. Celia was doing her set in pale blue wool, and both she and Grannie admired the result enormously. After tea was cleared away, Grannie and Celia would play spillikins, and after that cribbage, their faces serious and preoccupied, the classic phrases falling from their lips, 'One for his knob, two for his heel, fifteen two, fifteen four, fifteen six, and six are twelve.' 'Do you know why cribbage is such a good game, my dear?' 'No, Grannie.' 'Because it teaches you to *count*.'

Grannie never failed to make this little speech. She had been brought up never to admit enjoyment for enjoyment's sake. You ate your food because it was good for your health. Stewed cherries, of which Grannie was passionately fond, she had nearly every day because they were 'so good for the kidneys'. Cheese, which Grannie also loved, 'digested your food', the glass of port served with dessert 'I have been ordered by the doctor.' Especially was it necessary to emphasize the enjoyment of alcohol (for a member of the weaker sex). 'Don't you like it, Grannie?' Celia would demand. 'No, dear,' Grannie would reply, and would make a wry face as she took the first sip. 'I drink it for my health.' She could then finish her glass with every sign of enjoyment, having uttered the required formula. Coffee was the only thing for which Grannie admitted a partiality. 'Very Moorish, this coffee,' she would say, wrinkling up her eyelids in enjoyment. 'Very moreish,' and would laugh at her little joke as she helped herself to another cup.

On the other side of the hall was the morning-room, where sat Poor Miss Bennett, the sewing woman. Miss Bennett was never referred to without the poor in front of her name.

'Poor Miss Bennett,' Grannie would say. 'It's a charity to give her employment. I really don't believe the poor thing has enough to eat sometimes.'

If any special delicacies were served at table, a share was always sent in to Poor Miss Bennett.

Poor Miss Bennett was a little woman with a

wealth of untidy grey hair wreathed round her head till it looked like a bird's nest. She was not actually deformed, but she had a look of deformity. She spoke in a mincing and ultra-refined voice, addressing Grannie as Madam. She was quite incapable of making any article correctly. The dresses she made for Celia were always so much too large that the sleeves fell over her hands, and the armholes were halfway down her arms.

You had to be very, very careful not to hurt Poor Miss Bennett's feelings. The least thing did it, and then Miss Bennett would sit sewing violently with a red spot in each cheek and tossing her head.

Poor Miss Bennett had had an Unfortunate History. Her father, as she constantly told you, had been very well connected — 'In fact, though perhaps I ought not to say so, but this is entirely in confidence, he was a very Great Gentleman. My mother always said so. I take after him. You may have noticed my hands and my ears — always a sign of breeding, they say. It would be a great shock to him, I'm sure, if he knew I was earning my living this way. Not but that with you, madam, it is different from what I have had to bear from Some People. Treated almost like a Servant. You, madam, *understand*.'

So Grannie was careful always to see that Poor Miss Bennett was treated properly. Her meals went in on a tray. Miss Bennett treated the servants very haughtily, ordering them about, with the result that they disliked her intensely.

'Giving herself such airs,' Celia heard old

Sarah mutter. 'And her nothing but a come-by-chance with a father she doesn't even know the name of.'

'What's a come-by-chance, Sarah?'

Sarah grew very red.

'Nothing to hear about on the lips of a young lady, Miss Celia.'

'Is it a giblet?' asked Celia hopefully.

Kate, who was standing by, went off into peals of laughter and was wrathfully told by Sarah to hold her tongue.

Behind the morning-room was the drawing-room. It was cool and dim and remote in there. It was only used when Grannie gave a party. It was very full of velvety chairs and tables and brocaded sofas, it had big cabinets crammed to bursting point with china figures. In one corner was a piano with a loud bass and a weak sweet treble. The windows led into a conservatory, and from there into the garden. The steel grate and fire irons were the delight of old Sarah, who kept them bright and shining so that you could almost see your face in them.

Upstairs was the nursery, a low long room overlooking the garden, above it an attic which housed Mary and Kate, and up a few steps, the three best bedrooms and an airless slit of a room belonging to Sarah.

Celia privately considered the three best bedrooms much grander than anything at home. They had vast suites in them, one of a dappled grey wood, the other two of mahogany. Grannie's bedroom was over the dining-room. It had a vast four-poster bed, a huge mahogany

84

wardrobe which occupied the whole of one wall, a handsome washstand and dressing table, and another huge chest of drawers. Every drawer in the room was crammed to repletion with parcels of articles neatly folded. Sometimes when opened the drawers would not shut, and Grannie would have a terrible time with them. Everything was securely locked. On the inside of the door, besides the lock were a substantial bolt and two brass cabin hooks and eyes. Once securely fastened into her apartment, Grannie would retire for the night with a watchman's rattle and a police whistle within reach of her hand so as to be able to give an immediate alarm should burglars attempt to storm her fortress.

On the top of the wardrobe, protected by a glass case, was a large crown of white wax flowers, a floral tribute at the decease of Grannie's first husband. On the right-hand wall was the framed memorial service of Grannie's second husband. On the left-hand wall was a large photograph of the handsome marble tombstone erected to Grannie's third husband.

The bed was a feather one, and the windows were never opened.

The night air, Grannie said, was highly injurious. Air of all kinds, indeed, she regarded as something of a risk. Except on the hottest days of summer she rarely went into the garden, such outings as she made were usually to the Army and Navy Stores — a four-wheeler to the station, train to Victoria, and another four-wheeler to the stores. On such occasions she was well wrapped up in her 'mantle' and further protected by a feather boa wound tightly many times round her neck.

Grannie never went out to see people. They came to see her. When visitors arrived cake was brought in and sweet biscuits, and different kinds of Grannie's own home-made liqueur. The gentlemen were first asked what they would take. 'You must taste my cherry brandy — that's what all the gentlemen like.' Then the ladies were urged in their turn, 'A little drop — just to keep the cold out.' Thus Grannie, believing that no member of the female sex could admit publicly to liking alcoholic liquor. Or if it was in the afternoon: 'You'll find it digests your dinner, my dear.'

If an old gentleman who came should not already be in possession of a waistcoat, Grannie would display the waistcoat at present in hand and she would then say with a kind of sprightly archness: 'I'd offer to make *you* one if I were sure your wife wouldn't object.' The wife would then cry: 'Oh, do make him one. I shall be delighted.' Grannie would say waggishly: 'I mustn't cause trouble,' and the old gentleman would say something gallant about wearing a waistcoat worked 'with her own fair fingers'.

After a visit, Grannie's cheeks would be twice as pink, and her figure twice as upright. She adored the giving of hospitality in any form.

3

'Grannie, may I come and be with you for a little?'

'Why? Can't you find anything to do upstairs with Jeanne?'

Celia hesitated for a minute or two to find a phrase that satisfied her. She said at last:

'Things aren't very pleasant in the nursery this afternoon.'

Grannie laughed and said:

'Well, to be sure, that's one way of putting it.'

Celia was always uncomfortable and miserable on the rare occasions on which she fell out with Jeanne. This afternoon trouble had come out of the blue in the most unexpected manner.

They had been arguing about the correct disposition of the furniture in Celia's dolls' house, and Celia, arguing a point, had exclaimed: '*Mais, ma pauvre fille* — ' And that had done it. Jeanne had burst into tears and a voluble flood of French.

Yes, no doubt she was a *pauvre fille*, as Celia said, but her family, though poor, was honest and respectable. Her father was respected all over Pau. M. le Maire even was on terms of friendship with him.

'But I never said — ' began Celia.

Jeanne swept on.

'Doubtless *la petite* mees, so rich, so beautifully dressed, with her parents who voyaged, and her frocks of silk, considered her, Jeanne, as an equal with a mendicant in the street — '

'But I never said — ' began Celia again, more and more bewildered.

But even *les pauvres filles* had their feelings. She, Jeanne, had her feelings. She was wounded.

She was wounded to the core.

'But, Jeanne, I love you,' cried Celia desperately.

But Jeanne was not to be appeased. She got out some of her most severe sewing, a buckram collar for a gown she was making for Grannie, and stitched at it in silence, shaking her head and refusing to answer Celia's appeals. Naturally Celia knew nothing of certain remarks made by Mary and Kate at the midday meal as to Jeanne's people being indeed poor if they took all their daughter's earnings.

Faced by an incomprehensible situation, Celia retreated from it and trotted downstairs to the dining-room.

'And what do you want to do?' asked Grannie, peering over her spectacles and dropping a large ball of wool. Celia picked it up.

'Tell me about when you were a little girl — about what you said when you came down after tea.'

'We used all to come down together and knock on the drawing-room door. My father would say, 'Come in.' Then we would all go in, shutting the door behind us. Quietly, mind you, remember always to shut the door quietly. No lady bangs a door. Indeed, in my young days, no lady ever shut a door at all. It spoilt the shape of the hands. There was ginger wine on the table, and each of us children was given a glass.'

'And then you said — ' prompted Celia, who knew this story backwards.

'We each said in turn, 'My duty to you, Father and Mother.' '

'And they said?'

'They said, 'My love to you, children.' '

'Oh!' Celia wriggled in an ecstasy of delight. She could hardly have said why she enjoyed this particular story so much.

'Tell me about the hymns in church,' she prompted. 'About you and Uncle Tom.'

Crocheting vigorously, Grannie repeated the oft-told tale.

'There was a big board with hymn numbers on it. The clerk used to give them out. He had a fine booming great voice. 'Let us now sing to the honour and glory of God. Hymn No. — ' and then he stopped — because the board had been put up the wrong way round. He began again: 'Let us sing to the honour and glory of God. Hymn No. — ' Then he said it a third time: 'Let us sing to the honour and glory of God. Hymn No. — , 'ere, Bill, just you turn that 'ere board.' '

Grannie was a good actress. The cockney aside came out in an inimitable manner.

'And you and Uncle Tom laughed,' prompted Celia.

'Yes, we both laughed. And my father looked at us. Just looked at us, that was all. But when we got home we were sent straight to bed and had no lunch. And it was Michaelmas Sunday — with the Michaelmas goose.'

'And you had no goose,' said Celia, awestruck.

'And we had no goose.'

Celia pondered the calamity deeply for a minute or two. Then with a deep sigh, she said: 'Grannie, make me be a chicken.'

'You're too big a girl.'

'Oh, no, Grannie, make me be a chicken.'

Grannie laid aside her crochet and her spectacles.

The comedy was played through from the first moment of entering Mr Whiteley's shop, a demand to speak to Mr Whiteley himself: a specially nice chicken was required for a very special dinner. Would Mr Whiteley select a chicken himself? Grannie was in turn herself and Mr Whiteley. The chicken was wrapped up (business with Celia and a newspaper), carried home, stuffed (more business), trussed, skewered (screams of delight), popped in the oven, served up on a dish and then the grand climax: 'Sarah — Sarah, come here, this chicken's *alive*!'

Oh, certainly there were few playmates to equal Grannie. The truth of it was that Grannie enjoyed playing as much as you did. She was kind, too. In some ways kinder than Mummy. If you asked long enough and often enough, she would give in. She would even give you Things that Were Bad for You.

4

Letters came from Mummy and Daddy — written very clearly in print.

My Darling Little Popsy Wopsums: How is my little girl? Does Jeanne take you on nice walks? How do you enjoy dancing class? The people out here have very nearly black faces. I hear Grannie is going to take you to the

Pantomime. Is not that kind of her? I am sure you will be very grateful and do everything you can to be a helpful little girl to her. I am sure you are being a very good girl to dear Grannie who is so good to you. Give Goldie a hemp seed from me.

Your loving,
Daddy.

My Own Precious Darling: I do miss you so much, but I am sure you are having a very happy time with dear Grannie who is so good to you, and that you are being a good little girl and doing everything you can to please her. It is lovely hot sunshine out here and beautiful flowers. Will you be a very clever little girl and write to Rouncy for me? Grannie will address the envelope. Tell her to pick the Christmas roses and send them to Grannie. Tell her to give Tommy a big saucer of milk on Christmas Day.

A lot of kisses, my precious lamb, pigeony pumpkin, from,
Mother.

Lovely letters. Two lovely, lovely letters. Why did a lump rise in Celia's throat? The Christmas roses — in the bed under the hedge — Mummy arranging them in a bowl with moss — Mummy saying, 'Look at their beautiful wide-open faces.' Mummy's voice . . .

Tommy, the big white cat. Rouncy, munching, always munching.

Home, she wanted to go home.

Home, with Mummy in it . . . Precious lamb, pigeony pumpkin — that's what Mummy called her with a laugh in her voice and a sharp, short sudden hug.

Oh, Mummy — Mummy . . .

Grannie, coming up the stairs, said:

'What's this? Crying? What are you crying for? You've got no fish to sell.'

That was Grannie's joke. She always made it.

Celia hated it. It made her want to cry more. When she was unhappy, she didn't want Grannie. She didn't want Grannie at all. Grannie made it worse, somehow.

She slipped past Grannie down the stairs and into the kitchen. Sarah was baking bread.

Sarah looked up at her.

'Had a letter from your mammy?'

Celia nodded. The tears overflowed again. Oh, empty, lonely world.

Sarah went on kneading bread.

'She'll be home soon, love, she'll be home soon. You watch for the leaves on the trees.'

She began to roll the dough on the board. Her voice was remote, soothing.

She detached a small lump of the dough.

'Make some little loaves of your own, honey. I'll bake them along of mine.'

Celia's tears stopped.

'Twists and cottages?'

'Twists and cottages.'

Celia set to work. For twists you rolled out three long sausages and then plaited them in and out, pinching the ends well. Cottages were a big round ball and a smaller ball on top and then

— ecstatic moment — you drove your thumb sharply in, making a big round hole. She made five twists and six cottages.

'It's ill for a child away from her mammy,' murmured Sarah under her breath.

Her own eyes filled with tears.

It was not till Sarah died some fourteen years later that it was discovered that the superior and refined niece who occasionally came to visit her aunt was in reality Sarah's daughter, the 'fruit of sin', as in Sarah's young days the term went. The mistress she served for over sixty years had had no idea of the fact, desperately concealed from her. The only thing she could remember was an illness of Sarah's that had delayed her return from one of her rare holidays. That and the fact that she was unusually thin on her return. What agonies of concealment, of tight lacing, of secret desperation Sarah had gone through must forever remain a mystery. She kept her secret till death revealed it.

COMMENT BY J.L.

It's odd how words — casual, unconnected words — can make a thing live in your imagination. I'm convinced that I see all these people much more clearly than Celia did as she was telling me about them. I can visualize that old grandmother — so vigorous, so much of her generation, with her Rabelaisian tongue, her bullying of her servants, her kindness to the poor sewing woman. I can see further back still to her mother — that delicate, lovable creature 'enjoying her month'. Note, too, the difference of description between male and female. The wife dies of a decline, the husband of galloping consumption. The ugly word tuberculosis never intrudes. Women decline, men gallop to death. Note, too, for it is amusing, the vigour of these consumptive parents' progeny. Of those ten children, so Celia told me when I asked her, only three died early and those were accidental deaths, a sailor of yellow fever, a sister in a carriage accident, another sister in childbed. Seven of them reached the age of seventy. Do we really know anything about heredity?

It pleases me, that picture of a house with its Nottingham lace and its woolwork and its solid shining mahogany furniture. It has backbone. They knew what they wanted, that generation. They got it and they enjoyed it, and they took a keen, full-blooded active pleasure in the art of self-preservation.

You notice that Celia pictures that house, her grandmother's, far more clearly than her own home. She must have gone there just at the noticing age. Her home is more people than place — Nannie, Rouncy, the bouncing Susan, Goldie in his cage.

Then her discovery of her mother — funny, it seems, that she should not have discovered her before.

For Miriam, I think, had a very vivid personality. The glimpses I get of Miriam enchant me. She had, I fancy, a charm that Celia did not inherit. Even between the conventional lines of her letter to her little girl (such 'period pieces' those letters, full of stress on the moral attitude) — even, as I say, between the

94

conventional admonitions to goodness, a trace of the real Miriam peeps out. I like the endearment — precious lamb, pigeony pumpkin — and the caress — the short, sharp hug. Not a maudlin or a demonstrative woman — an impulsive one — a woman with strange flashes of intuitive understanding.

The father is dimmer. He appeared to Celia as a brown-bearded giant — lazy, good-humoured, full of fun. He sounds unlike his mother — probably took after his father, who is represented in Celia's narrative by a crown of wax flowers under glass. He was, I fancy, a friendly soul whom everybody liked — more popular than Miriam — but without her quality of enchantment. Celia, I think, took after him. Her placidity, her even temper, her sweetness.

But she inherited something from Miriam — a dangerous intensity of affection.

That's how I see it. But perhaps I invent . . . These people have, after all, become my creations.

4

Death

1

Celia was going home!

The excitement of it!

The train journey seemed endless. Celia had a nice book to read, they had the carriage to themselves — but her impatience made the whole thing seem interminable.

'Well,' said her father. 'Glad to be going home, poppet?'

He gave her a playful little nip as he spoke. How big and brown he looked — much bigger than Celia had thought. Her mother, on the other hand, was much smaller. Queer the way that shapes and sizes seemed to alter.

'Yes, Daddy, very pleased,' said Celia.

She spoke primly. This queer swelling, aching feeling inside wouldn't let her do anything else.

Her father looked a little disappointed. Her cousin Lottie, who was coming to stay with them and who was travelling with them, said:

'What a solemn little mite it is!'

Her father said:

'Oh, well, a child soon forgets . . . '

His face looked wistful.

Miriam said: 'She hasn't forgotten a bit. She's just boiling over inside.'

And she reached out her hand and gave Celia's a little squeeze. Her eyes smiled into Celia's — as though they two had a secret shared between them.

Cousin Lottie, who was plump and attractive, said:

'She hasn't much sense of humour, has she?'

'None at all,' said Miriam. 'No more have I,' she added ruefully. 'At least, John says I haven't.'

Celia murmured.

'Mummy, will it be soon — will it be soon, Mummy?'

'Will what be soon, pet?'

Celia breathed: 'The sea.'

'In about five minutes now.'

'I expect she'd like to live by the seaside and play on the sands,' said Cousin Lottie.

Celia did not speak. How to explain? The sea was the sign that one was getting near home.

The train ran into a tunnel and out again. Ah, there it was, dark blue and sparkling, on the left hand side of the train. They were running along beside it, popping in and out of tunnels. Blue, blue sea — so dazzling that it made Celia shut her eyes involuntarily.

Then the train twisted away inland. Very soon now they would be *Home*!

2

Sizes again! Home was enormous! Simply enormous! Great big rooms with hardly any furniture in them — or so it seemed to Celia after the house at Wimbledon. It was all so exciting she hardly knew what to do first . . .

The garden — yes, first of all it must be the garden. She ran madly along the steep path. There was the Beech Tree — funny she'd never thought about the Beech Tree before. It was almost the most important part of home. And there was the little arbour with the seat in the laurustinus — oh! it was nearly overgrown. Now to go up to the wood — perhaps the bluebells would be out. But they weren't. Perhaps they were over. There was the tree with the forked branch that you played Queen-in-hiding on. Oh! Oh! Oh! there was the Little White Boy.

The Little White Boy stood in an arbour in the wood. Three rustic steps led up to him. He carried a stone basket on his head, and into this basket you placed an offering and made a wish.

Celia had indeed quite a ritual. The proceedings were as follows. You started from the house and crossed the lawn, which was a flowing river. Then you tethered your river horse to the rose arch, picked your offering, and proceeded solemnly up the path to the wood. You made your offering and wished and dropped a curtsey and backed away. And your wish would come true. Only you mustn't have more than one wish a week. Celia had always wished the same wish — inspired by Nannie. Wishbones, boy in wood, piebald horse, it was always the same — she wished to be good! It wasn't right, Nannie said, to wish for *things*. The Lord would send you what was necessary for you to have, and since God had behaved with great generosity in the matter (via Grannie and Mummy and Daddy) Celia adhered honourably to her pious wish.

Now she thought: 'I must, I must, I must, I simply *must* bring him an offering.' She would do it the old way — across the river of the lawn on the sea horse, tether the horse to the rose arch, now up the path, and now lay the offering — two ragged dandelions, in the basket and wish . . .

But alas, shades of Nannie, Celia forsook that pious aspiration which had been hers so long.

'I want to be always happy,' wished Celia.

Then to the kitchen garden — ah! there was Rumbolt, the gardener — very gloomy-looking and cross.

'Hullo, Rumbolt, I've come home.'

'So I see, missie. And I'll trouble you not to stand on the young lettuces as you're doing at the minute.'

Celia shifted her feet.

'Are there any gooseberries to eat, Rumbolt?'

'They're over. Poor crop this year. There might be a raspberry or two — '

'Oh!' Celia danced off.

'But don't you be eating them all,' called Rumbolt after her. 'I want a nice dish for dessert.'

Celia was moving between the raspberry canes eating vigorously. A raspberry or two — why, there were hundreds!

With a final sigh of repletion Celia abandoned the raspberries. Next to visit her private niche by the wall looking down on the road. It was hard now to find the entrance to it, but she got it at last —

Next, to the kitchen and Rouncy. Rouncy looking very clean and larger than ever, her jaws, as always, moving rhythmically. Dear, dear Rouncy, smiling as though her face was cut in two, giving the old soft throaty chuckle . . .

'Well, I never, Miss Celia, you have got a big girl.'

'What are you eating, Rouncy?'

'I've just been making some rock cakes for the kitchen tea.'

'Oh! Rouncy, give me one!'

' 'Twill spoil your tea.'

Not a real protest that. Rouncy's bulk is moving towards the oven even as she speaks. She whips open the oven door.

'They're just done. Now, mind, Miss Celia, it's *hot*.'

Oh, lovely home! Back into the cool dim corridors of the house, and there, through the landing window, the green glow of the beech tree.

Her mother, coming out of her bedroom, found Celia standing ecstatically at the top of the stairs, her hands pressed firmly to her middle.

'What is it, child? Why are you holding your tummy?'

'It's the Beech Tree, Mummy. It's so beautiful.'

'I believe you feel everything in your tummy, Celia.'

'I get a sort of queer pain there. Not a *real* pain, Mummy, a sort of nice pain.'

100

'Then you're glad to be home again?'
'Oh, *Mummy*!'

3

'Rumbolt's gloomier than ever,' said Celia's father at breakfast.

'Oh, how I hate having that man,' cried Miriam. 'I wish we hadn't got him.'

'Well, my dear, he's a first-class gardener. The best gardener we've ever had. Look at the peaches last year.'

'I know. I know. But I never wanted him.'

Celia had hardly ever heard her mother so vehement. Her hands were pressed together. Her father was looking at her indulgently, rather in the same way that he looked at Celia herself.

'Well, I gave in to you, didn't I?' he said good-humouredly. 'I turned him down in spite of his references and took that lazy lout of a Spinaker instead.'

'It seems so extraordinary,' said Miriam. 'My dislike of him, and then our letting the house when we went to Pau, and Mr Rogers writing that Spinaker had given notice and that he was getting another gardener who had excellent references, and coming home to find this man installed, after all.'

'I can't think why you don't like him, Miriam. He's a little on the sad side, but a perfectly decent fellow.'

Miriam shivered.

'I don't know what it is. It's *something*.'

Her eyes stared out in front of her.

The parlourmaid entered the room.

'Please, sir, Mrs Rumbolt would like to speak to you. She's at the front door.'

'What does she want? Oh, well, I'd better go and see.'

He flung down his table napkin, went out. Celia was staring at her mother. How very funny Mummy looked — as though she were very frightened.

Her father came back.

'Seems Rumbolt never went home last night. Odd business. They've had several rows lately, I fancy.'

He turned to the parlourmaid who was in the room.

'Is Rumbolt here this morning?'

'I haven't seen him, sir. I'll ask Mrs Rouncewell.'

Her father left the room again. It was five minutes before he returned. As he opened the door and came in, Miriam uttered an exclamation, and even Celia was startled.

Daddy looked so queer — so very queer — like an old man. He seemed to have difficulty in getting his breath.

Like a flash her mother had jumped up off her seat and run round to him.

'John, John, what is it? Tell me. Sit down. You've had some terrible shock.'

Her father had gone a queer blue colour. He gasped out words with difficulty.

'Hanging — in the stable . . . I've cut him

down — but there's no — he must have done it last night . . . '

'The shock — it's so bad for you.' Her mother jumped up, fetched the brandy from the sideboard.

She cried:

'I knew — I *knew* there was *something* — '

She knelt down beside her husband, holding the brandy to his lips. Her glance caught Celia.

'Run upstairs, darling, to Jeanne. It's nothing to be frightened about. Daddy's not feeling very well.' She murmured in a lower tone to him: 'She mustn't know. That sort of thing might haunt a child for life.'

Very puzzled, Celia left the room. On the landing upstairs Doris and Susan were talking together.

'Carried on with her, he did, so they say, and his wife got wind of it. Well, it's always the quietest are the worst.'

'Did you see him? Was his tongue hanging out?'

'No, the master said no one was to go there. I wonder if I could get a bit of the rope — they say it's ever so lucky.'

'The master had a proper shock, and him with a weak heart and all.'

'Well, it's an awful thing to happen.'

'What's happened?' asked Celia.

'Gardener's hanged himself in the stables,' said Susan with relish.

'Oh!' said Celia not very impressed. 'Why do you want a bit of the rope?'

'If you have a bit of the rope a man's hanged

himself with it brings you luck all your life through.'

'That's so,' agreed Doris.

'Oh!' said Celia again.

She accepted Rumbolt's death as just one more of those facts that happened every day. She was not fond of Rumbolt, who had never been particularly nice to her.

That evening when her mother came to tuck her up in bed, she asked:

'Mummy, can I have a bit of the rope Rumbolt hanged himself with?'

'Who told you about Rumbolt?' Her mother's voice sounded angry. 'I gave particular orders.'

Celia's eyes opened very wide.

'Susan told me. Mummy, can I have a bit of the rope? Susan says it's very lucky.'

Suddenly her mother smiled — the smile deepened into a laugh.

'What are you laughing at, Mummy?' asked Celia suspiciously.

'Because it's so long since I was nine years old that I've forgotten what it feels like.'

Celia puzzled a little before she went to sleep. Susan had once been nearly drowned when she went to the sea for a holiday. The other servants had laughed and said: 'You're born to be hanged, my girl.'

Hanging and drowning — there must be some connection between them . . .

'I'd much, much, much rather be drowned,' thought Celia sleepily.

Darling Grannie [wrote Celia the next day]:

Thank you so much for sending me the Pink Fairy book. It is very good of you. Goldie is well and sends his love. Please give my love to Sarah and Mary and Kate and Poor Miss Bennett. There is an Iceland poppy come out in my garden. The gardener hanged himself in the stable yesterday. Daddy is in bed but not very ill Mummy says. Rouncy is going to let me make twists and cottages too.

Lots and lots and lots of love and kisses from
Celia.

4

Celia's father died when she was ten years old. He died in his mother's house at Wimbledon. He had been in bed for several months, and there had been two hospital nurses in the house. Celia had got used to Daddy being ill. Her mother was always talking of what they would do when Daddy was better.

That Daddy could *die* had never entered her head. She had just been coming up the stairs when the door of the sick-room opened and her mother came out. A mother she had never seen before . . .

Long afterwards she thought of it like a leaf driven before the wind. Her mother's arms were thrown up to heaven, she was moaning, and then she burst open the door of her own room and disappeared within. A nurse followed her out on to the landing, where Celia was staring open-mouthed.

'What has happened to Mummy?'

'Hush, my dear. Your father — your father has gone to Heaven.'

'Daddy? Daddy dead and gone to Heaven?'

'Yes, now you must be a good little girl. Remember, you'll have to comfort your mother.'

The nurse disappeared into Miriam's room.

Stricken dumb, Celia wandered out into the garden. It took her a long time to take it in. Daddy. Daddy gone — dead . . .

Momentarily her world was shattered.

Daddy — and everything looked just the same. She shivered. It was like the Gun Man — everything all right and then *he* was there . . . She looked at the garden, the ash tree, the paths — all the same and yet, somehow different. *Things could change — things could happen* . . .

Was Daddy in Heaven now? Was he happy?

Oh, Daddy . . .

She began to cry.

She went into the house. Grannie was there — she was sitting in the dining-room; the blinds were all down. She was writing letters. Occasionally a tear ran down her cheek, and she attended to it with a handkerchief.

'Is that my poor little girl?' she said when she saw Celia. 'There, there, my dear, you mustn't fret. It's God's will.'

'Why are the blinds down?' asked Celia.

She didn't like the blinds being down — it made the house dark and queer, as though it too were different.

'It's a mark of respect,' said Grannie.

She began rummaging in her pocket and produced a blackcurrant and glycerine jujube of which she knew Celia was fond.

Celia took it and said thank you. But she did not eat. She did not feel it would go down properly.

She sat there holding it and watching Grannie.

Grannie went on writing — writing — letter after letter on black-edged notepaper.

5

For two days Celia's mother was very ill. The starched hospital nurse murmured phrases to Grannie.

'The long strain — wouldn't allow herself to believe — shock all the worse in the end — must be roused.'

They told Celia she could go in and see Mummy.

The room was darkened. Her mother lay on her side, her brown hair with its grey strands lying wildly all around her. Her eyes looked queer, very bright — they stared at something — something beyond Celia.

'Here's your dear little girl,' said the nurse in her high irritating '*I know best*' voice.

Mummy smiled at Celia then — but not a real smile — not the kind of smile as if Celia were really there.

Nurse had talked to Celia beforehand. So had Grannie.

Celia spoke in her prim good little girl's voice.

'Mummy, darling, Daddy's happy — he's in

Heaven. You wouldn't want to call him back.'

Suddenly her mother laughed.

'Oh, yes, I would! If I could call him back, I'd never stop calling — never — day or night. John — John, come back to me.'

She had raised herself up on one elbow, her face was wild and beautiful but strange.

The nurse hustled Celia out of the room. Celia heard her go back to the bed and say:

'You've got to live for your children, remember, my dear.'

And she heard her mother say in a strange docile voice:

'Yes, I've got to live for my children. You needn't tell me that. I know it.'

Celia went downstairs and into the drawing-room, to a place on the wall where there hung two coloured prints. They were called The Distressed Mother and The Happy Father. Of the latter, Celia did not think much. The ladylike person in the print did not look in the least like Celia's idea of a father — happy or otherwise. But the distraught woman, her hair flying, her arms clasping children in every direction — yes, that was how Mummy had looked. The Distressed Mother. Celia nodded her head with a kind of queer satisfaction.

6

Things happened rapidly — some of them rather exciting things — like being taken by Grannie to buy black clothes.

Celia couldn't help rather enjoying those black clothes. Mourning! She was in mourning! It sounded very important and grown up. She fancied people looking at her in the street. 'See that child all dressed in black?' 'Yes, she's just lost her father.' 'Oh! dear, how sad. Poor child.' And Celia would strut a little as she walked and droop her head sadly. She felt a little ashamed of feeling like this, but she couldn't help feeling an interesting and romantic figure.

Cyril was at home. He was very grown up now, but occasionally his voice did peculiar things, and then he blushed. He was gruff and uncomfortable. Sometimes there were tears in his eyes, but he was furious if you noticed them. He caught Celia preening herself in front of the glass in her new clothes and was openly contemptuous.

'That's all a kid like you thinks of. New clothes. Oh, well, I suppose you're too young to take things in.'

Celia cried and thought he was very unkind.

Cyril shrank from his mother. He got on better with Grannie. He played the man of the family to Grannie, and Grannie encouraged him. She consulted him about the letters she wrote and appealed to his judgment about various details.

Celia was not allowed to go to the funeral, which she thought very unfair. Grannie did not go either. Cyril went with his mother.

She came down for the first time on the morning of the funeral. She looked very unfamiliar to Celia in her widow's bonnet

— rather sweet and small — and — and — oh, yes, *helpless* looking.

Cyril was very manly and protective.

Grannie said: 'I've got a few white carnations here, Miriam. I thought perhaps you might like to throw them on the coffin as it is being lowered.'

But Miriam shook her head, and said in a low voice:

'No, I'd rather not do anything like that.'

After the funeral the blinds were pulled up, and life went on as usual.

7

Celia wondered whether Grannie really liked Mummy and whether Mummy really liked Grannie. She didn't quite know what put the idea into her head.

She felt unhappy about her mother. She moved about so quietly, so silently, speaking very little.

Grannie spent a long part of the day receiving letters and reading them. She would say:

'Miriam, I'm sure you'd like to hear this. Mr Pike speaks so feelingly of John.'

But her mother would wince back, and say: 'Please, no, not now.'

And Grannie's eyebrows would go up a little and she would fold the letter, saying dryly: 'As you please.'

But when the next post came in the same thing would happen.

'Mr Clark is a truly good man,' she would say, sniffing a little as she read. 'Miriam, you really should hear this. It would help you. He speaks so beautifully of how our dead are always with us.'

And suddenly roused from her quiescence Miriam would cry out:

'No, no!'

It was that sudden cry that made Celia feel she knew what her mother was feeling. Her mother wanted to be let alone.

One day a letter came with a foreign stamp on it . . . Miriam opened it and sat reading it — four sheets of delicate sloping handwriting. Grannie watched her.

'Is that from Louise?' she asked.

'Yes.'

There was silence. Grannie watched the letter hungrily.

'What does she say?' she asked at last.

Miriam was folding up the letter.

'I don't think it's meant for any one but me to see,' she said quietly. 'Louise — understands.'

That time Grannie's eyebrows rose right up into her hair.

A few days later Celia's mother went away with Cousin Lottie for a change. Celia stayed with Grannie for a month.

When Miriam came back, she and Celia went home.

And life began again — a new life. Celia and her mother alone in the big house and garden.

5

Mother and Daughter

1

Her mother explained to Celia that things would be rather different now. While Daddy was alive they had thought they were comparatively rich. But now that he was dead the lawyers had found out that there was very little money left.

'We shall have to live very, very simply. I ought really to sell this house and take a little cottage somewhere.'

'Oh, no, Mummy — no.'

Miriam smiled at her daughter's vehemence.

'Do you love it so much?'

'Oh, yes.'

Celia was terribly in earnest. Sell *Home?* Oh, she couldn't bear it.

'Cyril says the same . . . But I don't know that I'm wise . . . It will mean being very, very economical — '

'Oh, please, Mummy. Please — please — please.'

'Very well, darling. After all, it's a happy house.'

Yes, it was a happy house. Looking back after long years Celia acknowledged the truth of that remark. It had, somehow an atmosphere. Happy home and happy years spent in it.

There were changes, of course. Jeanne went back to France. A gardener came only twice a week just to keep the place tidy, and the hothouses fell gradually to pieces. Susan and the parlourmaid left. Rouncy remained. She was unemotional but firm.

Celia's mother argued with her. 'But you know it will be much harder work. I shall only be able to afford a house-parlourmaid and no outside help for the boots and knives.'

'I'm quite willing, ma'am. I don't like change. I'm used to my kitchen here, and it suits me.'

No hint of loyalty — of affection. The mere suggestion of such a thing would have embarrassed Rouncy very much.

So Rouncy remained at reduced wages, and sometimes, Celia realized afterwards, her staying tried Miriam more than her going would have done. For Rouncy had been trained in the grand school. For her the recipes beginning 'Take a pint of rich cream and a dozen fresh eggs.' To cook plainly and economically and give small orders to the tradespeople was beyond the reach of Rouncy's imagination. She still made sheets of rock cakes for the kitchen tea and threw whole loaves into the pig tub when they went stale. To give large and handsome orders to the tradespeople was a kind of pride with her. It reflected credit on the House. She suffered acutely when Miriam took the ordering out of her hands.

As house-parlourmaid there came an elderly woman called Gregg. Gregg had been parlourmaid to Miriam when the latter was first married.

'And as soon as I saw your advertisement in the paper, ma'am, I gave in my notice and came along. I've never been so happy anywhere as I was here.'

'It will be very different now, Gregg.'

But Gregg was determined to come. She was a first-class parlourmaid, but her skill in that direction was not tested. There were no more dinner parties. As a housemaid she was slapdash, indifferent to cobwebs and indulgent to dust.

She would regale Celia with long tales of the glories in past days.

'Twenty-four your Pa and Ma would sit down to dinner. Two soups, two fish courses, four entrees, a joint — a sorbee as they call it, two sweets, lobster salad, and an ice pudding!'

'Those were the days,' Gregg implied as she reluctantly brought in the macaroni au gratin that represented Miriam's and Celia's supper.

Miriam got interested in the garden. She knew nothing about gardening and did not trouble to learn. She just made experiments — and the experiments were crowned with wild and quite unjustifiable success. She put flowers and bulbs in at the wrong time of year and in the wrong depth of soil, she sowed seeds wildly. Everything she touched bloomed and lived.

'Your Ma's got the live hand,' said old Ash gloomily.

Old Ash was the jobbing gardener who came twice a week. He really knew something about gardening, but was unfortunately gifted with a dead hand. Anything he put in always died. His pruning was unlucky, and the things that didn't 'damp off' were victims of the 'early frost'. He gave Miriam advice which she did not take.

It was his earnest wish to cut up the slope of the lawn into 'Some nice beds — crescent shape and diamond, and have some nice bedding-out plants.' He was chagrined by Miriam's indignant refusal. When she said she liked the unbroken sweep of green he would reply: 'Well, beds look like a gentleman's place. You can't deny it.'

Celia and Miriam 'did' flowers for the house — vying with each other. They would make great tall bouquets of white flowers, trailing jasmine, sweet-scented syringas, white phlox, and stocks. Then Miriam had a passion for little exotic posies, cherry pie and sweet flat-faced pink roses.

The smell of old-fashioned pink roses reminded Celia of her mother all through her life.

It annoyed Celia that her own arrangements could never equal her mother's, however much time and trouble she took over them. Miriam could fling flowers together with a wild grace. Her arrangements were original — they were not at all in accord with the flower arrangements of the period.

Lessons were a haphazard arrangement. Miriam said Celia must go on with her arithmetic by herself. She was no good at it herself. Celia did so conscientiously, working through the little brown book that she had started with her father.

Every now and then she stuck in a bog of uncertainty — uncertain in a problem as to whether the answer would be in sheep or men.

The papering of rooms so bewildered her that she skipped it altogether.

Miriam had theories of her own as to education. She was a good teacher, clear in explanation, and able to arouse enthusiasm over any subject she selected.

She had a passion for history, and under her guidance Celia was swept from one event to another in the world's life story. The steady progression of English history bored Miriam, but Elizabeth, the Emperor Charles the Fifth, Francis the First of France, Peter the Great — all these became living personages to Celia. The splendour of Rome lived again. Carthage perished. Peter the Great strove to raise Russia from barbarism.

Celia loved being read aloud to, and Miriam would select books dealing with the various historical periods they were studying. She skipped shamelessly when reading aloud — she had a complete impatience for anything tedious. Geography was rather bound up with history. Other lessons they had none, except that Miriam did her best to improve Celia's spelling, which was, for a girl of her age, nothing short of disgraceful.

A German woman was engaged to teach Celia the piano, and she showed an immediate aptitude and love for the study, practising long beyond the time Fräulein had indicated.

Margaret McCrae had left the neighbourhood, but once a week the Maitlands came to tea — Ellie and Janet. Ellie was older than Celia, Janet younger. They played Colours and

Grandmother's Steps, and they founded a Secret Society called the Ivy. After inventing passwords, a peculiar handclasp, and writing messages in invisible ink, the Ivy Society rather languished.

There were also the little Pines.

They were thick children, with adenoidy voices, younger than Celia. Dorothy and Mabel. Their only idea in life was eating. They always ate too much and were usually sick before they left. Sometimes Celia would go to lunch with them. Mr Pine was a great fat red-faced man; his wife was tall and angular with a terrific black fringe. They were very affectionate, and they too were devoted to food.

'Percival, this mutton is delicious — really delicious.'

'A little more, my love. Dorothy, a little more?'

'Thank you, Papa.'

'Mabel?'

'No, thank you, Papa.'

'Come, come, what's this? This mutton is delicious.'

'We must congratulate Giles, my love.' (Giles was the butcher.)

Neither the Pines nor the Maitlands made much impression on Celia's life. The games she played by herself were still the most real games to her.

As her piano playing improved she would spend long hours in the big schoolroom, turning out old dusty piles of music and reading them. Old songs — 'Down the Vale', 'A Song of Sleep', 'Fiddle and I'. She would sing them, her voice rising clear and pure.

She was rather vain about her voice.

When small she had declared her intention of marrying a duke. Nannie had concurred on the condition that Celia learned to eat her dinner faster.

'Because, my dear, in the grand houses the butler would take away your plate long before you'd finished.'

'Would he?'

'Yes, in the grand houses, the butler comes round, and he takes everyone's plate away whether they've finished or not!'

After this Celia fairly bolted her food to get into training for the ducal life.

Now, for the first time, her intention wavered. Perhaps she wouldn't marry a duke after all. No, she would be a prima donna — somebody like Melba.

Celia still spent much of her time alone. Although she had the Maitlands and the Pines to tea — they were not nearly so real to her as 'the girls'.

'The girls' were creations of Celia's imagination. She knew all about them — what they looked like, what they wore, what they felt and thought.

First there was Ethelred Smith — who was tall and very dark and very, *very* clever. She was good at games, too. In fact, Ethel was good at everything. She had a decided 'figure' and wore striped shirts. Ethel was everything that Celia was not. She represented what Celia would like to be. Then there was Annie Brown. Ethel's great friend. She was fair and weak and 'delicate'.

Ethel helped her with her lessons, and Annie looked up to and admired Ethel. Next came Isabella Sullivan, who had red hair and brown eyes and was beautiful. She was rich and proud and unpleasant. She always thought that she was going to beat Ethel at croquet, but Celia saw to it that she didn't, though she felt rather mean sometimes when she deliberately made Isabella miss balls. Elsie Green was her cousin — her poor cousin. She had dark curls and blue eyes and was very merry.

Ella Graves and Sue de Vete were much younger — only seven. Ella was very serious and industrious, with bushy brown hair and a plain face. She often won the arithmetic prize, because she worked so hard. She was very fair, and Celia was never quite sure what she looked like, and her character was variable. Vera de Vete, Sue's half sister, was the romantic personality of 'the school'. She was fourteen. She had straw-coloured hair and deep forget-me-not blue eyes. There was mystery about her past — and in the end Celia knew that she would turn out to have been changed at birth and that she was really the Lady Vera, the daughter of one of the proudest noblemen in the land. There was a new girl — Lena, and one of Celia's favourite plays was to be Lena arriving at the school.

Miriam knew vaguely about 'the girls' but she never asked questions about them — for which Celia was passionately grateful. On wet days 'the girls' gave a concert in the schoolroom, different pieces being allotted to them. It annoyed Celia very much that her fingers stumbled over Ethel's piece, which she was anxious to play well, and that though she always allotted Isabella the most difficult, it went perfectly. 'The girls' played cribbage against each other also, and here again Isabella always seemed to have an annoying run of luck.

Sometimes, when Celia went to stay with Grannie, she was taken by her to a musical comedy. They would have a four-wheeler to the station then train to Victoria, four-wheeler to lunch at the Army and Navy Stores, where Grannie would do immense lists of shopping in the grocery with the special old man who always attended to her. Then they would go up to the restaurant and have lunch, finishing with 'a small cup of coffee in a large cup', so that plenty of milk could be added. Then they would go to the confectionery department and buy half a pound of chocolate coffee creams, and *then* into another four-wheeler and off to the theatre, which Grannie enjoyed every bit as much as Celia did.

Very often, afterwards, Grannie would buy Celia the score of the music. That opened up a new field of activity to 'the girls'. They now blossomed into musical comedy stars. Isabella and Vera had soprano voices — Isabella's was bigger, but Vera's was sweeter. Ethel had a magnificent contralto — Elsie had a pretty little voice. Annie, Ella, and Sue had unimportant parts, but Sue gradually developed into taking the soubrette roles. *The Country Girl* was Celia's favourite. 'Under the Deodars' seemed to her the loveliest song that had ever been written.

She sang it until she was hoarse. Vera was given the part of the Princess, so that she could sing it and the heroine's role given to Isabella. *The Cingalee* was another favourite, because it had a good part for Ethel.

Miriam, who suffered from headaches and whose bedroom was below the piano, at last forbade Celia to play for more than three hours on end.

2

At last Celia's early ambition was realized. She had an accordion-pleated dancing dress, and she stayed behind for the skirt-dancing class.

She was now one of the elect. She would no longer dance with Dorothy Pine who only wore a plain white party frock. The accordion-pleated girls only danced with each other — unless they were being self-consciously 'kind'. Celia and Janet Maitland paired off. Janet danced beautifully. They were engaged for the waltz in perpetuity. And they also partnered each other for the march, but there they were sometimes torn apart, since Celia was a head and a half taller than Janet, and Miss Mackintosh liked her marching pairs to look symmetrical. The polka it was the fashion to dance with the little ones. Each elder girl took a tot. Six girls stayed behind for skirt dancing. It was a source of bitter disappointment to Celia that she always remained in the second row. Janet, Celia did not mind, because Janet danced better than anyone else, but Daphne danced badly and made lots of mistakes. Celia always felt it was very unfair, and the true solution of the mystery, that Miss Mackintosh put the shorter girls in front and the taller ones behind, never once occurred to her.

Miriam was quite as excited as Celia over what colour her accordion pleat should be. They had a long earnest discussion, taking into account what the other girls wore, and in the end they decided on a flame-coloured one. Nobody else had ever had a dress of that colour. Celia was enchanted.

Since her husband's death Miriam went out and entertained very little. She 'kept up' only with such people as had children of Celia's age, and a few old friends. All the same, the ease with which she dropped out of things made her a little bitter. The difference that money made. All those people who hadn't been able to make fuss enough of her and John! Nowadays they hardly remembered her existence. She didn't care for herself — she had always been a shy woman. It was for John's sake that she had been sociable. He loved people coming to the house; he loved going out. He had never guessed that Miriam hated it, so well had she played her part. She was relieved now, but all the same, she felt resentful on Celia's account. When the child grew up she would want social things.

The evenings were some of the happiest times mother and daughter spent together. They had supper early, at seven, and afterwards would go up to the schoolroom, and Celia would do fancy work, and her mother would read to her. Reading aloud would make Miriam sleepy. Her voice would go queer and blurry, her head would tilt forward . . .

'Mummy,' Celia would say accusingly, 'you're going to sleep.'

'I'm not,' Miriam would declare indignantly. She would sit very upright and read very clearly and distinctly for a couple of pages. Then she would say suddenly:

'I believe you're right,' and, shutting the book, she would drop fast asleep.

She only slept for about three minutes. Then she would wake up and start off again with renewed vigour.

Sometimes Miriam would tell stories of her early life instead of reading. Of how she had come, a distant cousin, to live with Grannie.

'My mother had died, and there was no money afterwards, so Grannie very kindly offered to adopt me.'

She was a little cool about the kindness, perhaps — a coolness that showed in tone, not in words. It masked a memory of childish loneliness, of a longing for her own mother. She had been ill at last, and the doctor called in. He had said: 'This child is fretting about something.' 'Oh, no,' Grannie had answered positively. 'She's quite a happy, merry little thing.' The doctor had said nothing, but when Grannie had gone out of the room he had sat on the bed talking to her in a kindly, confidential manner, and she had suddenly broken down and admitted to long bouts of weeping in bed at night.

Grannie had been very astonished when he had told her.

'Why, she never said anything to me about it.'

And after that, it had been better. Just the telling seemed to have taken the ache away.

'And then there was your father.' How her voice softened. 'He was always kind to me.'

'Tell me about Daddy.'

'He was grown up — eighteen. He didn't come home very often. He didn't like his stepfather very much.'

'And did you love him at once?'

'Yes, from the very first moment I saw him. I grew up loving him . . . I never dreamt he'd ever think of me.'

'Didn't you?'

'No. You see, he was always going about with smart grown-up girls. He was a great flirt — and then he was supposed to be a very good match. I was always expecting him to get married to someone else. He was very kind to me when he came — used to bring me flowers and sweets and brooches. I was just 'little Miriam' to him. I think he was pleased by my being so devoted to him. He told me once that an old lady, the mother of one of his friends, said to him, 'I think, John, you will marry the little cousin.' And he had said, laughing, 'Miriam? Why, she's only a child.' He was rather in love with a very handsome girl then. But somehow or other, it came to nothing . . . I was the only woman he ever asked to marry him . . . I remember — I used to think that if he married I should perhaps lie on a sofa pining away, and nobody would know what was the matter with me! I should just gradually fade away! That was the regular romantic idea in my young days — hopeless love — and lying on a sofa. I would die, and no one would ever know until they found a packet of his letters with pressed forget-me-nots in them all bound up in blue ribbon. All very silly — but I don't know, somehow — it helped — all that imagining . . .

'I remember the day when your father said suddenly, 'What lovely eyes the child has got.' I was so startled. I'd always thought I was terribly plain. I climbed up on a chair and stared and stared at myself in the glass to see what he had meant. In the end I thought perhaps my eyes *were* rather nice . . . '

'When did Daddy ask you to marry him?'

'I was twenty-two. He'd been away for a year. I'd sent him a Christmas card and a poem that I'd written for him. He kept that poem in his pocketbook. It was there when he died . . .

'I can't tell you how surprised I was when he asked me. I said, No.'

'But, Mummy, *why*?'

'It's difficult to explain . . . I'd been brought up to be very diffident about myself. I felt that I was 'dumpy' — not a tall, handsome person. I felt, perhaps, he'd be disappointed in me once we were married. I was dreadfully modest about myself.'

'And then Uncle Tom — ' prompted Celia who knew this part of the story almost as well as Miriam.

Her mother smiled.

'Yes, Uncle Tom. We were down in Sussex with Uncle Tom at the time. He was an old man then

— but very wise — very kindly. I was playing the piano, I remember, and he was sitting by the fire. He said: 'Miriam, John's asked you to marry him, hasn't he? And you've refused him.' I said, 'Yes.' 'But you love him, Miriam?' I said, 'Yes,' again. 'Don't say No next time,' he said. 'He'll ask you once more, but he won't ask you a third time. He's a good man, Miriam. Don't throw away your happiness.' '

'And he did ask you, and you said 'Yes.' '

Miriam nodded.

She had that kind of starry look in her eyes that Celia knew well.

'Tell me how you came to live here.'

That was another well-known tale.

Miriam smiled.

'We were staying down here in rooms. We had two young babies — your little sister Joy, who died, and Cyril. Your father had to go abroad to India on business. He couldn't take me with him. We decided that this was a very pleasant place and that we'd take a house for a year. I went about looking for one with Grannie.

'When your father came home to lunch, I said to him, 'John, I bought a house.' He said, '*What?*' Grannie said, 'It's all right, John, it will be quite a good investment.' You see, Grannie's husband, your father's stepfather, had left me a little money of my own. The only house I saw that I liked was this one. It was so peaceful — so happy. But the old lady who owned it wouldn't let — she would only sell. She was a Quaker — very sweet and gentle. I said to Grannie, 'Shall I buy it with my money?'

'Grannie was my trustee. She said, 'House property is a good investment. Buy it.'

'The old Quaker lady was so sweet. She said, 'I think of thee, my dear, being very happy here. Thee and thy husband, and thy children . . . ' It was like a blessing.'

How like her mother — that suddenness, that quick decision.

Celia said:

'And I was born here?'

'Yes.'

'Oh, Mother, don't let's ever sell it . . . '

Miriam sighed.

'I don't know if I've been wise . . . But you love it so . . . And perhaps — it will be something — always — for you to come back to . . . '

3

Cousin Lottie came to stay. She was married now and had a house of her own in London. But she needed a change and country air, so Miriam said.

Cousin Lottie was certainly not well. She stayed in bed and was terribly sick.

She talked vaguely about some food that had upset her.

'But she ought to be better now,' urged Celia, as a week passed and Cousin Lottie was still sick.

When you were 'upset' you had castor oil and stayed in bed, and the next day or the day after you were better.

Miriam looked at Celia with a funny

127

expression on her face. A sort of half-guilty, half-smiling look.

'Darling, I think I'd better tell you. Cousin Lottie is sick because she is going to have a baby.'

Celia had never been so astonished in her life. Since the dispute with Marguerite Priestman she had never thought of the baby question again.

She asked eager questions.

'But why does it make you sick? When will it be here? Tomorrow?'

Her mother laughed.

'Oh! No, not till next autumn.'

She told her more — how long a baby took to come — something of the process. It all seemed most astonishing to Celia — quite the most remarkable thing she had ever heard.

'Only don't talk about it before Cousin Lottie. You see, little girls aren't supposed to know about these things.'

Next day Celia came to her mother in great excitement.

'Mummy, Mummy, I've had a most exciting dream. I dreamt Grannie was going to have a baby. Do you think it will come true? Shall we write and ask her?'

She was astonished when her mother laughed.

'Dreams do come true,' she said reproachfully. 'It says so in the Bible.'

4

Her excitement over Cousin Lottie's baby lasted for a week. She still had a sneaking hope that the baby might arrive now and not next autumn. After all, Mummy might be wrong.

Then Cousin Lottie returned to town, and Celia forgot about it. It was quite a surprise to her the following autumn when she was staying with Grannie when old Sarah came suddenly out into the garden, saying: 'Your Cousin Lottie's got a little baby boy. Isn't that nice now?'

Celia had rushed into the house where Grannie was sitting with a telegram in her hand talking to Mrs Mackintosh, a crony of hers.

'Grannie, Grannie,' cried Celia, 'has Cousin Lottie really got a baby? How big is it?'

With great decision Grannie measured off the baby's size on her knitting pin — the big knitting pin — since she was making night socks.

'Only as long as that?' It seemed incredible.

'My sister Jane was so small she was put in a soap box,' said Grannie.

'A soap box, Grannie?'

'They never thought she'd live,' said Grannie with relish, adding to Mrs Mackintosh in a lowered voice, 'Five months.'

Celia sat quietly trying to visualize a baby of the required smallness.

'What kind of soap?' she asked presently, but Grannie did not answer. She was busy talking to Mrs Mackintosh in a low, hushed voice.

'You see, the doctors disagreed about Charlotte. Let the labour come on — that's what the specialist said. Forty-eight hours — the cord — actually round the neck . . . '

Her voice dropped lower and lower. She shot a glance at Celia and stopped.

What a funny way Grannie had of saying things. It made them sound, somehow, exciting . . . She had a funny way, too, of looking at you. As though there were all sorts of things she could tell you, if she liked.

5

When she was fifteen Celia became religious again. It was a different religion this time, very high church. She was confirmed, and she also heard the Bishop of London preach. She was seized immediately by a romantic devotion for him. A picture postcard of him was placed on her mantelpiece, and she scanned the newspapers eagerly for any mention of him. She wove long stories in which she worked in East End parishes, visiting the sick, and one day he noticed her, and finally they were married and went to live at Fulham Palace. In the alternative story she became a nun — there were nuns who weren't Roman Catholics, she had discovered — and she lived a life of great holiness and had visions.

After she was confirmed, she read a good deal in various little books and went to early church every Sunday. She was pained because her mother would not come with her. Miriam only went to church on Whitsunday. Whitsunday was to her the great festival of the Christian Church.

'The holy spirit of God,' she said. 'Think of it, Celia. That is the great wonder and mystery and beauty of God. The prayer books shy at it, and clergymen hardly ever speak about it. They're afraid to, because they are not sure what it is. The Holy Ghost.'

Miriam worshipped the Holy Ghost. It made Celia feel rather uncomfortable. Miriam didn't like churches much. Some of them, she said, had more of the Holy Spirit than others. It depended on the people who went there to worship, she said.

Celia, who was firmly and strictly orthodox, was distressed. She didn't like her mother being unorthodox. There was something of the mystic about Miriam. She had a vision, a perception of unseen things. It was on a par with her disconcerting habit of knowing what you were thinking.

Celia's vision of becoming the wife of the Bishop of London faded. She thought more and more about being a nun.

She thought at last that perhaps she had better break it to her mother. She was afraid her mother would, perhaps, be unhappy. But Miriam took the news very calmly.

'I see, darling.'

'You don't mind, Mummy?'

'No, darling. If, when you are twenty-one, you want to be a nun, of course you shall be one . . . '

Perhaps, Celia thought, she would become a Roman Catholic. Roman Catholic nuns were, somehow, more real.

Miriam said she thought the Roman Catholic religion a very fine one.

'Your father and I nearly became Catholics

once. Very nearly.' She smiled suddenly. 'I nearly dragged him into it. Your father was a good man — as simple as a child — quite happy in his own religion. It was I who was always discovering religions and urging him to take them up. I thought it mattered very much what religion you were.'

Celia thought that of course it mattered. But she did not say so, because if she did her mother would begin about the Holy Ghost, and Celia rather fought shy of the Holy Ghost. The Holy Ghost did not come much into any of the little books. She thought of the time when she would be a nun praying in her cell . . .

6

It was soon after that that Miriam told Celia it was time for her to go to Paris. It had always been understood that Celia was to be 'finished' in Paris. She was rather excited at the prospect.

She was well educated as to history and literature. She had been allowed and encouraged to read anything she chose. She was also thoroughly conversant with the topics of the day. Miriam insisted on her reading such newspaper articles as she thought essential to what she called 'general knowledge'. Arithmetic had been solved by her going twice a week to the local school for instruction in that subject for which she had always had a natural liking.

Of geometry, Latin, algebra, and grammar she knew nothing at all. Her geography was sketchy, being confined to the knowledge acquired through books of travel.

In Paris she would study singing, piano playing, drawing and painting, and French.

Miriam selected a place near the Avenue du Bois which took twelve girls and which was run by an Englishwoman and a Frenchwoman in partnership.

Miriam went to Paris with her and stayed until she was sure her child was going to be happy. After four days Celia had a violent attack of homesickness for her mother. At first she didn't know what was the matter with her — this queer lump in the throat — these tears that came into her eyes whenever she thought of her mother. If she put on a blouse her mother had made for her, the tears would come into her eyes as she thought of her mother stitching at it. On the fifth day she was to be taken out by her mother.

She went down outwardly calm but inwardly in a turmoil. No sooner were they outside and in the cab going to the hotel than Celia burst into tears.

'Oh, Mummy — Mummy.'

'What is it, darling? Aren't you happy? If you're not, I'll take you away.'

'I don't want to be taken away. I like it. It was just I wanted to see you.'

Half an hour later her recent misery seemed dreamlike and unreal. It was rather like seasickness. Once you recovered from it, you couldn't remember what you had felt like.

The feeling did not return. Celia waited for it, nervously studying her own feelings. But, no

— she loved her mother — adored her, but the mere thought of her no longer made a lump come in her throat.

One of the girls, an American, Maisie Payne, came up to her and said in her soft drawling voice:

'I hear you've been feeling lonesome. My mother's staying at the same hotel as yours. Are you feeling better now?'

'Yes, I'm all right now. It was silly.'

'Well, I reckon it was kind of natural.'

Her soft drawling voice reminded Celia of her friend in the Pyrenees, Marguerite Priestman. She felt a little tremor of gratitude towards this big black-haired creature. It was increased when Maisie said:

'I saw your mother at the hotel. She's very pretty. And more than pretty — she's kind of distanguay.'

Celia thought about her mother, seeing her objectively for the first time — her small eager face, her tiny hands and feet, her small delicate ears, her thin high-bridged nose.

Her mother — oh, there was no one like her mother in the whole world!

6

Paris

1

Celia stayed for a year in Paris. She enjoyed the time there very much. She liked the other girls, though none of them seemed very real to her. Maisie Payne might have done so, but she left the Easter after Celia arrived. Her best friend was a big fat girl called Bessie West who had the next room to hers. Bessie was a great talker, and Celia was a good listener, and they both indulged in a passion for eating apples. Bessie told long tales of her escapades and adventures between bites of apple — the stories always ending 'and then my hair came down'.

'I like you, Celia,' she said one day. 'You're sensible.'

'Sensible?'

'You're not always going on about boys and things. People like Mabel and Pamela get on my nerves. Every time I have a violin lesson they giggle and snigger and pretend I'm sweet on old Franz or he's sweet on me. I call that sort of thing common. I like a rag with the boys as well as anyone, but not all this idiotic sniggering business about the music masters.'

Celia, who had outgrown her passion for the Bishop of London, was now in the throes of one

135

for Mr Gerald du Maurier ever since she had seen him in *Alias Jimmy Valentine*. But it was a secret passion of which she never spoke.

The other girl she liked was one whom Bessie usually referred to as 'the Moron'.

Sybil Swinton was nineteen, a big girl with beautiful brown eyes and a mass of chestnut hair. She was extremely amiable and extremely stupid. She had to have everything explained to her twice. The piano was her great cross. She was bad at reading music, and she had no ear to hear when she played wrong notes. Celia would sit patiently beside her for an hour saying, 'No, Sybil, a sharp — your left hand's wrong now — D natural now. Oh, Sybil, can't you *hear?*' But Sybil couldn't. Her people were anxious for her to 'play the piano' like other girls, and Sybil did her best, but music lessons were a nightmare — incidentally they were a nightmare for the teacher also. Madame LeBrun, who was one of the two teachers who visited, was a little old woman with white hair and claw-like hands. She sat very close to you when you played so that your right arm was slightly impeded. She was very keen on sight-reading and used to produce big books of duets *a quatre mains*. Alternately you played the treble or the bass, and Madame LeBrun played the other. Things went most happily when Madame LeBrun was at the treble end of the piano. So immersed was she in her own performance that it would be some time before she discovered that her pupil was playing the accompanying bass some bars in front or behind herself. Then there would be an outcry '*Mais qu'est-ce que vous jouez là, ma petite? C'est affreux — c'est tout ce qu'il y a de plus affreux!*'

Nevertheless, Celia enjoyed her lessons. She enjoyed them still more when she was transferred to M. Kochter. M. Kochter took only those girls who showed talent. He was delighted with Celia. Seizing her hands and pulling the fingers mercilessly apart he would cry, 'You see the stretch here? This is the hand of a pianist. Nature is in your favour, Mademoiselle Celia. Now let us see what you can do to assist her.' M. Kochter himself played beautifully. He gave a concert twice a year in London, so he told Celia. Chopin, Beethoven, and Brahms were his favourite masters. He would usually give Celia a choice as to what she learnt. He inspired her with such enthusiasm that she willingly practised the six hours a day he required. Practising was no real fatigue to her. She loved the piano. It had been her friend always.

For singing lessons Celia went to M. Barré — an ex-operatic singer. She had a very high, clear soprano voice.

'Your high notes are excellent,' said M. Barré. 'They could not be better produced. That is the *voix de tête*. The low notes, the chest notes, they are too weak but not bad. It is the *médium* that we must improve. The *médium*, mademoiselle, comes from the roof of the mouth.'

He produced a tape measure.

'Let us now test the diaphragm. Breathe in — hold it — hold it now let the breath expire suddenly. Capital — capital. You have the breath of a singer.'

He handed her a pencil.

'Place that between the teeth — so — in the corner of the mouth. And do not let it fall out when you sing. You can pronounce every word and retain the pencil. Do not say that it is impossible.'

On the whole M. Barré was satisfied with her.

'But your French, it puzzles me. It is not the usual French with the English accent — ah, how I have suffered from that — *Mon Dieu*! nobody knows! No, it is, one would swear, an accent *méridional* that you have. Where did you learn French?'

Celia told him.

'Oh, and your maid she came from the South of France? That explains it. Well, well, we will soon get out of that.'

Celia worked hard at her singing. On the whole she pleased him, but occasionally he would rail at her English face.

'You are like all the rest of the English, you think that to sing is to open the mouth as wide as possible and let the voice come out! Not at all — there is the skin — the skin of the face — all round the mouth. You are not a little choir boy — you are singing the Habanera of Carmen which, by the way, you have brought me in the wrong key. This is transposed for soprano — an operatic song should always be sung in its original key — anything else is an abomination and an insult to the composer — remember that. I particularly want you to learn a mezzo song.

138

Now then, you are Carmen, you have a rose in your mouth, not a pencil, you are singing a song that is meant to allure this young man. Your face — your face — do not let your face be of wood.'

The lesson ended with Celia in tears. Barré was kind.

'There, there — it is not your song. No, I see it is not your song. You shall sing the 'Jerusalem' of Gounod. The 'Alléluia' from the Cid. Some day we will return to Carmen.'

Music occupied the time of most of the girls. There was an hour's French every morning, that was all. Celia, who could speak much more fluent and idiomatic French than any of the others, was always horribly humiliated at French. In dictation, while the other girls had two, three, or at most five faults, she would have twenty-five or thirty. In spite of reading innumerable French books, she had no idea of the spelling. Also she wrote much slower than the others. Dictation was a nightmare to her.

Madame would say:

'But it is impossible — *impossible* — that you should have so many faults, Celia! Do you not even know what a past participle is?'

Alas, that was exactly what Celia did not know.

Twice a week she and Sybil went to their painting lesson. Celia grudged the time taken from the piano. She hated drawing, and painting even worse. Flower painting was what the two girls were learning.

Oh, miserable bunch of violets in a glass of water!

'The shadows, Celia, put in the shadows first.'

But Celia could never see the shadows. Her best hope was surreptitiously to look at Sybil's painting and try to make hers look like it.

'You seem to see where these beastly shadows are, Sybil. I don't — I never do. It's just a blob of lovely purple.'

Sybil was not particularly talented, but certainly at painting it was Celia who was 'the Moron'.

Something deep down in her hated this copying business — this tearing the secrets out of flowers and scratching and blobbing it down on paper. Violets should be left to grow in gardens or arranged droopingly in glasses. This making something out of something else — it went against her.

'I don't see why you've got to draw things,' she said to Sybil one day. 'They're there already.'

'What do you mean?'

'I don't know quite how to say it, but why make things that are like other things? It's such a waste. If one could draw a flower that didn't exist — imagine one — then it might be worth while.'

'You mean make up a flower out of your head?'

'Yes, but even then it wouldn't be right. I mean it would still be a flower, and you wouldn't have made a flower — you'd have made a thing on paper.'

'But, Celia, pictures, real pictures, art — they're very beautiful.'

'Yes, of course — at least — ' She stopped. 'Are they?'

'Celia!' cried Sybil, aghast at such heresy.

Had they not been taken to the Louvre to look at old masters only yesterday?

Celia felt she had been too heretical. Everybody spoke reverently of Art.

'I expect I'd had too much chocolate to drink,' she said. 'That's why I thought them stuffy. All those saints looking exactly alike. Of course, I don't mean it,' she added. 'They're wonderful, really.'

But her voice sounded a little unconvinced.

'You *must* be fond of art, Celia, you're so fond of music.'

'Music's different. Music's *itself*. It's not copy cat. You take an instrument — the violin, or the piano, or the 'cello, and you make sounds — lovely sounds all woven together. You haven't got to get it like anything else. It's just itself.'

'Well,' said Sybil, 'I think music is just a lot of nasty noises. And very often when I'm playing the wrong notes it sounds to me better than when I play the right ones.'

Celia gazed despairingly at her friend.

'You can't be able to *hear* at all.'

'Well, from the way you were painting those violets this morning nobody would think you were able to see.'

Celia stopped dead — thereby blocking the path of the little *femme de chambre* who accompanied them and who chattered angrily.

'Do you know, Sybil,' said Celia, 'I believe you're right. I don't think I do see things — not *see* them. That's why I can't spell. And that's why I don't really know what anything is like.'

'You always walk straight through puddles,' said Sybil. Celia was reflecting.

'I don't see that it matters — not really — except spelling, I suppose. I mean, it's the feeling a thing gives you that matters — not just its shape and how it happens to be made.'

'What *do* you mean?'

'Well, take a rose.' Celia nodded towards a flower-seller they were passing. 'What does it matter how many petals it has and exactly what the shape of them is — it's just the oh, sort of whole thing that matters — the velvetyness and the smell.'

'You couldn't draw a rose without knowing its shape.'

'Sybil, you great ass, haven't I told you I don't want to draw? I don't like roses on paper. I like them real.'

She stopped in front of the flower woman and for a few sous bought a bunch of drooping dark-red roses.

'Smell,' she said, thrusting them in front of Sybil's nose. 'Now, doesn't that give you a heavenly sort of pain just here?'

'You've been eating too many apples again.'

'I haven't. Oh, Sybil, don't be so literal. Isn't it a heavenly smell?'

'Yes, it is. But it doesn't give me a pain. I don't see why one should want it to.'

'Mummy and I tried to do botany once,' said Celia. 'But we threw the book away, I hated it so. Knowing all the different kinds of flowers and classifying them — and pistils and stamens — horrid, like undressing the poor things. I think it's disgusting. It's — it's indelicate.'

'Do you know, Celia, that if you go to a convent, the nuns make you have your bath with a chemise on. My cousin told me.'

'Do they? Why?'

'They don't think it's nice to look at your own body.'

'Oh.' Celia thought a minute. 'How do you manage with the soap? You wouldn't get awfully clean if you soaped yourself through a chemise.'

2

The girls at the Pensionnat were taken to the opera, and to the Comédie Francaise, and to skate at the Palais de Glace in winter. Celia enjoyed it all, but it was the music that really filled her life. She wrote to her mother that she wanted to take up the piano professionally.

At the end of the term Miss Schofield gave a party, at which the more advanced of the girls played and sang. Celia was to do both. The singing went off quite all right, but over playing she broke down and stumbled badly through the first movement of Beethoven's Sonate Pathétique.

Miriam came over to Paris to fetch her daughter, and at Celia's wish she asked M. Kochter to tea. She was not at all anxious for Celia to take up music professionally, but she thought she might as well hear what M. Kochter had to say on the matter. Celia was not in the room when she asked him about it.

143

'I will tell you the truth, madame. She has the ability — the technique — the feeling. She is the most promising pupil I have. But I do not think she has the temperament.'

'You mean she has not the temperament to play in public?'

'That is exactly what I do mean, madame. To be an artist one must be able to shut out the world — if you feel it there listening to you, then you must feel it as a stimulus. But Mademoiselle Celia, she will give of her best to an audience of one — of two people — and she will play best of all to herself with the door closed.'

'Will you tell her what you have told me, M. Kochter?'

'If you wish, madame.'

Celia was bitterly disappointed. She fell back on the idea of singing.

'Though it won't be the same thing.'

'You don't love singing as you love your piano?'

'Oh, no.'

'Perhaps that's why you're not nervous when you sing?'

'Perhaps it is. A voice seems somehow something apart from one's self — I mean, it isn't you doing it — like it is with your fingers on the piano. Do you understand, Mummy?'

They had a serious discussion with M. Barré.

'She has the ability and the voice, yes. Also the temperament. She has as yet very little expression in her singing — it is the voice of a boy, not a woman. That' — he smiled — 'will come. But the voice is charming — pure

144

— steady — and her breathing is good. She can be a singer, yes. A singer for the concert stage — her voice is not strong enough for opera.'

When they were back in England, Celia said:

'I've thought about it, Mummy. If I can't sing in opera, I don't want to sing at all. I mean, not professionally.'

Then she laughed.

'You didn't want me to, did you, Mummy?'

'No, I certainly didn't want you to become a professional singer.'

'But you'd have let me? Would you let me do anything I wanted to if I wanted it enough?'

'Not anything,' said Miriam with spirit.

'But nearly anything?'

Her mother smiled at her.

'I want you to be happy, my pet.'

'I'm sure I shall always be happy,' said Celia with great confidence.

3

Celia wrote to her mother that autumn that she wanted to be a hospital nurse. Bessie was going to be one, and she wanted to be one too. Her letters had been very full of Bessie lately.

Miriam did not reply directly, but towards the end of the term she wrote and told Celia that the doctor had said it would be a good thing for her to winter abroad. She was going to Egypt, and Celia was coming with her.

Celia arrived back from Paris to find her mother staying with Grannie and in the full bustle of departure. Grannie was not at all pleased at the Egyptian idea. Celia heard her talking about it to Cousin Lottie, who had come in to lunch.

'I can't understand Miriam. Left as badly off as she is. The idea of rushing off to Egypt — Egypt — about the most expensive place she could go to! That's Miriam all over — no idea of money. And Egypt was one of the last places she went to with poor John. It seems most unfeeling.'

Celia thought her mother looked both defiant and excited. She took Celia to shop and bought her three evening dresses.

'The child's not out. You're absurd, Miriam,' said Grannie.

'It wouldn't be a bad idea for her to come out there. It's not as though she could have a London season — we can't afford it.'

'She's only sixteen.'

'Nearly seventeen. My mother was married before she was seventeen.'

'I don't suppose you want Celia to marry before she's seventeen.'

'No, I don't, but I want her to have her young girl's time.'

The evening dresses were very exciting — though they emphasized the one crumpled roseleaf in Celia's life. Alas, the figure that Celia had never ceased to look forward to so eagerly had never materialized. No swelling mounds for Celia to encase in a striped shirt. Her disappointment was bitter and acute. She had wanted 'a chest' so badly. Poor Celia — had she only been born twenty years later — how

146

admired her shape would have been! No slimming exercises necessary for that slender yet well-covered frame.

As it was, 'plumpers' were introduced into the bodices of Celia's evening dresses — delicate ruchings of net.

Celia longed for a black evening dress, but Miriam said No, not until she was older. She bought her a white taffeta gown, a dress of pale green net with lots of little ribbons running across it and a pale pink satin with rosebuds on the shoulder.

Then Grannie unearthed from one of the bottom mahogany drawers a piece of brilliant turquoise blue taffeta with suggestions that Poor Miss Bennett should try her hand at it. Miriam managed to suggest tactfully that perhaps Poor Miss Bennett would find a fashionable evening dress a little beyond her. The blue taffeta was made up elsewhere. Then Celia was taken to a hairdresser and given a few lessons in the art of putting up her own hair — a somewhat elaborate process, since it was trained over a 'hair frame' in front and arranged in masses of curls behind. Not an easy style for anyone who had, like Celia, long thick hair falling far below her waist.

It was all very exciting, and it never occurred to Celia that her mother seemed rather better than worse in health than usual.

It did not escape Grannie.

'But there,' she said, 'Miriam's got a bee in her bonnet over this business.'

It was many years later that Celia realized exactly what her mother's feelings were at the time. She had had a dull girlhood herself — she was passionately eager that her darling should have all the gaieties and excitements that a young girl's life could hold. And it was going to be difficult for Celia to have a 'good time' living buried in the country with few young people of her own age around.

Hence, Egypt — where Miriam had many friends from the time when she and her husband had been there together. To obtain the necessary funds she did not hesitate to sell out some of the few stocks and shares she possessed. Celia was not to be envious of other girls having 'good times' which she had never had.

Also, so she confided some years later to Celia, she had been afraid of her friendship for Bessie West.

'I've seen so many girls get interested in another girl and refuse to go out or take any interest in men. It's unnatural — and not right.'

'Bessie? But I was never very fond of Bessie.'

'I know that now. But I didn't know it then. I was afraid. And all that hospital nurse nonsense. I wanted you to have a good time and pretty clothes and enjoy yourself in a young, natural way.'

'Well,' said Celia, 'I did.'

7

Grown Up

1

Celia enjoyed herself, it is true, but she also went through a lot of agony through being handicapped by the shyness that she had had ever since she was a baby. It made her tongue-tied and awkward, and utterly unable to show when she was enjoying herself.

Celia seldom thought about her appearance. She took it for granted that she was pretty — and she *was* pretty — tall, slender and graceful, with very fair flaxen hair and Scandinavian fairness and delicacy of colouring. She had an exquisite complexion, though she went pale through nervousness. In the days when to 'make up' was shameful, Miriam put a touch of rouge on her daughter's cheeks every evening. She wanted her to look her best.

It was not her appearance that worried Celia. What weighed her down was the consciousness of her stupidity. She was not clever. It was awful not to be clever. She never could think of anything to say to the people she danced with. She was solemn and rather heavy.

Miriam ceaselessly urged her daughter to talk.

'Say something, darling. Anything. It doesn't matter what silly thing it is. But it's such uphill work for a man to talk to a girl who says nothing but yes and no. Don't let the ball drop.'

Nobody appreciated Celia's difficulties more than her mother who had been hampered herself by shyness all her life.

Nobody ever realized that Celia was shy. They thought she was haughty and conceited. Nobody realized how humble this pretty girl was feeling — how bitterly conscious of her social defects.

Because of her beauty Celia had a good time. Also, she danced well. At the end of the winter she had been to fifty-six dances and had at last acquired a certain amount of the art of small talk. She was less gauche now, more self-assured, and was at last beginning to be able to enjoy herself without being tortured by constantly recurring shyness.

Life was rather a haze — a haze of dancing and golden light, and polo and tennis and young men. Young men who held her hand, flirted with her, asked if they might kiss her, and were baffled by her aloofness. To Celia only one person was real, the dark bronzed colonel of a Scottish regiment, who seldom danced and who never bothered to talk to young girls.

She liked jolly little red-haired Captain Gale who always danced three times with her every evening. (Three was the largest number of dances permissible with one person.) It was his joke that she didn't need teaching to dance, but did need teaching to talk.

Nevertheless, she was surprised when Miriam said on the way home:

'Did you know that Captain Gale wanted to marry you?'

'Me?' Celia was very surprised.

'Yes, he talked to me about it. He wanted to know whether I thought he had any chance.'

'Why didn't he ask me?' Celia felt a little resentful about it.

'I don't quite know. I think he found it difficult.' Miriam smiled. 'But you don't want to marry him, do you, Celia?'

'Oh, *no* — but I think I ought to have been asked.'

That was Celia's first proposal. Not, she thought, a very satisfactory one.

Not that it mattered. She would never want to marry anyone except Colonel Moncrieff, and he would never ask her. She would remain an old maid all her life, loving him secretly.

Alas for the dark, bronzed Colonel Moncrieff! In six months he had gone the way of Auguste, of Sybil, of the Bishop of London and Mr Gerald du Maurier.

2

Grown-up life was difficult. It was exciting but tiring. You always seemed to be in agonies about something or other. The way your hair was done, or your lack of figure, or your stupidity in talking, and people, especially men, made you feel uncomfortable.

All her life Celia never forgot her first country-house visit. Her nervousness in the train, which made pink blotches come out all down her neck. Would she behave properly? Would she (ever recurring nightmare) be able to *talk?* Would she be able to roll up her curls on the back of her head? Miriam usually did the very back ones for her. Would they think her very stupid? Had she got the right clothes with her?

Nobody could have been kinder than her host and hostess. She was not shy with them.

It felt very grand to be in this big bedroom with a maid unpacking for her and coming in to do her dress up down the back.

She wore a new pink net dress and went down to dinner feeling terribly shy. There were lots of people there. It was awful. Her host was very nice. He talked to her, chaffed her, called her the Pink 'Un because he said she always wore pink dresses.

There was a lovely dinner, but Celia couldn't really enjoy it because she had to be thinking what to say to her neighbours. One was a little fat round man with a very red face, the other a tall man with a quizzical expression and a touch of grey hair.

He talked to her gravely about books and theatres, and then about the country and asked her where she lived. When she told him, he said he might be coming down that way at Easter. He would come and see her if she would allow it. Celia said that would be very nice.

'Then why not look as though it would be nice?' he asked, laughing.

Celia got red.

'You ought to,' he said. 'Especially as I've made

up my mind only a minute ago to go there.'

'The scenery's beautiful,' said Celia earnestly.

'It isn't the scenery I'm coming to see.'

How she wished people wouldn't say things of that kind. She crumbled her bread desperately. Her neighbour looked at her with amusement. What a child she was! It amused him to embarrass her. He gravely proceeded to pay her the most extravagant compliments.

Celia was terribly relieved when at last he turned to the lady on his other side and left her to the little fat man. His name was Roger Raynes, so he told her, and very soon they had got on to the subject of music. Raynes was a singer — not a professional, though he had often sung professionally. Celia became quite happy chatting to him.

She had hardly noticed what there had been to eat, but now an ice cream was coming round — a slender apricot-coloured pillar studded with crystalized violets.

It collapsed just before being handed to her. The butler took it to the sideboard and rearranged it. Then he resumed his round, but, alas, his memory failed him. He missed out Celia!

She was so bitterly disappointed that she hardly heard what the little fat man was saying. He had taken a large helping and seemed to be enjoying it very much. The idea of asking for some ice cream never occurred to Celia. She resigned herself to disappointment.

After dinner they had music. She played Roger Raynes's accompaniments. He had a splendid tenor voice. Celia enjoyed playing for him. She was a good and sympathetic accompanist. Then it was her turn to sing. Singing never made her nervous. Roger Raynes said kindly that she had a charming voice and then continued to talk about his own. He asked Celia to sing again, but she said, Wouldn't he? And he accepted with alacrity.

Celia went to bed quite happy. The house party was not being so dreadful after all.

The next morning passed pleasantly. They went out and looked at the stables and tickled the pigs' backs, and then Roger Raynes asked Celia if she would come and try over some songs with him. She did. After he had sung about six he produced a song called 'Love's Lilies', and when they had finished he said:

'Now, tell me your candid opinion — what do you really think of that song?'

'Well — ' Celia hesitated — 'well, really, I think it's rather dreadful.'

'So do I,' said Roger Raynes. 'At least, I wasn't sure. But you've settled it. You don't like it — so here goes.'

And he tore the song in half and flung it into the grate. Celia was very much impressed. It was a brand-new song which, he told her, he had only bought the day before. And because of her opinion he had torn it up relentlessly.

She felt quite grown up and important.

3

The big fancy-dress ball for which the party was assembled was to take place that night. Celia was to go as Marguerite from *Faust* — all in white with her hair in two plaits hanging down each side. She looked very fair and Gretchen-like, and Roger Raynes told her that he had the music of *Faust* with him, and that they would try over one of the duets tomorrow.

Celia felt rather nervous as they set off for the ball. She always found her programme a difficulty. She always seemed to manage badly — to dance with the people she didn't much like, and then when the people she did like came along, there weren't any dances left. But if one pretended to be engaged then the people one liked mightn't come along after all, and then one might have to 'sit out' (horror). Some girls seemed to manage cleverly but, Celia realized for the hundredth time gloomily, she *wasn't* clever.

Mrs Luke looked after Celia well, introducing people to her.

'Major de Burgh.'

Major de Burgh bowed. 'Have you a dance?'

He was a big man, rather horsey-looking, long fair moustache, rather red face, about forty-five.

He put down his name for three dances and asked Celia to go in to supper with him.

She did not find him very easy to talk to. He said little, but he looked at her a good deal.

Mrs Luke left the ball early. She was not strong.

'George will look after you and bring you home,' she said to Celia. 'By the way, child, you seem to have made quite a conquest of Major de Burgh.'

Celia felt heartened. She was afraid she had

155

bored Major de Burgh horribly.

She danced every dance, and it was two o'clock when George came up to her, and said:

'Hallo, Pink 'Un, time to take the stable home.'

It was not till Celia was in her room that she realized that she was quite unable to extricate herself unaided from her evening frock. She heard George's voice in the corridor still saying good nights. Could she ask him? Or couldn't she? If she didn't she would have to sit up in her frock till morning. Her courage failed her. When the morning dawned Celia was lying on her bed fast asleep in her evening dress.

4

Major de Burgh came over that morning. He wasn't hunting today, he said, to the chorus of astonishment that greeted him. He sat there saying very little. Mrs Luke suggested that he might like to see the pigs. She sent Celia with him. At lunch Roger Raynes was very sulky.

The next day Celia went home. She had a quiet morning alone with her host and hostess. The others left in the morning, but she was going by an afternoon train. Somebody called 'dear Arthur, so amusing' came to lunch. He was (in Celia's eyes) a very elderly man, and he did not seem amusing. He spoke in a low tired voice.

After lunch, when Mrs Luke had left the room

and he was alone with Celia, he began stroking her ankles.

'Charming,' he murmured. 'Charming. You don't mind, do you?'

Celia did mind. She minded very much. But she endured it. She supposed that this was a regular part of house parties. She did not want to appear gauche or immature. She set her teeth and sat very stiff.

Dear Arthur slipped a practised arm round her waist and kissed her. Celia turned on him furiously and pushed him away.

'I can't — oh, please, I can't.'

Manners were manners, but there were some things she couldn't endure.

'Such a sweet little waist,' said Arthur advancing the practised arm again.

Mrs Luke came into the room. She noticed Celia's expression and flushed face.

'Did Arthur behave himself?' she asked on the way to the station. 'He's not really to be trusted with young girls — can't leave him alone. Not that there's any real harm in him.'

'Have you *got* to let people stroke your ankles?' demanded Celia.

'Got to? Of course not, you funny child.'

'Oh,' said Celia with a deep sigh. 'I'm *so* glad.'

Mrs Luke looked amused and said again:

'You funny child!'

She went on: 'You looked charming at the dance. I fancy you'll hear something more of Johnnie de Burgh.' She added: 'He's extremely well off.'

157

5

The day after Celia got home a big pink box of chocolates arrived addressed to her. There was nothing inside to show whom they came from. Two days later a little parcel came. It contained a small silver box. Engraved on the lid were the words 'Marguerite' and the date of the ball.

Major de Burgh's card was enclosed.

'Who is this Major de Burgh, Celia?'

'I met him at the ball.'

'What is he like?'

'He's rather old and got rather a red face. Quite nice, but difficult to talk to.'

Miriam nodded thoughtfully. That night she wrote to Mrs Luke. The answer was quite frank — Mrs Luke was by nature the complete matchmaker.

'He's very well off — very well off indeed. Hunts with the B'. George doesn't like him very much but *there's nothing against him*. He seems to have been *quite* bowled over by Celia. She is a dear child — very naïve. She is certainly going to be attractive to men. Men do admire fairness and sloping shoulders so much.'

A week later Major de Burgh 'happened to be in the neighbourhood'. Might he come over and call on Celia and her mother?

He did so. He seemed as tongue-tied as ever — sat and stared at Celia a good deal, and tried clumsily to make friends with Miriam.

For some reason, after he had gone, Miriam was upset. Her conduct puzzled Celia. Her mother made disjointed remarks that Celia could not make head or tail of.

'I wonder if it's wise to pray for a thing . . . How hard it is to know what is right . . . ' Then suddenly, 'I want you to marry a good man — a man like your father. Money isn't everything — but comfortable surroundings do mean a lot to a woman . . . '

Celia accepted and replied to these remarks without in any way connecting them with the late visit of Major de Burgh. Miriam was in the habit of making remarks out of the blue, as it were. They had ceased to surprise her daughter.

Miriam said: 'I should like you to marry a man older than yourself. They take more care of a woman.'

Celia's thoughts flew momentarily to Colonel Moncrieff — now a fast fading memory. She had danced at the ball with a young soldier of six feet four and was inclined at the moment to idealize handsome young giants.

Her mother said: 'When we go to London next week, Major de Burgh wants to take us to the theatre. That will be nice, won't it?'

'Very nice,' said Celia.

6

When Major de Burgh proposed to Celia he took her completely by surprise. Mrs Luke's remarks, her mother's, none of them had made any impression upon her. Celia saw clearly her own thoughts — she never saw coming events, and not usually her own surroundings.

Miriam had asked Major de Burgh to come for the weekend. Actually he had practically asked himself, and, a little troubled, Miriam had uttered the necessary invitation.

On the first evening Celia was showing the guest the garden. She found him very hard work. He never seemed to be listening to what she was saying. She was afraid that he must be terribly bored ... Everything that she was saying was rather stupid, of course — but if only he would *help* —

And then, breaking into what she was saying, he had suddenly seized her hands in his and in a queer, hoarse, utterly unrecognizable voice had said:

'Marguerite — my Marguerite. I want you so. Will you marry me?'

Celia stared. Her face went quite blank — her eyes were blue and wide and astonished. She was quite incapable of speech. Something was affecting her — affecting her powerfully — something that was being communicated through those trembling hands that held her. She felt enveloped in a storm of emotion. It was rather frightening — rather terrible.

She stammered out:

'I — no. I don't know. Oh, no, I can't.'

What was he making her feel, this man, this elderly quiet stranger whom as yet she had hardly noticed, save to feel flattered because he 'liked her'?

'I've startled you, my darling. My little love. You're so young — so pure. You can't understand what I feel for you. I love you so.'

160

Why didn't she take her hands away and say at once, firmly and truthfully, 'I'm very sorry, but I don't care for you in that way'?

Why, instead, just stand there, helpless, looking at him — feeling those currents beating round her head?

He drew her gently towards him, but she resisted — only half resisted — did not draw completely away.

He said gently: 'I won't worry you now. Think it over.'

He released her. She walked away slowly to the house, went upstairs to her bed, lay down there, her eyes closed, her heart beating.

Her mother came to her there half an hour later.

She sat down on the bed, took Celia's hand.

'Did he tell you, Mother?'

'Yes. He cares for you very much. What — what do you feel about it?'

'I don't know. It's — it's all so queer.'

She couldn't say anything else. It was all queer — everything was queer — complete strangers could turn into lovers — all in a minute. She didn't know what she felt or what she wanted.

Least of all did she understand or appreciate her mother's perplexities.

'I'm not very strong. I've been praying so that a good man would come along and give you a good home and make you happy . . . There's so little money . . . and I've had dreadful expenses over Cyril lately . . . There will be so little for you when I am gone. I don't want you to marry anyone rich if you don't care for him. But you're so romantic, and a Fairy Prince — that sort of thing doesn't happen. So few women can marry the man they are romantically in love with.'

'You did.'

'*I* did — yes — but even then — it isn't always wise — to care too much. It's a thorn in your side always . . . To be cared for — it's better . . . You can take life more easily — I've never taken it easily enough. If I knew more about this man . . . If I was sure I liked him. He might drink . . . He might be — anything. Would he take care of you — look after you? Be good to you? There *must* be someone to take care of you when I'm gone.'

Most of it passed Celia by. Money meant nothing to her. When Daddy had been alive they had been rich; when he had died they had been poor; but Celia had found no difference between the two states. She had had home and the garden and her piano.

Marriage to her meant love — poetical, romantic love — and living happily ever afterwards. All the books she had read had taught her nothing of the problems of life. What puzzled and confused her was that she did not know whether she loved Major de Burgh — Johnnie — or not. A minute before his proposal she would have said if asked that most certainly she did not. But now? He had roused in her something — something hot and exciting and uncertain.

Miriam had decreed that he was to go away and leave Celia to think it over for two months. He had obeyed — but he wrote — and the inarticulate Johnnie de Burgh was a master of the love letter. His letters were sometimes short, sometimes long, never twice the same, but they were the love letters a young girl dreams of getting. By the end of two months Celia had decided that she was in love with Johnnie. She went up to London with her mother prepared to tell him so. When she saw him, a sudden revulsion of feeling swept over her. This man was a stranger whom she did not love. She refused him.

7

Johnnie de Burgh did not take his defeat easily. He asked Celia five times more to marry him. For over a year he wrote to her, accepted 'friendship' with her, sent her pretty trifles, and laid persistent siege to her, and his perseverance nearly won the day.

It was all so romantic — so much the way Celia's fancy inclined to being wooed. His letters, the things he said — they were all so exactly right. That was, indeed, Johnnie de Burgh's forte. He was a born lover. He had been the lover of many women, and he knew what appealed to women. He knew how to attack a married woman and how to attract a young girl. Celia was very nearly swept off her feet into marriage with him, but not quite. Somewhere in her was something calm that knew what it wanted and was not to be deceived.

It was at this time that Miriam urged the reading of a course of French novels upon her daughter. To keep up your French, she said.

They included the works of Balzac and other French realists.

And there were some modern ones that few English mothers would have given to their daughters.

But Miriam had a purpose.

She was determined that Celia — so dreamy — so much in the clouds — should not be ignorant of life . . .

Celia read them with great docility and very little interest.

9

Celia had other suitors, Ralph Graham, the original freckled-faced boy of the dancing class. He was now a tea planter in Ceylon. He had always been attracted by Celia, even when she was a child. Returning to find her grown up, he asked her to marry him during the first week of his leave. Celia refused him without hesitation. He had had a friend staying with him, and later the friend wrote to Celia. He had not wanted to 'queer Ralph's pitch,' but he had fallen in love with her at first sight. Was there any hope for him? But neither Ralph nor his friend made any impression on Celia's consciousness.

But during the year of Johnnie de Burgh's

wooing she made a friend — Peter Maitland. Peter was some years older than his sisters. He was a soldier and had been stationed abroad for many years. Now he returned to England for a period of home service. His return coincided with Ellie Maitland's engagement. Celia and Janet were to be bridesmaids. It was at the wedding that Celia got to know Peter.

Peter Maitland was tall and dark. He was shy, but concealed it under a lazy pleasant manner. The Maitlands were all much the same, good-natured, companionable, and easy-going. They never hurried themselves for anyone or anything. If they missed a train — well, there would be another one some time. If they were late in getting home for lunch — well, they supposed someone would have kept them something to eat. They had no ambitions and no energies. Peter was the most marked example of the family traits. No one had ever seen Peter hurry. 'All the same a hundred years hence,' was his motto.

Ellie's wedding was a typical Maitland affair. Mrs Maitland, who was large and vague and good-natured, never got up till midday and frequently forgot to order any meals. 'Getting Mum into her wedding garments' was the chief business of the morning. Owing to Mum's distaste for trying on, her oyster satin was found to be uncomfortably tight. The bride fussed round her — and all was made comfortable by a judicious use of the scissors and a spray of orchids to cover the deficiency. Celia was at the house early — to help — and it certainly seemed at one point as though Ellie was never going to get married that day. At the moment she should have been putting the final touches to her appearance, she was sitting in a chemise placidly manicuring her toenails.

'I meant to have done this last night,' she explained. 'But somehow I didn't seem to have time.'

'The carriage has come, Ellie.'

'Has it? Oh, well, somebody had better telephone to Tom and tell him I shall be about half an hour late.'

'Poor little Tom,' she added reflectively. 'He's such a dear little fellow. I shouldn't like him to be dithering in the church thinking I'd changed my mind.'

Ellie had grown very tall — she was nearly six foot. Her bridegroom was five foot five, and as Ellie described it, 'such a merry little fellow — and a sweet little nature.'

While Ellie was finally being induced to finish her toilet, Celia wandered into the garden, where Captain Peter Maitland was smoking a placid pipe, not in the least concerned by the tardiness of his sister.

'Thomas is a sensible fellow,' he said. 'He knows what she is like. He won't expect her to be on time.'

He was a little shy talking to Celia, but, as is often the case when two shy people get together, they soon found it easy to talk to each other.

'Expect you find us a rum family?' said Peter.

'You don't seem to have much sense of time,' said Celia laughing.

166

'Well, why spend your life rushing? Take it easy — enjoy yourself.'

'Does one ever get anywhere that way?'

'Where is there to get to? One thing is very like another in this life.'

When he was at home on leave, Peter Maitland usually refused all invitations. He hated 'poodle faking' he said. He did not dance, and he played tennis or golf with men or his own sisters. But after the wedding he seemed to adopt Celia as an extra sister. He and she and Janet used to do things together. Then Ralph Graham, recovering from Celia's refusal, began to be attracted to Janet, and the trio became a foursome. Finally it split into couples — Janet and Ralph and Celia and Peter.

Peter used to instruct Celia in the game of golf.

'We won't hurry ourselves, mind. Just a few holes and take it easy — and sit down and smoke a pipe if it gets too hot.'

The programme suited Celia very well. She had no 'eye' for games — which fact depressed her only a little less than her lack of 'a figure'. But Peter made her feel that it didn't matter.

'You don't want to be a pro — or a pot hunter. Just get a little fun out of it — that's all.'

Peter himself was extraordinarily good at all games. He had a natural flair for athletics. He could have been in the front rank but for his constitutional laziness. But he preferred, as he said, to treat games as games. 'Why make a business of the thing?'

He got on very well with Celia's mother. She

was fond of all the Maitland family, and Peter, with his lazy, easy charm, his pleasant manners, and his undoubted sweetness of disposition, was her favourite.

'You don't need to worry about Celia,' he said when he suggested that they should ride together. 'I'll look after her. I will — really — look after her.'

Miriam knew what he meant. She felt Peter Maitland was to be trusted.

He knew a little of how the land lay between Celia and her major. Vaguely, in a delicate way, he gave her advice.

'A girl like you, Celia, ought to marry a fellow with a bit of the 'oof'. You're the kind that wants looking after. I don't mean you ought to marry a beastly Jew boy — nothing like that. But a decent fellow who's fond of sport and all that — and who could look after you.'

When Peter's leave was up and he rejoined his regiment, which was stationed at Aldershot, Celia missed him very much. She wrote to him, and he to her — easy colloquial letters that were very much like the way he talked.

When Johnnie de Burgh finally accepted his dismissal, Celia felt rather flat. The effort to withstand his influence had taken more out of her than she knew. No sooner had the final break occurred than she wondered whether, after all, she didn't regret . . . Perhaps she did care for him more than she thought. She missed the excitement of his letters, of his presents, of his continual siege.

She was uncertain of her mother's attitude.

Was Miriam relieved or disappointed? Sometimes she thought one and sometimes the other, and as a matter of fact was not far from the truth in so thinking.

Miriam's first sensation had been one of relief. She had never really liked Johnnie de Burgh — she had never quite trusted him — though she could never put her finger on exactly where the distrust lay. Certainly he was devoted to Celia. His past had been nothing outrageous — and indeed Miriam had been brought up in the belief that a man who has sown his wild oats is likely to make a better husband.

The thing that worried her most was her own health. The heart attacks that she once suffered from at long distant intervals were becoming more frequent. From the humming and hawing and diplomatic language of doctors she had formed the conclusion that while she might have long years of life in front of her — she might equally well die suddenly. And then, what was to become of Celia? There was so little money. How little only Miriam knew.

So little — little — money.

COMMENT BY J.L.

It would strike us in these days: 'But why on earth, if there was so little money, didn't she train Celia for a profession?'

But I don't think that would ever have occurred to Miriam. She was, I should imagine, intensely receptive to new thought and new ideas — but I don't think that that particular idea had come her way. And if it had, I don't think she would have taken to it readily.

169

I take it that she knew the peculiar vulnerability of Celia. You may say that that might have been altered with a different training, but I don't believe that that is so. Like all people who live chiefly by the inner vision, Celia was peculiarly impervious to influences from outside. She was stupid when it came to realities.

I think Miriam was aware of her daughter's deficiencies. I think her choice of reading — her insisting on Balzac and other French novelists — was done with an object. The French are great realists. I think she wanted Celia to realize life and human nature for what it is, something common, sensual, splendid, sordid, tragic, and intensely comic. She did not succeed, because Celia's nature matched her appearance — she was Scandinavian in feeling. For her the long Sagas, the heroic tales of voyages and heroes. As she clung to fairy tales in childhood, so she preferred Maeterlinck and Fiona MacLeod and Yeats when she grew up. She read the other books, but they seemed as unreal to her as fairy stories and fantasies seem annoying to a practical realist.

We are as we are born. Some Scandinavian ancestor lived again in Celia. The robust Grannie, the merry and jovial John, the mercurial Miriam — one of these passed on the secret strain that they possessed unknown to themselves.

It is interesting to see how completely her brother drops out of Celia's narrative. And yet Cyril must often have been there — on holidays — on leave.

Cyril went into the army and had gone abroad to India before Celia came out. He never loomed very large in her life — or in Miriam's. He was, I gather, a great source of expense when he was first in the army. Later he married, left the army, and went to Rhodesia to farm. As a personality he faded from Celia's life.

8

Jim and Peter

1

Both Miriam and her daughter believed in prayer. Celia's prayers had been first conscientious and conscious of sin, and later had been spiritual and ascetic. But she never broke herself of her little-girl habit of praying over everything that happened. Celia never went into a ballroom without murmuring: 'Oh, God, don't let me be shy. Oh, please God, don't let me be shy. And don't let my neck get red.' At dinner parties she prayed: 'Please, God, let me think of something to say.' She prayed that she might manage her programme well and dance with the people she wanted to. She prayed that it might not rain when they started on a picnic.

Miriam's prayers were more intense and more arrogant. She was, in truth, an arrogant woman. For her darling she did not ask, she demanded things of God! Her prayers were so intense, so burning, that she could not believe they would not be answered. And perhaps most of us, when we say our prayers have been unanswered, really mean that the answer has been No.

She had not been sure whether Johnnie de Burgh was an answer to prayer or not, but she was quite sure that Jim Grant was.

Jim was keen on taking up farming, and his people sent him to a farm near Miriam on purpose. They felt that she would keep an eye on the boy. It would help him to keep out of mischief.

Jim at twenty-three was almost exactly like Jim at thirteen had been. The same good-humoured, high-cheekboned face, the same round, intensely dark blue eyes, the same good-humoured, efficient manner. The same dazzling smile, and the same way of throwing back his head and laughing.

Jim was twenty-three and heart whole. It was spring and he was a strong, healthy young man. He came often to Miriam's house, and Celia was young and fair and beautiful, and since nature is nature, he fell in love.

To Celia, it was another friendship like her friendship with Peter Maitland, only that she admired Jim's character more. She had always felt that Peter was almost too 'slack'. He had no ambition. Jim was full of ambition. He was young and intensely solemn about life. The words 'life is real, life is earnest', might have been written for Jim. His desire to take up farming was not rooted in a love of the soil. He was interested in the practical scientific side of farming. Farming in England ought to be made to pay much better than it did. It only needed science and will power. Jim was very strong on will power. He had books about it which he lent to Celia. He was very fond of lending books. He was also interested in theosophy, bimetallism, economics, and Christian Science.

He liked Celia because she listened so attentively. She read all the books and made intelligent comments on them.

If Johnnie de Burgh's courtship of Celia had been physical, Jim Grant's was almost entirely intellectual. At this time in his career, he was simply bursting with serious ideas — almost to the point of being priggish. When Celia liked him best was not when he was seriously discussing ethics or Mrs Eddy, but when he threw back his head and laughed.

Johnnie de Burgh's love-making had taken her by surprise, but she realized Jim was going to ask her to marry him some time before he did.

Sometimes Celia felt life was a pattern: you wove in and out of it like a shuttle, obedient to the design imposed upon you. Jim, she began to suppose, was her pattern. He was her destiny, appointed from the beginning. How happy her mother looked nowadays.

Jim was a dear — she liked him immensely. Some day soon he would ask her to marry him and then she would feel as she had felt with Major de Burgh (she always thought of him as that in her mind, never as Johnnie) — excited and troubled — her heart beating fast . . .

Jim proposed to her one Sunday afternoon. He had planned to do so some weeks beforehand. He liked making plans and keeping to them. He felt it was an efficient way of living.

It was a wet afternoon. They were sitting in the schoolroom after tea. Celia had been playing and singing. Jim liked Gilbert and Sullivan.

After the singing they sat on the sofa and

discussed socialism and the Good of Man. After that, there was a pause. Celia said something about Mrs Besant, but Jim answered rather at random.

There was another pause, and then Jim got rather red and said:

'I expect you know I am awfully fond of you, Celia. Would you like to be engaged, or would you rather wait a bit? I think we should be very happy together. We've got so many tastes in common.'

He was not so calm as he sounded. If Celia had been older she would have realized this. She would have seen the significance of the slight tremble of his lips, the nervous hand that plucked at a sofa cushion.

As it was — well, what was she to say?

She didn't know — so she said nothing.

'I think you like me?' said Jim.

'I do — oh, I do,' cried Celia eagerly.

'That's the most important thing,' said Jim. 'That people should really like each other. That lasts. Passion' — he got a little pink as he said the word — 'doesn't. I think you and I would be ideally happy, Celia. I want to marry young.' He paused, then said: 'Look here, I think the fairest thing would be for us to be engaged on trial, as it were, for six months. We needn't tell anyone except your mother and mine. Then, at the end of six months, you can make up your mind definitely.'

Celia reflected a minute.

'Do you think that's fair? I mean, I mightn't — even then — '

'If you don't — then of course we oughtn't to marry. But you will. I know it's going to be all right.'

What comfortable assurance there was in his voice. He was so sure. He *knew*.

'Very well,' said Celia and smiled.

She expected him to kiss her, but he didn't. He wanted to badly, but he felt shy. They went on discussing socialism and man — not perhaps quite so logically as they might have done.

Then Jim said it was time to go, and got up.

They stood for a minute awkwardly.

'Well,' said Jim, 'so long. I'll be over next Sunday — perhaps before. And I'll write.' He hesitated. 'I — shall — will you give me a kiss, Celia?'

They kissed. Rather awkwardly . . .

It was exactly like kissing Cyril, Celia thought. Only, she reflected, Cyril never wanted to kiss anybody . . .

Well, that was that. She was engaged to Jim.

2

Miriam's happiness was so overflowing that it made Celia feel quite enthusiastic over her engagement.

'Darling, I'm so happy about you. He's such a dear boy. Honest and manly, and he'll take care of you. And they are such old friends and were so fond of your dear father. It seems so wonderful that it should have come about like this — their son and our daughter. Oh, Celia, I

176

was so unhappy all the time with Major de Burgh. I felt somehow that it wasn't *right* . . . not the thing for you.'

She paused and said suddenly:

'And I've been afraid of myself.'

'Of yourself?'

'Yes, I've wanted so badly to keep you with me . . . Not to have you marry. I've wanted to be selfish. I've said that you would lead a more sheltered life — no cares, no children, no troubles . . . If it hadn't been that I could have left you so little — so very little to live upon, I would have been sorely tempted . . . It's very hard, Celia, for mothers not to be selfish.'

'Nonsense,' said Celia. 'You would have been dreadfully humiliated when other girls got married.'

She had noted with some amusement her mother's intense jealousy on her behalf. Were another girl better dressed, more amusing in conversation, Miriam immediately displayed a frenzied annoyance quite unshared by Celia. Her mother had hated it when Ellie Maitland got married. The only girls Miriam would speak kindly of were girls so plain or so dowdy as not in any way to rival Celia. This trait in her mother sometimes annoyed Celia but more often warmed her heart towards her. Darling thing, what a ridiculous mother bird she was with her ruffled plumage! So absurdly illogical . . . But it was sweet of her, all the same. Like all Miriam's actions and feelings, it was so violent.

She was glad her mother was so happy. It had indeed all come about in a very wonderful way.

177

It was nice to be marrying into a family of 'old friends'. And she certainly did like Jim better than anyone else she knew — much, *much* better. He was just the kind of man she had always imagined having as a husband. Young, masterful, full of ideals.

Did girls always feel depressed when they got engaged? Perhaps they did. It was so final — so irrevocable.

She yawned as she picked up Mrs Besant. Theosophy depressed her too. A lot of it seemed so silly . . .

Bimetallism was better . . .

Everything was rather dull — much duller than it had been two days ago.

3

There was a letter on her plate next morning addressed in Jim's handwriting. A little flush rose in Celia's cheek. A letter from Jim. Her first letter since . . .

She felt, for the first time, a little excited. He hadn't said much, but perhaps in a letter . . .

She took it out in the garden and opened it.

Dearest Celia [wrote Jim]: I got back very late for supper. Old Mrs Cray was rather annoyed but old Cray was rather amusing. He told her not to fuss — I'd been courting, he said. They really are awfully nice, simple people — their jokes are good-natured. I wish they were a little more receptive to new ideas — in farming, I mean. He doesn't seem to have read *anything* on the subject and to be quite content to run the farm just like his great-grandfather did. I suppose agriculture is always more reactionary than anything else. It's the peasant instinct rooted in the soil.

I feel I ought, perhaps, to have spoken to your mother before I left last night. However, I have written to her. I hope she won't mind my taking you away from her. I know you mean a lot to her, but I think she likes me all right.

I might come over on Thursday — it depends on the weather. If not, Sunday next,

Lots of love,

Yours affectionately,

Jim.

After the letters of Johnnie de Burgh, it was not an epistle calculated to produce great elation of spirits in a girl!

Celia felt annoyed with Jim.

She felt that she could love him quite easily — if only he were a little different!

She tore the letter into small pieces and threw it into a ditch.

4

Jim was not a lover. He was too self-conscious. Besides, he had very definite theories and opinions.

Moreover, Celia was not really the kind of woman to stir in him all that was there to be stirred. An experienced woman, whom Jim's bashfulness would have piqued, could have made him lose his head — with beneficial results.

As it was, his relations with Celia were vaguely unsatisfactory. They seemed to have lost the easy camaraderie of their friendship and to have gained nothing in exchange.

Celia continued to admire Jim's character, to be bored by his conversation, to be maddened by his letters, and to be depressed by life in general.

The only thing she found real pleasure in was her mother's happiness.

She got a letter from Peter Maitland, to whom she had written telling her news under a promise of secrecy.

All the best to you, Celia [wrote Peter]. He sounds a thoroughly sound fellow. You don't say whether's he's got any of the ready. I hope so. Girls don't think of a thing like that, but I assure you, Celia dear, it matters. I'm much older than you and I've seen women trailing round with their husbands fagged out and worried to death over money problems. I'd like you to live like a queen. You're not the sort than can rough it.

Well, there's not much more to say. I shall have a squint at your young man when I come home in September and see whether he's worthy of you. Not that I should ever think anyone was that!

All the best to you, old girl, and may your

shadow never grow less.
    Yours always,
    Peter.

It was a strange fact, yet true nevertheless, that the thing Celia enjoyed most about her engagement was her prospective mother-in-law.

Her old childish admiration for Mrs Grant resumed its sway. Mrs Grant, she thought now as then, was lovely. Grey-haired now, she had still the same queen-like grace, the same exquisite blue eyes and swaying figure, the same well-remembered, clear, beautiful voice, the same dominating personality.

Mrs Grant realized Celia's admiration for her and was pleased by it. Possibly she was not quite satisfied about the engagement — something may have seemed to her lacking. She quite agreed with what the young people had decided — to be openly engaged at the end of six months and married a year later.

Jim adored his mother, and he was pleased that Celia should so obviously adore her also.

Grannie was very pleased that Celia was engaged but felt constrained to throw out many dark hints as to the difficulties of married life, ranging from poor John Godolphin who developed cancer of the throat on his honeymoon, to old Admiral Collingway who 'gave his wife a bad disease, and then carried on with the governess, and at last, my dear, she couldn't keep a maid in the house, poor thing. He used to jump out at them from behind doors — and not a stitch on. Naturally they wouldn't stay.'

Celia felt that Jim was much too healthy to get cancer of the throat ('Ah, my dear, but it's the healthy ones who get it,' interpolated Grannie), and not even the wildest imagination could picture the sedate Jim as an elderly satyr leaping on maidservants.

Grannie liked Jim but was, secretly, a little disappointed in him. A young man who didn't drink or smoke and who looked embarrassed when jokes were made — what sort of a young man was that? Frankly, Grannie preferred a more virile generation.

'Still,' she said hopefully, 'I saw him pick up a handful of gravel off the terrace last night, and I thought that pretty — the place where your feet had trodden.'

In vain Celia explained that it had been a matter of geological interest. Grannie would hear of no such explanation.

'That's what he told you, dear. But I know young men. Why, young Planterton wore my handkerchief next his heart for seven years, and he only met me once at a ball.'

Through the indiscretion of Grannie the news leaked through to Mrs Luke.

'Well, child, I hear you've fixed things up with a young man. I'm glad you turned Johnnie down. George said I wasn't to say anything to put you off, as he was such a good match. But I always did think he looked exactly like a codfish.'

Thus Mrs Luke.

182

She went on:

'Roger Raynes is always asking about you. I put him off. Of course, he's quite well off — that's why he never really does anything with his voice. A pity — because he could be a professional. But I don't suppose you'd fancy him — he's such a little roundabout. And he eats steak for breakfast and always cuts himself shaving. I hate men who cut themselves shaving.'

6

One day in July, Jim came over in a state of great excitement. A very rich man, a friend of his father's was going on a trip round the world with the special view of studying agriculture. He had offered to take Jim with him.

Jim talked excitedly for some time. He was grateful to Celia for her prompt interest and acquiescence. He had had a half guilty feeling that she might be annoyed at his going.

A fortnight later he started off in boisterous spirits, sending Celia a farewell telegram from Dover:

BEST OF LOVE TAKE CARE OF YOURSELF — JIM.

How beautiful an August morning can be . . .

Celia came out on the terrace in front of the house and looked round her. It was early — there was still dew on the grass — that long green slope that Miriam had refused to have cut up into beds. There was the beech tree — bigger than ever, heavily, deeply green. And the sky was blue — blue — blue like deep sea water.

Never, Celia thought, had she felt so happy. The old familiar 'pain' clutched at her. It was so lovely — so lovely — it hurt . . .

Oh, beautiful, beautiful world! . . .

The gong sounded. She went in to breakfast.

Her mother looked at her. 'You look very happy, Celia.'

'I am happy. It's such a lovely day.'

Her mother said quietly:

'It's not only that . . . It's because Jim's gone away, isn't it?'

Celia had hardly known it herself till that minute. Relief — wild, joyous relief. She wouldn't have to read theosophy or economics for nine months. For nine glorious delirious months she could live as she pleased — feel as she pleased. She was free — free — free . . . She looked at her mother, and her mother looked back at her.

Miriam said gently:

'You mustn't marry him. Not if you feel like that . . . I didn't know . . . '

Words poured from Celia.

'I didn't know myself . . . I thought I loved him — yes — he's so much the nicest person I ever met — and so splendid in every way.'

Miriam nodded sadly. It was the ruin of all her newfound peace.

'I knew you didn't love him at first — but I thought that you might grow to love him if you were engaged. It's been the other way . . . You

184

mustn't marry anybody who bores you.'

'Bores me!' Celia was shocked. 'But he's so clever — he couldn't bore me.'

'That's just what he does do, Celia.' She sighed and added: 'He's very young.'

Perhaps the thought came to her that minute that if only these two had not met until Jim was older all might have been well. She was always to feel that Jim and Celia missed love by a very little — but they did miss it . . .

And secretly, in spite of her disappointment and her fear for Celia's future, a little thread ran singing joyfully, 'She will not leave me yet. She will not leave me yet . . . '

7

Once Celia had written to Jim to tell him she could not marry him she felt as though a load of care had slipped off her back.

When Peter Maitland came down in September he was amazed at her good spirits and her beauty.

'So you gave that young fellow the chuck, Celia?'

'Yes.'

'Poor chap. Still, I dare say you'll soon find someone more to your mind. I suppose people are always asking you to marry them?'

'Oh, not very many.'

'How many?'

Celia thought.

There was that funny little man, Captain Gale,

in Cairo, and a silly boy on the boat coming back (if that counted), and Major de Burgh, of course, and Ralph and his tea-planter friend (who was married to another girl now, by the way), and Jim — and then there had been that ridiculous business with Roger Raynes only a week ago.

Mrs Luke had no sooner heard that Celia's engagement was off than she had telegraphed for Celia to come and stay. Roger was coming, and Roger was always asking George to arrange for him to meet Celia again. Things had really looked quite promising. They had sung together in the drawing-room by the hour.

'If only he could sing his proposal, she might take him,' thought Mrs Luke hopefully.

'Why shouldn't she take him? Raynes is a jolly good chap,' said George reproachfully.

It was no good explaining to men. They never could understand what women 'saw' or did not 'see' in a man.

'A bit of a roundabout, of course,' admitted George. 'But looks don't matter in a man.'

'A man invented that saying,' snapped Mrs Luke.

'Well, come now, Amy, you women don't want a barber's block.'

He insisted that 'Roger should have his chance.'

Roger's best chance would have been to propose to Celia in song. He had a magnificent, moving voice. Listening to him singing, Celia would easily have thought she loved him. But when the music was over, Roger resumed his everyday personality.

186

Celia was a little nervous of Mrs Luke's matchmaking. She saw the look in her eye and carefully manoeuvred not to be alone with Roger. She didn't want to marry him. Why let him speak at all?

But the Lukes were determined to 'give Roger his chance', and Celia found herself being compelled to drive with Roger in the dogcart to a certain picnic.

It had not been an auspicious drive. Roger had talked of the delights of a home life and Celia had said a hotel was more fun. Roger said he had always fancied living somewhere not more than an hour from London — but in country surroundings.

'Where would you hate living most?' asked Celia.

'London. I couldn't live in London.'

'Fancy,' said Celia. 'It's the only place I could bear to live.'

She looked at him coolly after uttering this untruth.

'Oh, I dare say I *could* do it,' said Roger, sighing, 'if I found the ideal woman. I think I have found her. I — '

'I must tell you something so funny that happened the other day,' said Celia desperately.

Roger did not listen to the anecdote. As soon as it was over he resumed:

'Do you know, Celia, ever since I met you the first time — '

'Do you see that bird? I do believe it's a goldfinch.'

But there was no hope. Between a man who is

determined to propose and a woman who is determined not to let him, the man always wins. The wilder Celia's red herrings, the more determined Roger became to keep to the point. He was then bitterly hurt by the curtness of Celia's refusal. She was angry because she had not managed to stave it off and also annoyed with Roger for his genuine surprise at her refusal to marry him. The drive finished in cold silence. Roger said to George that, after all, perhaps he had had a lucky escape — she seemed to have quite a temper . . .

All this passed through Celia's mind as she meditated Peter's question.

'I suppose seven,' she said at last doubtfully. 'But only two real ones.'

They were sitting on the grass under a hedge on the golf course. From there you looked out over a panorama of cliffs and sea.

Peter had let his pipe go out. He was snapping off daisies' heads with his fingers.

'You know, Celia,' he said, and his voice sounded odd and strained, 'you can — add me to that list any time you like.'

She looked at him in astonishment.

'You, Peter?'

'Yes, didn't you know?'

'No, I never thought of it. You never — seemed like that.'

'Well, it's been that way with me almost since the beginning . . . I think I knew even at Ellie's wedding. Only, you see, Celia, I'm not the right sort of fellow for you. You want a go-ahead, brainy chap — oh, yes, you do. I know what your

188

ideal man is like. He's not a lazy, easygoing fellow like me. I shan't get on in life. I'm not made that way. I shall amble through the service and retire. No fireworks. And I've very little of the ready. Five or six hundred a year — that's all we'd have to live upon.'

'I wouldn't mind that.'

'I know you wouldn't. But I mind for you. Because you don't know what it's like — and I do. You ought to have the best, Celia — absolutely the best. You're a very lovely girl. You could marry anybody. I'm not going to have you throw yourself away on a tuppeny halfpenny soldier. No proper home, always packing up and moving on. No, I always meant to keep my mouth shut and let you make the kind of marriage a beautiful girl like you ought to make. I just thought that supposing you didn't — then — well, some day, there might be a chance for me . . . '

Very timidly Celia laid her slender pink hand on the brown one. It closed round hers, held it warmly. How nice it felt — Peter's hand . . .

'I don't know that I ought to have spoken now. But we're ordered abroad again. I thought I'd like you to know before I go. Supposing Mr Right doesn't turn up — I'm there — always — waiting . . . '

Peter — dear, dear Peter . . . Somehow, Peter belonged to the nursery and the garden and Rouncy and the beech tree. Safety — happiness — home . . .

How happy she was, sitting here looking out over the sea, with her hand in Peter's. She would

189

always be happy with Peter. Dear, easygoing, sweet-tempered Peter.

He had never looked at her all this time. His face looked rather grim — rather tense . . . very brown and dark.

She said:

'I'm very fond of you, Peter. I'd like to marry you . . .'

He turned then — slowly, as he did everything. He put his arm around her . . . those dark, kind eyes looked into hers.

He kissed her — not awkwardly like Jim — not passionate like Johnnie — but with a deep, satisfying tenderness.

'My little love,' he said. 'Oh, my little love . . .'

8

Celia wanted to marry Peter at once and go out to India with him. But Peter refused point-blank.

He insisted obstinately that she was still very young — only nineteen now — and that she must still have every chance.

'I'd feel the most awful swine, Celia, if I went and snatched at you greedily. You may change your mind — you may meet someone you like a lot better than me.'

'I shan't — I shan't.'

'You don't know. Lots of girls are keen about a fellow when they're nineteen and wonder what they could have seen in him by the time they're twenty-two. I'm not going to rush you. You must have lots of time — you've got to be quite sure you're not making a mistake.'

Lots of time. The Maitland habit of thought — never rushing a thing — plenty of time. And so the Maitlands missed trains and trams and appointments and meals and, sometimes, more important things.

Peter talked in the same way to Miriam.

'You know how I love Celia,' he said. 'You've always known, I think. That's why you trusted me to go about with her. I know I'm not the sort of fellow you thought of her marrying — '

Miriam interrupted.

'I want her to be happy. I think she would be happy with you.'

'I'd give my life to make her happy — you know that. But I don't want to rush her. Some fellow with money might come along and if she liked him — '

'Money is not everything. It is true that I hoped Celia would not be poor. Still, if you and she are fond of each other — you have enough to live on by being careful.'

'It's a dog's life for a woman. And it's taking her away from you.'

'If she loves you — '

'Yes, there's an if about it. You feel that. Celia's got to have every chance. She's too young to know her own mind. I shall have leave in two years' time. If she still feels the same — '

'I hope she will.'

'She's so beautiful, you know. I feel she ought to do better. I'm a rotten match for her.'

'Don't be too humble,' said Miriam suddenly. 'Women don't appreciate it.'

191

'No, perhaps you're right.'

Celia and Peter were very happy together during the fortnight spent at home. Two years would soon pass.

'And I promise you I'll be faithful to you, Peter. You'll find me waiting for you.'

'Now, Celia, that's just what you're not to do — consider yourself promised to me. You're absolutely free.'

'I don't want to be.'

'Never mind, you are.'

She said with sudden resentment:

'If you really loved me, you'd want me to marry you at once and come with you.'

'Oh, my love, my little love, don't you understand that it's because I love you so much?'

Seeing his stricken face she knew that he did indeed love her, with a love that feared to grasp at a treasure much desired.

Three weeks later Peter sailed.

A year and three months later Celia married Dermot.

9

Dermot

1

Peter came gradually into Celia's life; Dermot came with a rush.

Except that he too was a soldier, no greater contrast could have been imagined between two men than between Dermot and Peter.

Celia met him at a regimental ball at York to which she went with the Lukes.

When she was introduced to this tall young man with the intensely blue eyes he said: 'I'd like three dances, please.'

After they had danced the second, he asked for three more. Her programme was full up. He said:

'Never mind. Cut somebody.'

He took her programme from her and crossed out three names at random.

'There,' he said, 'don't forget. I'll be early so as to snatch you in time.'

Dark, tall, with dark curling hair; very blue eyes that slanted, faun-like, and glanced at you and away quickly. A decided manner, an air of being able to get his own way always — under any circumstances.

At the end of the ball he asked how long Celia was going to be in this part of the world. She told him she was leaving the next day. He asked if she ever went to London.

She told him that she was going to stay with her grandmother next month. She gave him the address.

He said: 'I may be in town about then. I'll come and call.'

Celia said: 'Do.'

But she never thought seriously that he would. A month is a long time. He fetched her a glass of lemonade, and she sipped it, and they talked about life, and Dermot said that he believed you could always get everything you wanted if only you wanted it enough.

Celia felt rather guilty over the dances she had cut — it wasn't a habit of hers — only, somehow, she hadn't been able to help it . . . He was like that.

She felt sorry that she would probably never see him again.

But, to be truthful, she had forgotten all about him when on entering the house at Wimbledon one day she found Grannie leaning forward animatedly in her big chair, talking to a young man whose face and ears were rather pink with embarrassment.

'I hope you haven't forgotten me,' mumbled Dermot.

He was by now very shy indeed.

Celia said of course she hadn't, and Grannie, always sympathetic to young men, asked him to stay on to dinner, which he did. And after dinner they went into the drawing-room, and Celia sang to him.

Before he left he propounded a plan for the morrow. He had tickets for a matinèe — would Celia come in to town and go with him to it? When it turned out that he meant alone, Grannie demurred. She didn't think Celia's mother would like it. The young man, however, managed to get round Grannie. So Grannie gave in, but she said on no account was he to take Celia anywhere to tea afterwards. She was to come straight home.

So that was settled, and Celia met him at the matinèe and enjoyed it more than any theatre she had ever seen, and they had tea at the buffet at Victoria, because Dermot said that didn't count.

He came twice again before Celia returned home.

The third day after Celia had returned she was having tea with the Maitlands when she was summoned to the telephone. Her mother spoke:

'Darling, you simply must come home. Some young man of yours has turned up on a motor bicycle — and you know it worries me to have to talk to young men. Come home quickly and look after him yourself.'

Celia went home wondering who it was. Her mother had said that he had mumbled his name so that she hadn't been able to hear it.

It was Dermot. He had a desperate, determined, miserable look, and he seemed quite unable to talk to Celia when he did see her. He just sat muttering monosyllables and not looking at her.

The motor bicycle was a borrowed one, he

told her. He had thought it would be refreshing to get out of London and do a few days' tour round. He was putting up at the inn. He had to go off tomorrow morning. Would she come for a walk with him first?

He was in much the same mood the next day — silent — miserable — unable to look at her. Suddenly he said:

'My leave's over, I've got to go back to York. Something's got to be settled. I must see you again. I want to see you always — all the time. I want you to marry me.'

Celia stood stock still — utterly startled. While she had recognized that Dermot liked her, it had never entered her head that a young subaltern of twenty-three would contemplate marriage.

She said: 'I'm sorry — very sorry — but I couldn't — oh, no, I couldn't.'

How could she? She was going to marry Peter. She loved Peter. Yes, she still loved Peter — just the same — but she loved Dermot also . . .

She realized that she wanted to marry Dermot more than anything in the world.

Dermot was going on:

'Well, I've got to see you, anyway . . . I expect I've asked you too soon . . . I couldn't wait . . . '

Celia said:

'You see — I'm — engaged to someone else . . . '

He looked at her — one of those quick sidelong glances. He said:

'That doesn't matter. You must give him up. You do love me?'

'I — think I do.'

Yes, she loved Dermot better than anything in the world. She would rather be unhappy with Dermot than happy with anyone else. But why put it like that? Why should she be unhappy with Dermot? Because, she supposed, she didn't know at all what he was like . . . He was a stranger . . .

Dermot was stammering.

'I — I oh! that's splendid — we'll get married at once. I can't wait . . . '

Celia thought: 'Peter. I can't bear to hurt Peter . . . '

But she knew that Dermot could bear to hurt any number of Peters and she knew that what Dermot told her to do she would do.

For the first time she looked right into his eyes which no longer gave a glance and flashed away.

Very, very blue eyes . . .

Shyly — uncertainly — they kissed . . .

2

Miriam was lying on the sofa in her bedroom, resting, when Celia came in. One glance at her daughter's face told her that something unusual had happened. Like a flash it went through Miriam's mind. 'That young man — I don't like him.'

She said, 'Darling — what is it?'

'Oh, Mother — he wants to marry me — and I want to marry him, Mother . . . '

Straight into Miriam's arms — her face buried on Miriam's shoulder.

And above the agonizing beating of her strained heart, Miriam's thought ran frenziedly:

'I don't like it — I don't like it . . . But that's selfishness — because I don't want her to go.'

3

There were difficulties almost at once. Dermot could not override Miriam high-handedly as he overrode Celia. He kept his temper because he did not want to put Celia's mother against him, but he was annoyed at any hint of opposition.

He admitted that he had no money — a bare eighty pounds a year beyond his pay. But he was annoyed when Miriam asked how he and Celia proposed to live. He said he hadn't had time to think yet. Surely they could manage — Celia wouldn't mind being poor. When Miriam said that it wasn't usual for subalterns to marry, he said impatiently that he couldn't help what was usual.

He said, rather bitterly, to Celia: 'Your mother seems determined to bring everything down to pounds, shillings, and pence.'

He was like an eager child denied the thing it had set its heart on and unwilling to listen to 'reason'.

When he had gone, Miriam felt very depressed. She saw the prospect of a long engagement with very little hope of marriage for many years to come. Perhaps, she felt, she ought not to have let them be engaged at all . . . But she loved Celia too dearly to cause her pain.

Celia said: 'Mother, I must marry Dermot. I must. I shall never love anybody else. It will come right some day — oh, say it will.'

'It seems so hopeless, my darling. You've neither of you got anything. And he's so young . . . '

'But, some day — if we wait . . . '

'Well, perhaps . . . '

'You don't like him, Mother. Why?'

'I do like him. I think he's very attractive — very attractive indeed. But not considerate . . . '

At night Miriam lay awake going over her small income. Could she make Celia an allowance — however small? If she sold the house . . .

But, at any rate, she was living rent free — running expenses had been reduced to a minimum. The house was in bad repair, and there was very little demand for such properties at the minute.

She lay awake, tossing and turning. How to get her child her heart's desire?

4

It was awful, having to write to Peter and tell him.

Such a lame letter, too — for what could she say to excuse her treachery?

When Peter's answer came it was exactly like Peter. So like Peter that Celia cried over it.

Don't blame yourself, Celia [wrote Peter]. It was my fault entirely. My fatal habit of putting things off. We're like that. That's why, as a family, we always miss the bus. I meant it for the best — to give you a chance of marrying some rich fellow. And now you've fallen in love with someone poorer than I am.

The truth of it is you feel he's got more guts than I had. I ought to have taken you at your word when you wanted to marry me and come out with me here . . . I was a cursed fool. I've lost you, and it's my own fault. He's a better man than I am — your Dermot . . . He must be a good sort, or you wouldn't have taken a fancy to him. Best of luck to you both — always. And don't grieve about me. It's my funeral, not yours . . . I could kick myself all round the town for being such a confounded fool. God bless you, my dear . . .

Dear Peter — dear, dear, Peter . . .
She thought: 'I should have been happy with Peter. Very happy always . . . '
But with Dermot life was high adventure!

5

The year of Celia's engagement was a stormy period. She would get a letter from Dermot suddenly:

I see now — your mother was perfectly right. We are too poor ever to marry. I

200

shouldn't have asked you. Forget me as soon as you can.

And then, two days later, he would arrive on the borrowed motor bicycle, take a tear-stained Celia in his arms, and declare that he couldn't give her up. Something *must* happen.

What happened was the war.

6

The war came to Celia as to most people like an utterly improbable thunderbolt. A murdered archduke, a 'war scare' in the newspapers — such things barely entered her consciousness.

And then, suddenly, Germany and Russia were actually at war — Belgium was invaded. The fantastically improbable became possible.

Letter from Dermot:

It looks as though we're going to be in it. Everyone says if we are it will be over by Christmas. They say I'm a pessimist, but I think it will be a jolly sight more like two years . . .

And then the accomplished fact — England at war . . .

Meaning to Celia one thing only — *Dermot may be killed* . . .

A telegram — he couldn't get away to say goodbye to her — could she and her mother come to him?

The banks were closed but Miriam had a couple of five-pound notes (Grannie's training: 'Always have a five-pound note in your bag, dear'). The ticket office at the station refused to take the notes. They went round through the goods yard, crossed the line, and entered the train. Ticket collector after ticket collector — no tickets? 'No, ma'am, can't take a five-pound note — ' endless writing down of names and address.

All a nightmare — nothing was real but Dermot . . .

Dermot in khaki — a different Dermot — very jerky and flippant, with haunted eyes. No one knows about this new war — it's the kind of war where *no one might come back* . . . New engines of destruction. The air — nobody knows about the air . . .

Celia and Dermot were two children clinging together . . .

'Let me come through . . . '

'Oh, God, let him come back to me . . . '

Nothing else mattered.

7

The awful suspense of those first weeks. The postcards faintly scrawled in pencil.

'*Not allowed to say where we are. Everything goes well. Love.*'

Nobody knew what was happening.

The shock of the first casualty lists.

Friends. Boys that you had danced with — killed . . .

But Dermot was safe — and that was all that mattered.

War, for most women, is the destiny of one person . . .

8

After that first week and fortnight of suspense there were things to be done at home. A Red Cross hospital was being opened near Celia's home, but she must pass her First Aid and Nursing exam. There were classes going on near Grannie, and Celia went up to stay.

Gladys, the new, pretty young house-parlourmaid, opened the door. She and a young cook now ran the establishment. Poor old Sarah was no more.

'How are you, miss?'

'Very well. Where's Grannie?'

A giggle.

'She's out, Miss Celia.'

'*Out?*'

Grannie — now just on ninety years of age — more particular than ever about letting injurious fresh air touch her. Grannie *out?*

'She went to the Army and Navy Stores, Miss Celia. She said she'd be back before you came. Oh, I believe there she is now.'

An aged four-wheeler had drawn up at the gate. Assisted by the cabman, Grannie descended cautiously on to her good leg.

She came with a firm step up the drive. Grannie looked jaunty, positively jaunty — the bugles on her mantle were swaying and glinting in the September sunshine.

'So you've arrived, Celia darling.'

Such a soft old face — like crinkled rose leaves. Grannie was very fond of Celia — and was knitting bed socks for Dermot, to keep his feet warm in the trenches.

Her voice changed as she looked at Gladys. More and more did Grannie enjoy bullying 'the maids' (well able to take care of themselves nowadays, and keeping bicycles whether Grannie liked it or not!).

'Now then, Gladys,' sharply, 'why can't you go and help the man with the things? And no taking them into the kitchen, mind. Put them in the morning-room.'

No longer did Poor Miss Bennett reign in the morning-room.

Piled inside the door were flour, biscuits, dozens of tins of sardines, rice, tapioca, sago. Grinning from ear to ear the cabman appeared. He was carrying five hams. Gladys followed with more hams. Sixteen in all were deposited in the treasure chamber.

'I may be ninety,' said Grannie (who wasn't, yet, but anticipated the event as more dramatic), 'but I shan't let the Germans starve *me* out!'

Celia was taken with hysterical laughter.

Grannie paid the cabman, gave him an enormous tip, and directed him to feed his horse better.

'Yes, mum, thank you, mum.'

He touched his hat and, still grinning, departed.

'Such a day as I've had,' said Grannie, untying her bonnet strings. She displayed no signs of fatigue and had obviously enjoyed herself.

'The Stores were packed, my dear.'

Apparently with other old ladies, all carrying off hams in four-wheeled cabs.

9

Celia never took up Red Cross work.

Several things happened. First, Rouncy broke up and went home to live with her brother. Celia and her mother did the work of the house with the disapproving aid of Gregg, who 'didn't hold' with war and ladies doing things they weren't meant to do.

Then Grannie wrote to Miriam.

Dearest Miriam: You suggested some years ago that I should make my home with you. I refused then, as I felt too old to make a move. But Dr Holt (such a *clever* man — and enjoys a good story — I'm afraid his wife doesn't really appreciate him) says my eyesight is failing and that nothing can be done about it. That is God's will and I accept it, but I do not fancy being left *at the mercy of maids*. Such wicked things as one reads of nowadays — *and I have missed several things lately*. Do not mention this when you write — they may *open my letters*. I am posting this *myself*. So I think that it will be best for me to come to you. It will make things easier, as my income will help. I do not like the idea of Celia doing things in the house. The dear child should *reserve her strength*. You remember Mrs Pinchin's Eva? Just that same delicate complexion. She *overdid things* and is now in a Sanatorium in Switzerland. You and Celia must come and help me to *move*. It will be a terrible business, I'm afraid.

It *was* a terrible business. Grannie had lived in the house at Wimbledon for fifty years, and, true product of a thrifty generation, she had never thrown away anything that might possibly 'come in'.

There were vast wardrobes and chests of drawers of solid mahogany, each drawer and shelf crammed with neatly rolled bundles of materials and odds and ends put away safely by Grannie and forgotten. There were innumerable 'remnants', odd lengths of silks and satins, and prints and cottons. There were dozens of needle books 'for the maids at Christmas', with the needles rusted in them. There were old scraps and pieces of gowns. There were letters and papers and diaries and recipes and newspaper cuttings. There were forty-four pin-cushions and thirty-five pairs of scissors. There were drawers and drawers full of fine linen underclothes all gone into holes, but preserved because of 'the good embroidery, my dear'.

Saddest of all there was the store cupboard (memory of Celia's youth). The store cupboard had defeated Grannie. She could no longer penetrate into its depths. Stores had lain there undisturbed while fresh stores accumulated on top of them. Weevily flour, crumbling biscuits, mouldy jams, liquescent mass of preserved fruits — all these were disinterred from the depths and thrown away while Grannie sat and wept and lamented the 'shameful waste'. 'Surely, Miriam, they would do very nicely for puddings for the kitchen?'

Poor Grannie — so able and energetic and thrifty a housewife — defeated by age and failing sight, and forced to sit and see alien eyes surveying her defeat . . .

She fought tooth and nail for every one of her treasures that this ruthless younger generation wanted to throw away.

'Not my brown velvet. That's my brown *velvet*. Madame Bonserot made it for me in Paris. So Frenchy! Everyone admired me in it.'

'But it's all worn, dear, the nap has gone. It's in holes.'

'It would do up. I'm sure it would do up.'

Poor Grannie — old, defenceless, at the mercy of these younger folk — so scornful, so full of their 'That's no good, throw it away.'

She had been brought up never to throw away anything. It might come in some day. They didn't know that, these young folk.

They tried to be kind. They yielded so far to her wishes as to fill a dozen old-fashioned trunks with bits and pieces of stuffs and old moth-eaten furs — all things that could never be used, but why upset the old lady more than need be?

Grannie herself insisted on packing various

faded pictures of old-fashioned gentlemen.

'That's dear Mr Harty — and Mr Lord — such a handsome couple as we made dancing together! Everyone remarked on it.'

Alas, for Grannie's packing! Mr Harty and Mr Lord arrived with the glass shattered in the frames. And yet, once Grannie's packing had been celebrated. Nothing she packed was ever broken.

Sometimes, when she thought no one was looking, Grannie would surreptitiously retrieve little bits of trimming, a jet ornament, a little piece of net ruching, a crochet motif. She would stuff them into that capacious pocket of hers, and would secretly transfer them to one of the great ark-like trunks that stood in her bedroom ready for her personal packing.

Poor Grannie. Moving nearly killed her, but it didn't quite. She had the will to live. It was the will to live that was driving her out of the home she had lived in so long. The Germans were not going to starve her out — and they were not going to get her in an air raid, either. Grannie meant to live and enjoy life. When you had reached ninety years you knew how extraordinarily enjoyable life was. That was what the young people didn't understand. They spoke as though anyone old were half dead and sure to be miserable. Young people, thought Grannie, remembering an aphorism of her youth, thought the old people fools, but old people *knew* that young people were fools! Her aunt Caroline had said that at the age of eighty-five and her aunt Caroline had been right.

Anyway, Grannie didn't think much of young

people nowadays. They had no stamina. Look at the furniture removers — four strapping young men — and they actually asked her to empty the drawers of her big mahogany chest of drawers.

'It was carried up with every drawer locked,' said Grannie.

'You see, ma'am, it's solid mahogany. And there's heavy stuff in the drawers.'

'So there was when it came up! There were men in those days. You're all weaklings nowadays. Making a fuss about a little weight.'

The young men grinned, and with some difficulty the chest was got down the stairs and out to the van.

'That's better,' said Grannie approvingly. 'You see, you don't know what you can do until you try.'

Among the various things removed from the house were thirty demijohns of Grannie's home-made liqueurs. Only twenty-eight were unloaded the other end . . .

Was this, perhaps, the revenge of the grinning young men?

'Rogues,' said Grannie. 'That's what they are — rogues. And call themselves teetotallers too. The impudence of it.'

But she tipped them handsomely and was not really displeased. It was, after all, a subtle compliment to her home-made liqueur . . .

10

When Grannie was installed, a cook was found to replace Rouncy. This was a girl of twenty-eight called Mary. She was good-natured and pleasant to elderly people, and chattered to Grannie about her young man and her relations who suffered from an agreeable number of complaints. Grannie delighted ghoulishly in the bad legs, varicose veins, and other ailments of Mary's relations. She gave her bottles of patent medicines and shawls for them.

Celia began to think once more about taking up war work, though Grannie combated the idea vigorously, prophesying the most dire disasters if Celia 'over-strained' herself.

Grannie loved Celia. She gave her mysterious warnings against all the dangers of life, and five-pound notes. One of Grannie's fixed beliefs in life was that you should always have a five-pound note 'handy'.

She gave Celia fifty pounds in five-pound notes and told her to 'keep it by her'.

'Don't even let your husband know you've got it. A woman never knows when she may need a little nest egg . . .

'Remember, dear, men are not to be trusted. Gentlemen can be very agreeable, but you can't trust one of them — unless he's such a namby-pamby fellow that he's no good at all.'

11

The move and all that had gone with it had successfully distracted Celia's mind from the war and Dermot.

Now that Grannie was settled in, Celia began

to chafe at her own inactivity.

How to keep herself from thinking of Dermot — out there?

In desperation she married off 'the girls'! Isabella married a rich Jew, Elsie married an explorer. Ella became a school teacher. She married an elderly man, somewhat of an invalid, who was charmed by her young chatter. Ethel and Annie kept house together. Vera had a romantic morganatic alliance with a royal prince, and they both died tragically in a motor accident on their wedding day.

Planning the weddings, choosing the bridesmaids' gowns, arranging the funeral music for Vera — all this helped to keep Celia's mind from realities.

She longed to be hard at work at something. But it meant leaving home . . . Could Miriam and Grannie spare her?

Grannie required a good deal of attention. Celia felt she couldn't desert her mother.

But it was Miriam herself who urged Celia to leave home. She understood well enough that work, hard physical work, was the thing that would help Celia at the present time.

Grannie wept, but Miriam stood firm.

'Celia must go.'

But, after all, Celia didn't take up any war work.

Dermot got wounded in the arm and came home to a hospital. On his recovery he was passed fit for home service and was sent to the War Office. He and Celia were married.

10

Marriage

1

Celia's ideas about marriage were limited in the extreme.

Marriage, for her, was the 'living happily ever afterwards' of her favourite fairy tales. She saw no difficulties in it, no possibilities of shipwreck. When people loved each other they were happy. Unhappy marriages, and of course she knew there were many such, were because people didn't love each other.

Neither Grannie's Rabelaisian descriptions of the male character, nor her mother's warnings (so old-fashioned they sounded to Celia) that you had to 'keep a man', nor any amount of realistic literature with sordid and unhappy endings really made any impression on Celia at all. 'The men' of Grannie's conversation never struck her as being the same species as Dermot. People in books were people in books, and Miriam's warnings struck Celia as peculiarly amusing considering the extraordinary happiness of her mother's own married life.

'You know, Mummy, Daddy never looked at anybody but you.'

'No, but then he'd spent a very gay life as a young man.'

212

'I don't believe you like Dermot or trust him.'

'I do like him,' said Miriam. 'I find him extremely attractive.'

Celia laughed, and said:

'But you wouldn't think anybody I married good enough for ME — your precious pet lamb pigeony pumpkin — come now, would you? Not the superest of supermen.'

And Miriam had to confess that perhaps that was true.

And Celia and Dermot were so happy together.

Miriam told herself that she had been unduly suspicious and hostile towards the man who had taken her daughter away from her.

2

Dermot as a husband was quite different from what Celia had imagined. All the boldness, the masterfulness, the audacity of him fell from him. He was young, diffident, very much in love, and Celia was his first love.

In some ways, indeed, he was rather like Jim Grant. But whereas Jim's diffidence had annoyed Celia because she was not in love with him, Dermot's diffidence made him still dearer to her.

She had been, half-consciously, a little afraid of Dermot. He had been a stranger to her. She had felt that though she loved him she knew nothing about him.

Johnnie de Burgh had appealed to the physical side of her, Jim to the mental. Peter was woven

213

into the very stuff of her life, but in Dermot she found what she had never yet had — a playmate.

There was something that was to be eternally boyish in Dermot — it found and met the child in Celia. Their aims, their minds, their characters were poles apart, but they each wanted a playfellow and found that playfellow in the other.

Married life to them was a game — they played at it enthusiastically.

3

What are the things one remembers in life? Not the so-called important things. No — little things — trivialities . . . staying persistently in the memory — not to be shaken off.

Looking back on her early married life, what did Celia remember?

Buying a frock in a dressmaker's — the first frock Dermot bought her. She tried them on in a little cubicle with an elderly woman to help her. Then Dermot was called in to say which he would like.

They both enjoyed it hugely.

Dermot pretended, of course, that he had often done this before. They weren't going to admit they were newly married before the shop people — not likely!

Dermot even said nonchalantly:

'That's rather like the one I got you in Monte two years ago.'

They decided at last on a periwinkle blue with

a little bunch of rosebuds on the shoulder.

Celia kept that frock. She never threw it away.

4

House-hunting! They must, of course, have a furnished house or flat. There was no knowing when Dermot would be ordered abroad again. And it must be as cheap as possible.

Neither Celia nor Dermot knew anything about neighbourhoods or prices. They started confidently in the heart of Mayfair!

The next day they were in South Kensington, Chelsea, and Bayswater. They reached West Kensington, Hammersmith, West Hampstead, Battersea, and other outlying neighbourhoods the day after.

In the end they were undecided between two. One was a self-contained flat at three guineas a week. It was in a block of mansions in West Kensington. It was scrupulously clean and belonged to an awe-inspiring maiden lady called Miss Banks. Miss Banks radiated efficiency.

'No plate or linen? That simplifies things. I never permit agents to make the inventory. I am sure you will agree with me that it is a sheer waste of money. You and I can check over things together.'

It was a long time since anyone had frightened Celia as much as Miss Banks did. Every question she asked served to expose anew Celia's complete lack of knowledge where flat-taking was concerned.

Dermot said they would let Miss Banks know, and they got away into the street.

'What do you think?' asked Celia breathlessly. 'It's very clean.'

She had never thought about cleanliness before, but two days' investigation of cheap furnished flats had brought the matter home to her.

'Some of those other flats simply *smelt*,' she added.

'I know — and it's quite decently furnished, and Miss Banks says it's a good shopping neighbourhood. I'm not quite sure I like Miss Banks herself. She's such a tartar.'

'She is.'

'I feel she knows too much for us.'

'Let's go and look at the other again. After all, it's cheaper.'

The other was two and a half guineas a week. It was the top floor of an old decayed house that had known better days. There were only two rooms and a large kitchen, but they were big rooms, nobly proportioned, and they looked out over a garden which actually had two trees in it.

It was, undeniably, not nearly as clean as the flat of the efficient Miss Banks, but it was, Celia said, quite a nice kind of dirt. The wallpaper showed damp, and the paint was peeling, and the boards needed restaining. But the cretonne covers were clean, though so faded as hardly to show the pattern, and it had big, comfortable, shabby armchairs.

There was another great attraction to it in Celia's eyes. The woman who lived in the

216

basement would be able to cook for them. And she looked a nice woman, fat, good-natured, with a kindly eye that reminded Celia of Rouncy.

'We shouldn't have to look for a servant.'

'That's true. You're sure it will be all right for you, though? It's not shut off from the rest of the house, and it isn't — well, it isn't what you've been accustomed to, Celia. I mean your home is so lovely.'

Yes, home was lovely. She realized now how lovely it was. The mellow dignity of the Chippendale and the Hepplewhite, the china, the fresh cool chintzes . . . Home might be getting shabby — the roof leaked, the range was old-fashioned, the carpets were showing wear, but it was still beautiful . . .

'But as soon as the war is over' — Dermot stuck out his chin in his determined way — 'I mean to set to at something and make money for you.'

'I don't want money. And besides, you're a captain already. You wouldn't have been a captain for ten years if it hadn't been for the war.'

'A captain's pay is no good, really. There's no future in the army. I shall find something better. Now I've got you to work for, I feel I could do anything. And I shall.'

Celia felt a thrill at his words. Dermot was so different from Peter. He didn't accept life. He set out to change it. And she felt he would succeed.

She thought:

'I was right to marry him. I don't care what

217

anyone says. Some day they'll admit that I was right.'

Because, of course, there *had* been criticism. Mrs Luke, in particular, had shown heartfelt dismay.

'But, darling Celia — your life will be too *dreadful*. Why, you won't even be able to have a kitchenmaid. You'll have simply to pig it.'

Farther than no kitchenmaid Mrs Luke's imagination refused to go. It was, for her, the supreme catastrophe. Celia magnanimously forbore to break it to her that they mightn't even have a cook!

Then Cyril, who was fighting in Mesopotamia, had written a long disapproving letter on hearing of her engagement. He said it was an absurd business.

But Dermot was ambitious. He would succeed. He had a quality in him — a driving power — that Celia felt and admired. It was so different from anything she possessed herself.

'Let's have this flat,' she said. 'I like it best — I really do. And Miss Lestrange is much nicer than Miss Banks.'

Miss Lestrange was an amiable woman of thirty with a twinkle in her eye and a good-natured smile.

If this serious young house-hunting couple amused her, she did not show it. She agreed to all their suggestions, imparted a certain amount of tactful information and explained the working of the geyser to an awe-stricken Celia who had never met such a thing before.

'But you can't have baths often,' she said

218

cheerfully. 'The ration of gas is only forty thousand cubic feet — and you've got to cook, remember.'

So Celia and Dermot took 8 Lanchester Terrace for six months, and Celia started her career as a housewife.

5

The thing that Celia suffered from most in her early married life was loneliness.

Dermot went off to the War Office every morning, and Celia was left with a long empty day on her hands.

Pender, Dermot's batman, served up a breakfast of bacon and eggs, cleaned up the flat, and left to draw the rations. Mrs Steadman then came up from the basement to discuss the evening meal with Celia.

Mrs Steadman was warm-hearted, talkative, and a willing if somewhat uncertain cook. She was, she admitted herself, 'heavy in hand with the pepper'. There seemed to be no halfway course with her between completely unseasoned food or something that brought the tears to your eyes and made you choke.

'I've always been like that — ever since a girl,' said Mrs Steadman cheerfully. 'Curious, isn't it? And I've no hand for pastry, either.'

Mrs Steadman took motherly command of Celia, who was anxious to be economical and was uncertain how to do it.

'You'd better let me shop for you. A young

lady like you would get taken advantage of. You'd never think to stand a herring up on its tail to test its freshness. And some of these fish salesmen are that artful.'

Mrs Steadman shook her head darkly.

Housekeeping was complicated by its being wartime. Eggs were eightpence each. Celia and Dermot lived a good deal on 'egg substitutes', soup squares which, no matter what their advertised flavour, Dermot always referred to as 'brown-sand soup', and their meat ration.

The meat ration excited Mrs Steadman more than anything had done for a long time. When Pender returned with the first huge chunk of beef, Celia and Mrs Steadman walked admiringly round it, while Mrs Steadman gave tongue freely.

'Isn't that a beautiful sight now? Fairly makes my mouth water. I haven't seen a bit of meat like that since the war began. A picture, that's what I call it. I wish Steadman were at home, I'd get him up to see it — you not objecting, ma'am. It would be a treat for him to see a bit of meat like that. If you're wanting to roast it, I don't think it will go in that tiny gas oven. I'll cook it downstairs for you.'

Celia pressed Mrs Steadman to accept some slices of it when cooked, and after a proper reluctance Mrs Steadman consented.

'Just for once — though not wishing to impose on you.'

So free had been Mrs Steadman's admiration that Celia herself felt quite excited when 'the joint' was placed proudly on the table.

For lunch Celia usually went out and fetched something from a national kitchen near by. She did not dare to use up the gas ration too early in the week. By using the gas stove only morning and evening, and reducing baths to twice a week, they could just keep within it and allow for firing in the sitting-room.

In the matter of butter and sugar Mrs Steadman was a valuable ally producing supplies of these commodities much in excess of the ration tickets.

'They know me, you see,' she said to Celia. 'Young Alfred, he always tips me the wink when I come in. 'Plenty for you, Ma,' he says. But he doesn't go handing it out to every fine lady that comes in. He and I know each other.'

Thus cared for by Mrs Steadman, Celia had her whole day practically to herself.

And she found it increasingly difficult to know what to do with it!

At home there had been the garden, the flowers to do, her piano. There had been Miriam . . .

Here there was nobody. Such friends as she had in London were either married or gone elsewhere or were engaged in war work. Most of them, too, were frankly too rich now for Celia to keep up with. As an unmarried girl she had been asked freely to houses, to dances, to parties at Ranelagh and Hurlingham. But now, as a married woman, all that ceased. She and Dermot could not entertain people in return. People had never meant much to Celia, but she did feel the inactivity of her days. She proposed to Dermot taking up hospital work.

He negatived the idea violently. He hated the idea of it. Celia gave in to him. In the end he agreed to her taking up a course of typewriting and shorthand. Also bookkeeping which, as Celia pointed out, would be useful to her if she wanted a job afterwards.

She found life much pleasanter now she had some work to do. She took an extreme pleasure in bookkeeping — the neatness and accuracy of which pleased her.

And then there was the joy of Dermot's return. They were both so excited and happy in their new life together.

Best of all was the time when they would sit in front of the fire before going to bed, Dermot with a cup of Ovaltine, Celia with a cup of Bovril.

They could as yet hardly believe it was true — that they were really together for always.

Dermot was not demonstrative. He never said, 'I love you,' hardly ever attempted a spontaneous caress. When he did break through his reserve and say something, Celia treasured it up as something to remember. It was so obviously difficult for him that she prized these chance words and sayings all the more. They always startled her when they came.

They would be sitting talking of the oddities of Mrs Steadman when suddenly Dermot would clutch her to him and stammer:

'Celia — you're so beautiful — so beautiful. Promise me you'll always be beautiful.'

'You'd love me just the same if I weren't.'

'No. Not quite. It wouldn't be quite the same. Promise me. Say you'll always be beautiful . . . '

6

Three months after settling in, Celia went home for a week's visit. She found her mother looking ill and tired. Grannie, on the other hand, was looking blooming and had a splendid repertoire of German atrocity stories.

Miriam was like a drooping flower placed in water. The day after Celia's return she had revived — was her old self again.

'Have you missed me so terribly, Mummy?'

'Yes, darling. Don't talk about it. It had to come some day. And you're happy — you look happy.'

'Yes, oh, Mummy, you were quite wrong about Dermot. He's kind — he's so kind that nobody could be kinder . . . And we have such fun. You know how I adore oysters. For a joke he got a dozen and put them in my bed — said it was an oyster bed — oh, it sounds silly told, but we laughed and laughed. He's such a dear. And so good. I don't think he's ever done a mean or dishonourable thing in his life. Pender, that's his batman, thinks the world of 'the captain'. He's rather critical of me. I don't believe he thinks I'm good enough for his idol. He said the other day, 'The captain's very fond of onions, but we never seem to have them here.' So we had fried ones at once. Mrs Steadman's on my side. She always wants me to have the food I like. She says men are all very well, but if she once gave in to Steadman where would she be? she'd like to know.'

Celia sat on her mother's bed, chatting happily.

It was lovely to be home — home looked so much lovelier than she remembered. It was so *clean* — the spotless cloth for lunch, and the shining silver and the polished glasses. How much one took for granted!

The food, too, though very plain, was delicious, appetizingly cooked and served.

Mary, her mother told her, was going to join the WAACS.

'I think it's quite right that she should. She's young.'

Gregg had proved unexpectedly difficult since the war. She grumbled unceasingly at the food.

'A hot meat dinner every day is what I've been used to — these insides and this fish — it's not right and it's not nourishing.'

In vain Miriam tried to explain the restrictions in war time. Gregg was too old to take it in.

'Economy's one thing — proper food's another. And margarine I never have eaten and never will. My father would turn in his grave if he knew his daughter was eating margarine — and in a proper gentleman's house too.'

Miriam laughed when telling this to Celia.

'At first I was rather weak and used to give her the butter and eat margarine myself. Then, one day, I wrapped the butter in the margarine paper, and the margarine in the butter paper. I took them both out and told her this was unusually good margarine — just like butter — would she taste it? She did and pulled a face at once. No, indeed, she couldn't eat stuff like that. So then I produced the real margarine in the butter paper and said did she like that better? She tasted it and said, 'Ah, yes, that was the right thing.' So then I told her the truth and I was rather fierce — and since then we share the butter and margarine equally, and we've had no fuss.'

Grannie was also adamant on the subject of food.

'I hope, Celia, you take plenty of butter and eggs. They're *good* for you.'

'Well, one can't get very much butter, Grannie.'

'Nonsense, my dear, it's good for you. You must have it. That beautiful girl, Mrs Riley's daughter, died only the other day. Starved herself. Out working all day — and all these scraps at home. Pneumonia on top of influenza. I could have told her how it would be.'

And Grannie nodded cheerfully over her knitting needles.

Poor Grannie, her sight was failing badly. She only knitted on big pins now, and even then she often dropped a stitch or made a mistake in the pattern. Then she would sit weeping quietly — the tears running down her old roseleaf cheeks.

'It's the waste of time,' she would say. 'It makes me so mad.'

She was getting increasingly suspicious of her surroundings.

When Celia came into her bedroom in the morning she would often find the old lady crying.

'It's my earrings, dearie, my diamond earrings your grandfather gave me. That girl has taken them.'

'Which girl?'

'Mary. She tried to poison me too. She put something in my boiled egg. I tasted it.'

'Oh, no, Grannie, you couldn't put anything in a *boiled* egg.'

'I tasted it, my dear. Bitter on my tongue.' Grannie made a face. 'A servant girl poisoned her mistress only the other day, I heard about it in the paper. She knows I know about her taking my things. Several things I've missed. And now my beautiful earrings.'

Grannie wept again.

'Are you sure, Grannie? Perhaps they're in the drawer all the time.'

'It's no use your looking, dear, they're gone.'

'Which drawer was it?'

'The right-hand one — where she passed with the tray. I rolled them up in my mittens. But it's no use. I looked carefully.'

Then Celia would produce the earrings rolled up in a strip of lace, and Grannie would express delighted surprise and say that Celia was a good, clever girl, but her suspicions of Mary remained unabated.

She would lean forward in her chair and hiss excitedly.

'Celia — your bag. Your handbag. Where is it?'

'In my room, Grannie.'

226

'They're up there now. I heard them.'

'Yes, they're doing the room.'

'They've been a long time. They're looking for your bag. Always keep it with you.'

Writing cheques was another thing Grannie found very difficult with her failing eyesight. She would get Celia to stand over her and tell her where to start and when she was reaching the end of the paper.

Then, with a sigh, the cheque written, she would give it to Celia to take to the bank to cash.

'You'll notice I've made it out for ten pounds, although the bills come to just under nine. But never make out a cheque for nine pounds, Celia, remember that. It's so easily altered into ninety.'

Since Celia herself was cashing the cheque, she was the only person who could have had the opportunity of altering it, but Grannie had not perceived that. It was merely part of her fury for self-preservation.

Another thing that upset her was when Miriam gently told her that she must have some more dresses made.

'You know, Mother, the one you've got on is almost frayed through.'

'My velvet? My beautiful velvet?'

'Yes, you can't see. But it's really in a terrible state.'

Grannie would sigh piteously, and tears would come into her eyes.

'My velvet. My good velvet; I got this velvet in Paris.'

Grannie was suffering from having been uprooted from her surroundings. She found the

country terribly dull after Wimbledon. So few
people dropped in, and there was nothing going
on. She never went outside into the garden, for
fear of the air. She sat in the dining-room as she
had sat in Wimbledon. Miriam read the papers
to her, and after that the days passed slowly for
both of them.

Almost Grannie's only relaxation was the
ordering in of large quantities of foodstuffs, and
after they had arrived the discussion and
selection of a good hiding place for them so that
they should not be convicted of 'hoarding'. The
tops of the cabinets were filled with tins of
sardines and biscuits; tinned tongues and
packets of sugar were concealed in unexpected
cupboards. Grannie's own trunks were full of
tins of golden syrup.

'But, Grannie, you really oughtn't to hoard
food.'

'Tchah!' Grannie gave a good-humoured
laugh. 'You young people don't know about
things. In the siege of Paris people ate rats. *Rats.*
Forethought, Celia, I was brought up to have
forethought.'

And then Grannie's face would go suddenly
alert.

'The servants — *they're in your room again.*
What about your jewellery?'

7

Celia had been feeling slightly sick for some
days. Finally she took to her bed and was

228

prostrate with violent nausea.

She said:

'Mummy, do you think this means I'm going to have a baby?'

'I'm afraid so.'

Miriam looked worried and depressed.

'Afraid?' Celia was surprised. 'Don't you want me to have a baby?'

'No, I didn't. Not yet. Do you want one yourself very much?'

'Well — ' Celia considered — 'I hadn't thought about it. We've never talked about having a baby, Dermot and I. I suppose we knew we might have one. I wouldn't like not to have one. I should feel I'd missed something . . . '

Dermot came down for the week-end.

It was not at all like in books. Celia was still being violently sick the whole time.

'Why are you so sick, do you think, Celia?'

'Well, I expect I'm going to have a baby.'

Dermot was terribly upset.

'I didn't want you to have one. I feel a brute — an absolute brute. I can't bear you to be sick and miserable.'

'But, Dermot, I'm very pleased about it. We'd hate not to have a baby.'

'I wouldn't care. I don't want a baby. You'll think of it all the time and not of me.'

'I shan't. I shan't.'

'Yes, you will. Women do. They're forever being domestic and messing about with a baby. They forget about their husbands altogether.'

'I shan't. I shall love the baby because it's your baby — don't you understand? It's because it's

229

your baby that it's exciting — not because it's *a* baby. And I shall always love you best — always — always — always . . . '

Dermot turned away — tears in his eyes.

'I can't bear it. I've done this to you. I could have prevented it. You might even die.'

'I shan't die. I'm frightfully strong.'

'Your grandmother says you're very delicate.'

'Oh, that's just Grannie. She can't bear to believe anyone enjoys rude health.'

Dermot took a lot of comforting. His anxiety and misery on her behalf touched Celia deeply.

When they returned to London he waited on her hand and foot, urging her to take patent foods and quack medicines to stop the sickness.

'It gets better after three months. The books say so.'

'Three months is a long time. I don't want you to be sick for three months.'

'It is rather beastly, but it can't be helped.'

Expectant motherhood, Celia felt, was distinctly disappointing. It was so different in books. She had visualized herself sitting sewing little garments while she thought beautiful thoughts about the coming child.

But how could one think beautiful thoughts when one was in the condition of one on a Channel steamer? Intense nausea blots out all thought! Celia was just a healthy but suffering animal.

She was sick not only in the early morning, but all day long at irregular intervals. Apart from the discomfort, it made life somewhat of a nightmare to her, since she never knew when the fit would seize her. Twice she jumped off a bus in the nick of time and was sick in the gutter. Under these circumstances, invitations to people's houses could not safely be accepted.

Celia stayed at home feeling miserably ill, occasionally going for a walk for exercise. She had to give up her secretarial training. Sewing made her giddy. She lay in a chair and read, or listened to the rich obstetric reminiscences of Mrs Steadman.

'It was when I was carrying Beatrice, I remember. It come over me in the greengrocer's sudden like (I'd dropped in for a half of sprouts). *I've got to have that pear!* Big and juicy, it was — the expensive kind that rich people has for dessert. Before you could say knife, I'd up and ate it! The lad who was serving me, he stared — and no wonder. But the proprietor, he was a family man, he knew what it was. 'That's all right, son,' he said. 'Don't you take no notice.' 'I'm ever so sorry,' I said. 'That's all right,' he said. 'I've got seven myself, and the missus had a fancy for nothing but pickled pork the last time.''

Mrs Steadman paused for breath, and added:

'I wish your Ma could be with you, but of course there's the old lady, your grandmother, to be considered.'

So did Celia wish her mother could come to her. The days were a nightmare. It was a foggy winter — day after day of fog. So terribly long till Dermot returned.

But he was so sweet when he did. So anxious about her. He had usually some new book he had bought on pregnancy. After dinner he used to read out extracts from it.

'*Women sometimes have a craving for strange and exotic food at these times. In olden days such cravings were always supposed to be satisfied. Nowadays they should be controlled when of a harmful character.* Do you feel any longings for strange exotic foods, Celia?'

'I don't care what I eat.'

'I've been reading up about twilight sleep. It seems quite the thing to have.'

'Dermot, when do you think I shall stop being sick? It's past four months.'

'Oh, it's bound to stop soon. All the books say so.'

But in spite of what the books said, it didn't. It went on and on.

Dermot, of his own accord, suggested that Celia should go home.

'It's so dreadful for you here all day.'

But Celia refused. He would, she knew, feel hurt if she went. And she didn't want to go. Of course, it was going to be all right; she wouldn't die, as Dermot so absurdly suggested, but — just in case — after all, women sometimes did — she wasn't going to miss a minute of her time with Dermot . . .

Sick as she was, she still loved Dermot — more than ever.

And he was so sweet to her — and so funny.

Sitting one evening, she watched his lips moving.

'What is it, Dermot? What are you saying to yourself?'

232

Dermot looked rather sheepish.

'I was just imagining that the doctor said to me, 'We can't save both the mother and the child.' And I said, 'Hack the child in pieces.' '

'Dermot, how brutal of you.'

'I hate him for what he's doing to you — if it is a he. I want it to be a she. I wouldn't mind having a blue-eyed long-legged daughter. But I hate the thought of a beastly little boy.'

'It's a boy. I want a boy. A boy just like you.'

'I shall beat him.'

'How horrid you are.'

'It's the duty of fathers to beat their children.'

'You're jealous, Dermot.'

He was jealous, horribly jealous.

'You're beautiful. I want you all to myself.'

Celia laughed and said:

'I'm particularly beautiful just now!'

'You will be again. Look at Gladys Cooper. She's had two children, and she's just as lovely as ever. It's a great consolation to me to think of that.'

'Dermot, I wish you wouldn't insist so on beauty. It — it frightens me.'

'But why? You're going to be beautiful for years and years and years . . . '

Celia gave a slight grimace and moved uncomfortably.

'What is it? Pain?'

'No, a sort of stitch in my side — very tiresome. Like something knocking.'

'It isn't it, I suppose. It says in that last book that after the fifth month — '

'Oh, but, Dermot, do you mean that 'flutter

233

under the heart'? It always sounded so poetical and lovely. I thought it would be a lovely feeling. It can't be this.'

But it was this!

Her child, Celia said, must be a very active one. It spent its time kicking.

Because of this athletic activity they christened him Punch.

'Punch been very active today?' Dermot would ask as he returned.

'Terrible,' Celia would reply. 'Not a minute's peace, but I think he's gone to sleep for a bit now.'

'I expect,' said Dermot, 'that he's going to be a professional pugilist.'

'No, I don't want his nose broken.'

What Celia wished for most was that her mother should come to her, but Grannie had not been well — a touch of bronchitis (attributed by her to having inadvertently opened a window in her bedroom), and though longing to come to Celia, Miriam did not like to leave the old lady.

'I feel I am responsible for Grannie and mustn't leave her — especially as she mistrusts the servants, but — oh, my darling, I want to be with you so much. Can't you come here?'

But Celia would not leave Dermot — at the back of her mind that faint shadowy fear — 'I might die.'

It was Grannie who took the matter into her own hands. She wrote to Celia in her thin spidery handwriting — now erratically astray on the paper owing to her failing sight.

Dearest Celia: I have insisted on your mother going to you. It is very bad for you in your condition to have desires that are not satisfied. Your dear mother wants to go, I know, but doesn't like leaving me alone with servants. I will not say anything about that, as *one never knows who reads one's letters.*

Be sure, dear child, to keep your feet up a good deal, and remember not to put your hand to your skin if you are looking at a piece of salmon or lobster. My mother put her hand to her neck when she was expecting and was looking at a piece of salmon at the time, and so your aunt Caroline was born with a mark like a piece of salmon on the side of her neck.

I enclose a five-pound note (half — the other half follows separately), and be sure you buy yourself any little delicacy you fancy.

With fond love,
Your loving Grannie.

Miriam's visit was a great delight to Celia. They made her a bed in the sitting-room on the divan, and Dermot was particularly charming to her. It was doubtful if that would have affected Miriam, but his tenderness to Celia did.

'I think perhaps it was jealousy that made me not like Dermot,' she confessed. 'You know, darling, even now, I can't like anyone who has taken you away from me.'

On the third day of her visit Miriam got a

telegram and hurried home. Grannie died a day later — almost her last words being to tell Celia never to jump off or on a bus. 'Young married women never think of these things.'

Grannie had no idea that she was dying. She fretted because she was not getting on with the little bootikins she was knitting for Celia's baby . . . She died without it having entered her head that she would not live to see her great grandchild.

8

Grannie's death made little difference financially to Miriam and Celia. The larger part of her income had been a life interest from her third husband's estate. Of the remaining money, various small legacies accounted for more than half of it. The remainder was left to Miriam and Celia. While Miriam was worse off (since Grannie's income had helped to keep up the house) Celia was the possessor of a hundred a year of her own. With Dermot's consent and approval she turned this over to Miriam to help with the upkeep of 'home'. More than ever, now, she hated the idea of selling it, and her mother agreed. A country home to which Celia's children could come — so Miriam visualized it.

'And besides, darling, you may need it yourself one of these days — when I am gone. I should like to feel it was there to be a refuge to you.'

Celia thought refuge was a funny word to use, but she liked the idea of some day going to live at home with Dermot.

Dermot, however, saw the matter differently.

'Naturally you're fond of your own home, but, all the same, I don't suppose it will ever be of much use to us.'

'We might go and live there some day.'

'Yes, when we're about a hundred and one. It's too far from London to be any practical use.'

'Not when you retire from the army?'

'Even then I shan't want to sit down and stagnate. I shall want a job. And I'm not so sure about staying in the army after the war, but we needn't talk about that now.'

Of what use to look forward? Dermot might still be ordered out to France again at any minute. He might be killed . . .

'But I shall have his child,' thought Celia.

But she knew that no child could replace Dermot in her heart. Dermot meant more to her than anyone in the world and always would.

11

Motherhood

1

Celia's child was born in July, and it was born in the same room where she had been born twenty-two years ago.

Outside the deep green branches of the beech tree tapped against the window.

Putting his fears (curiously intense ones) for Celia out of sight, Dermot had resolutely regarded the role of an expectant mother as a highly amusing one. No attitude could so well have helped Celia through the weary time. She remained strong and active but obstinately seasick.

She went home about three weeks before the baby was due. At the end of that time Dermot got a week's leave and joined her. Celia hoped her baby would be born while he was there. Her mother hoped it would be born after he departed. Men, in Miriam's opinion, were nothing more nor less than a nuisance at such times.

The nurse had arrived and was so briskly cheerful and reassuring that Celia was devoured by secret terrors.

One night at dinner Celia dropped her knife and fork and cried: 'Oh, Nurse!'

They went out of the room together. Nurse came back in a minute or two. She nodded to Miriam.

'Very punctual,' she said smiling. 'A model patient.'

'Aren't you going to telephone for the doctor?' demanded Dermot fiercely.

'Oh, there's no hurry. He won't be needed for many hours yet.'

Celia came back and went on with her dinner. Afterwards Miriam and the nurse went off together. They murmured of linen, and jingled keys . . .

Celia and Dermot sat looking at each other desperately. They had joked and laughed, but now their fear was upon them:

Celia said: 'I'll be all right. I know I'll be all right.'

Dermot said violently: 'Of course you will.'

They stared at each other miserably.

'You're very strong,' said Dermot.

'Very strong. And women have babies every day — one a minute isn't it?'

A spasm of pain contorted her face. Dermot cried out: 'Celia!'

'It's all right. Let's go out. The house seems like a hospital somehow.'

'It's that damned nurse does it.'

'She's very nice, really.'

They went out into the summer night. They felt curiously isolated. Inside the house was bustle, preparation — they heard Nurse at the telephone, her 'Yes, Doctor . . . No, Doctor . . . Oh, yes, about ten o'clock will do nicely . . . Yes, quite satisfactory.'

Outside the night was cool and green . . . The beech tree rustled . . .

Two lonely children wandered there hand in hand — not knowing how to console each other . . .

Celia said suddenly:

'I just want to say — not that anything will happen — but in case it did — that I've been so wonderfully happy that nothing in the world matters. You promised you'd make me happy, and you have . . . I didn't dream anyone *could* be so happy.'

Dermot said brokenly:

'I've brought this on you . . . '

'I know. It's worse for you . . . But I'm terribly happy about it — about everything . . . '

She added:

'And afterwards — we'll always love each other.'

'Always, all our lives . . . '

Nurse called from the house.

'You'd better come in now, my dear.'

'I'm coming.'

It was upon them now. They were being torn apart. That was the worst of it, Celia felt. Having to leave Dermot to face this new thing alone.

They clung together — all the terror of separation in their kiss.

Celia thought: 'We'll never forget this night — never . . . ' It was the fourteenth of July.

She went into the house.

2

So tired . . . so tired . . . so very tired . . .

The room, spinning, hazy — then broadening

240

out and settling into reality. The nurse smiling at her, the doctor washing his hands in a corner of the room. He had known her all her life, and he called out to her jocularly:

'Well, Celia, my dear, you've got a baby.'

She had got a baby, had she?

It didn't seem to matter.

She was so tired.

Just that . . . tired . . .

They seemed to be expecting her to do or say something . . .

But she couldn't.

She just wanted to be let alone . . .

To rest . . .

But there was something . . . someone . . .

She murmured: 'Dermot?'

3

She had dozed off. When she opened her eyes he was there.

But what had happened to him? He looked different — so queer. He was in trouble — had had bad news or something.

She said: 'What is it?'

He answered in a queer, unnatural voice: 'A little daughter.'

'No, I mean — you? What's the matter?'

His face crumpled up — puckered queerly. He was crying — Dermot crying!

He said brokenly: 'It's been so awful — so long . . . You don't know how ghastly it's been . . . '

He knelt by the bed, burying his face there. She laid a hand on his head.

How much he cared . . .

'Darling,' she said. 'It's all right now . . . '

4

Here was her mother. Instinctively, at the sight of that sweet smiling face, Celia felt better — stronger. As in nursery days she felt 'everything would be all right now that Mummy was here.'

'Don't go away, Mummy.'

'No, darling. I'm going to sit here by you.'

Celia fell asleep holding her mother's hand. When she woke up, she said:

'Oh, Mummy, it feels just *wonderful* not to be sick!'

Miriam laughed.

'You're going to see your baby now. Nurse is bringing her.'

'Are you sure it isn't a boy?'

'Quite sure. Girls are much nicer, Celia. You've always meant much more to me than Cyril has.'

'Yes, but I was so sure it was a boy . . . Well, Dermot will be pleased. He wanted a girl. He's got his own way.'

'As usual,' said Miriam dryly. 'Here comes Nurse.'

Nurse came in very starched and stiff and important — carrying something on a pillow.

Celia steeled herself. New-born babies were

very ugly — frightfully ugly. She must be prepared.

'Oh!' she said in a tone of great surprise.

Was this little creature her baby? She felt excited and frightened as Nurse laid her gently within the crook of her arm. This funny little Red Indian squaw with her dark thatch of hair? Nothing raw beef-like about her. A funny, adorable, comic little face.

'Eight and a half pounds,' said Nurse with great satisfaction.

As often before in her life, Celia felt unreal. She was now definitely playing the part of the Young Mother.

But she did not feel at all like either a wife or a mother. She felt like a little girl come home after an exciting but tiring party.

5

Celia called the baby Judy — as being the next best thing to Punch!

Judy was a most satisfactory baby. She put on the requisite weight every week and indulged in the minimum amount of crying. When she did cry it was the angry roar of a miniature tigress.

Having, as Grannie would have put it, 'taken her month', Celia left Judy with Miriam and went up to London to look about for a suitable home.

Her reunion with Dermot was particularly joyous. It was like a second honeymoon. Part of Dermot's satisfaction arose from the fact (Celia

discovered) that she had left Judy to come up to
him.

'I've been so afraid you'd get all domestic and
not bother about me any longer.'

His jealousy allayed, Dermot joined her
energetically in flat hunting whenever he could.
Celia now felt quite experienced in the
house-hunting business — no longer was she the
complete nincompoop who had been frightened
away by the efficiency of Miss Banks. She might
have been renting flats all her life.

They were going to take an unfurnished flat. It
would be cheaper, and Miriam could easily
supply them with nearly all the furniture they
needed from home.

Unfurnished flats, however, were few and far
between. They nearly always had a snag attached
to them in the shape of a monstrous premium.
As day followed day, Celia got more and more
depressed.

It was Mrs Steadman who saved the situation.

She appeared at breakfast one morning with a
mysterious air of engaging in a conspiracy.

'Apologizing, I'm sure, to you, sir,' said Mrs
Steadman, 'for intruding at such a time, but it
came to Steadman's ears last night that No. 18
Lauceston Mansions — just round the corner
— is to Be Had. They wrote to the agents about
it last night, so if you was to nip round now,
ma'am, before anybody Got Wind of it, so to
speak — '

There was no need for more. Celia sprang up
from the table, pulled on a hat, and departed
with the eagerness of a dog on the scent.

At 18 Lauceston Mansions also breakfast was in progress. To the announcement by a slatternly maid of 'Somebody to see over the flat, ma'am,' Celia, standing in the hall, heard an agitated wail: 'But they can hardly have got my letter yet. It's only half-past eight.'

A young woman in a kimono came out of the dining-room, wiping her mouth. A smell of kipper accompanied her.

'Do you really want to see over the flat?'

'Yes, please.'

'Oh, well, I suppose . . . '

Celia was taken round. Yes, it would do excellently. Four bedrooms, two sitting-rooms — everything pretty dirty, of course. Rent £80 a year (marvellously cheap). A premium (alas) of a hundred and fifty pounds, and the 'lino' (Celia abhorred lino) to be taken at a valuation. Celia offered a hundred premium. The young woman in the kimono refused scornfully.

'Very well,' said Celia firmly. 'I'll take it.'

As she descended the stairs she was glad of her decision. Two separate women came up, each with a house agent's order to view in her hand!

Within three days Celia and Dermot had been offered a premium of two hundred to abdicate their right.

But they stuck to it, paid over their hundred and fifty pounds, and entered into possession of 18 Lauceston Mansions. At last they had a home (a very dirty one) of their own.

In a month's time you would hardly have known the place. Dermot and Celia did all the decorating themselves — they could not afford anything else. They learnt by experience interesting facts about distempering, painting, and papering. The finished result was charming, they thought. Cheap chintz papers brightened up the long dingy passages. Yellow distempered walls gave a sunny look to the rooms facing north. The sitting-rooms were pale cream — a background for pictures and china. The 'lino surrounds' were torn up and presented to Mrs Steadman, who received them greedily. 'I do like a bit of nice lino, ma'am . . . '

6

In the meantime Celia had successfully passed through another ordeal — that of Mrs Barman's Bureau. Mrs Barman's Bureau provided children's nurses.

Arriving at this awe-inspiring establishment, Celia was received by a haughty yellow-haired creature, required to fill in thirty-four answers to questions on an imposing form — the questions being of a kind to induce acute humility in the filler in. She was then conducted to a small cubicle, rather medical in appearance, and there, curtained in, she was left to await those nurses whom the yellow-haired one saw fit to send her.

By the time the first one came in, Celia's sense of inferiority had deepened to complete abasement, not relieved by the first applicant, a big starched massive woman, aggressively clean and majestic in demeanour.

'Good morning,' said Celia weakly.

'Good morning, madam.' The majestic one took the chair opposite Celia and gazed at her steadily, conveying somehow as she did so, her sense that Celia's situation was not likely to suit anyone who respected one's self.

'I want a nurse for a young baby,' began Celia wishing that she did not feel and (she was afraid) sound amateurish.

'Yes, madam. From the month?'

'Yes, at least two months.'

One mistake already — 'from the month' was a technical term — not a period of time. Celia felt she had gone down in the majestic one's estimation.

'Quite so, madam. Any other children?'

'No.'

'A first baby. How many in family?'

'Er — me and my husband.'

'And what establishment do you keep, madam?'

Establishment? What a word to describe one general servant not yet acquired.

'We live very simply,' said Celia, blushing. 'One maid.'

'Nurseries cleaned and waited on?'

'No, you would have to do your own nursery.'

'Ah!' The majestic one rose and said more in sorrow than in anger: 'I'm afraid, madam, your situation is not quite what I am looking for. At Sir Eldon West's, I had a nurserymaid, and the nurseries were attended to by the under housemaid.'

Celia cursed the yellow-haired one in her heart. Why fill up a paper of your requirements

247

and your household and then be sent someone who would clearly only accept a post with the Rothschilds if they happened to please her fancy?

A stern black-browed woman came next.

'One baby? Taken from the month? You understand, madam, I take *entire charge*. I do not tolerate interference.'

She glared at Celia.

'I'll teach young mother to come bothering me,' said the glare.

Celia said she was afraid she would not do.

'I am devoted to children, madam. I worship them, but I cannot have a mother always interfering.'

The black-browed one was got rid of.

There came next a very untidy old woman who described herself as a 'Nannie'.

As far as Celia could make out she could neither see, hear, nor understand what was said to her.

Rout of the Nannie.

Next came a bad-tempered-looking young woman who scoffed at the idea of doing her own nurseries, followed by an amiable red-cheeked girl who had been a housemaid but thought she'd 'get on better with children'.

Celia was getting desperate when a woman of about thirty-five came in. She had pince-nez, was extremely neat, and had pleasant blue eyes.

She displayed none of the usual reactions when it came to 'doing your own nursery'.

'Well, I don't object to that — except the grate. I don't like doing a grate — it musses up your hands — and you don't want rough hands looking after a baby. But otherwise I don't mind seeing to things. I've been to the colonies, and I can turn my hand to anything.'

She showed Celia various snapshots of her charges, and Celia ended by engaging her if her references were satisfactory.

With a sigh of relief Celia left Mrs Barman's Bureau.

Mary Denman's references proved most satisfactory. She was a careful, thoroughly experienced nurse. Celia had next to engage a servant.

This proved to be almost more trying than finding a nurse. Nurses at least were plentiful. Servants were practically non-existent. They were all in munition factories or in the WAACS or WRENS. Celia saw a girl she liked very much, a plump good-humoured damsel called Kate. She did her utmost to persuade Kate to come to them.

Like all the others, Kate jibbed at a nursery.

'It isn't the baby I object to, ma'am. I like children. It's the nurse. After my last place I vowed I'd never go where there was a nurse again. Wherever there's a nurse there's trouble.'

In vain Celia represented Mary Denman as a mine of all the virtues. Kate repeated solidly:

'Wherever there's a nurse, there's trouble. That's my experience.'

In the end it was Dermot who turned the scale. Celia turned him on to the obdurate Kate, and Dermot, the adept at getting his own way, was successful in getting Kate to give them a trial.

'Though whatever came over me I don't know, because go where there is a nursery I said I never would again. But the captain spoke so nicely, and him knowing the regiment my boy's in in France and everything. Well, I said, we can but try.'

So Kate was secured, and on a triumphant October day Celia, Dermot, Denman, Kate, and Judy all moved in to 18 Lauceston Mansions, and family life began.

7

Dermot was very funny with Judy. He was afraid of her. When Celia tried to make him hold her in his arms, he backed away nervously.

'No, I can't. I simply can't. I won't hold the thing.'

'You'll have to some day, when she's older. And she's not a thing!'

'She'll be better when she's older. Once she can talk and walk, I dare say I shall like her. She's so awfully fat now. Do you think she'll ever get right?'

He refused to admire Judy's curves or her dimples.

'I want her to be thin and bony.'

'Not now — at three months old.'

'You really think she will be thin some day?'

'Sure to be. We're both thin.'

'I couldn't bear it if she grew up fat.'

Celia had to fall back upon the admiration of Mrs Steadman, who walked round and round the baby rather as she had done round the joint of meat of glorious memory.

'The image of the captain, isn't she? Ah, you can see she was made at home — if you'll pardon the old saying.'

On the whole, Celia found domesticity rather fun. It was fun because she did not take it seriously. Denman proved an excellent nurse, capable and devoted to the baby, and extraordinarily pleasant and willing so long as there was a lot of work to do and everything was at sixes and sevens. The moment the household had settled down and things were running smoothly, Denman showed she had another side to her character. She had a fierce temper — directed not towards Judy, whom she adored, but towards Celia and Dermot. All employers were to Denman natural enemies. The most innocent remark would create a sudden storm. Celia would say, 'You had your electric light on last night. I hope baby was all right?'

Immediately Denman flared up.

'I suppose I can turn on the light to see the time in the night? I may be treated like a black slave, but there are limits. I've had slaves myself under me in Africa — poor ignorant heathen — but they weren't grudged necessities. If you think I'm wasting the light, I'll trouble you to say so straight out.'

Kate, in the kitchen, used to giggle sometimes when Denman talked of slaves.

'Nurse won't never be satisfied — not till she's got a dozen niggers under her. She's always talking of the niggers in Africa, I wouldn't have a nigger in my kitchen — nasty black things.'

251

Kate was a great comfort. Good-humoured, placid, and untroubled by storms, she went her way, cooking, cleaning, and indulging in reminiscences of 'places'.

'I'll never forget my first place — no, never. A slip of a girl I was — not seventeen. They starved me something cruel. A kipper, that's all they'd let me have for lunch, and margarine instead of butter. I got so thin you could hear my bones rubbing together. Mother was in a way about me.'

Looking at the robust and daily increasing plumpness of Kate, Celia could hardly believe this story.

'I hope you get enough to eat here, Kate?'

'Don't you worry, ma'am, that's all right — and you've no call to do things yourself. You'll only muss yourself up.'

But Celia had acquired a guilty passion for cooking. Having made the startling discovery that cooking was mainly following a recipe carefully, she plunged headlong into the sport. Kate's disapproval forced her to confine most of her activities to Kate's days out, when she would go and have an orgy in the kitchen and produce exciting delicacies for Dermot's tea and dinner.

It was in the nature of the unsatisfactory quality of life that Dermot should frequently arrive home on these days with indigestion and demand weak tea and thin toast instead of lobster cutlets and vanilla soufflè.

Kate herself kept firmly to plain cooking. She was unable to follow a recipe because she scorned to measure any quantities.

252

'A bit of this, and that — that's what I take,' she said. 'That's the way my mother did. Cooks never measure.'

'Perhaps it would be better if they did,' suggested Celia.

'You've got to do it by eye,' said Kate firmly. 'That's the way I've always seen my mother do.'

What fun it was, thought Celia.

A house (or rather a flat) of one's very own — a husband — a baby — a servant.

At last, she felt, she was being grown up — a real person. She was even learning the correct jargon. She had made friends with two other young wives in the mansions. These were very earnest over the qualities of good milk, where you got the cheapest Brussels sprouts, and the iniquities of servants.

'I looked her straight in the face, and I said, 'Jane, I never permit insolence,' just like that. Such a look she gave me.'

They never seemed to talk about anything except these subjects.

Secretly, Celia felt afraid that she would never be truly domestic.

Luckily Dermot didn't mind. He often said he hated domestic women. Their homes, he said, were always so uncomfortable.

And, really there seemed to be something in what he said. Women who talked of nothing but servants seemed to be always having 'insolence' from them and their 'treasures' departed at inconvenient moments and left them to do all the cooking and the housework. And women who spent the whole morning shopping and selecting edibles seemed to have worse food than anybody else.

There was, Celia thought, a lot too much fuss made over all this business of domesticity.

People like her and Dermot had far more fun. She wasn't Dermot's housekeeper — she was his playmate.

And some day Judy would run about and talk, and adore her mother like Celia adored Miriam.

And in summer, when London got hot and stuffy, she would take Judy home, and Judy would play in the garden and invent games of princesses and dragons, and Celia would read her all the old fairy stories in the nursery bookcase . . .

12

Peace

1

The armistice came as a great surprise to Celia. She had got so used to the war that she had felt it would never end . . .

It was just a part of life . . .

And now the war was over!

While the war had been on it hadn't been any use making plans. You had to let the future take care of itself and live for the day — just hoping and praying that Dermot wouldn't be sent out to France again.

But now — it was different.

Dermot was full of plans. He wasn't going to stay in the army. There wasn't any future in the army. As soon as possible he would get demobilized and would go into the City. He knew of an opening in a very good firm.

'But, Dermot isn't it safer to stay in the army? I mean, there's the pension and all that.'

'I should stagnate if I stayed in the army. And what good is a miserable pension? I mean to make money — a good deal of money. You don't mind taking a risk, do you, Celia?'

No, Celia didn't mind. That disposition to take risks was what she admired most about Dermot. He was not afraid of life.

Dermot would never run away from life. He would face it and force it to do his will.

Ruthless, her mother had called him once. Well, that was true in a way. He *was* ruthless to life — no sentimental considerations would ever influence him. But he was not ruthless to her. Look how tender he had been before Judy was born . . .

2

Dermot took his risk.

He left the army and went into the City, starting on a small salary, but with a prospect of good money in the future.

Celia had wondered whether he would find office life irksome, but he did not seem to do so. He seemed entirely happy and satisfied in his new life.

Dermot liked doing new things.

He liked new people too.

Celia was sometimes shocked that he never wanted to go and see the two old aunts in Ireland who had brought him up.

He sent them presents and wrote to them regularly once a month, but he never wanted to see them.

'Weren't you fond of them?'

'Of course I was — especially of Aunt Lucy. She was just like a mother to me.'

'Well, then, don't you want to see them? We could have them to stay, if you liked.'

'Oh, that would be rather a nuisance.'

'A nuisance? If you're fond of them?'

'Well, I know they're all right. Quite happy and all that. I don't exactly want to see them. After all, when you grow up, you grow out of your relations. That's only nature. Aunt Lucy and Aunt Kate don't really mean anything to me now. I've outgrown them.'

Dermot was extraordinary, Celia thought.

But perhaps he thought her equally extraordinary for being so attached to places and people she had known all her life.

As a matter of fact, he didn't think her extraordinary. He didn't think about it at all. Dermot never thought about what people were like. Talking about thoughts and feelings seemed to him a waste of time.

He liked realities — not ideas.

Sometimes Celia would ask him questions like, 'What would you do if I ran away with someone?' or 'What would you do if I died?'

Dermot never knew what he would do. How could he know till it happened?

'But can't you just sort of imagine?'

No, Dermot couldn't. Imagining things that weren't so seemed to him a great waste of time.

Which, of course, was quite true.

Nevertheless, Celia couldn't stop doing it. She was made that way.

3

One day Dermot hurt Celia.

They had been to a party. Celia was still rather

257

scared of parties in case a fit of tongue-tied shyness should come over her. Sometimes it did and sometimes it didn't.

But this party (or so she thought) had gone remarkably well. She *had* been a little tongue-tied at first, and then she had ventured on a remark that had made the man she was talking to laugh.

Emboldened, Celia had found her tongue, and after that she fairly chattered. Everybody had laughed and talked a great deal, Celia as much as anybody. She had said things that sounded to her quite witty and which even seemed to have appeared witty to other people. She came home in a happy glow.

'I'm not so stupid. I'm not so stupid after all,' she said to herself happily.

She called through the dressing-room door to Dermot.

'I think that was a nice party. I enjoyed it. How lucky that I caught that ladder in my stocking in time.'

'It wasn't too bad.'

'Oh, Dermot didn't you like it?'

'Well, I've got a bit of indigestion.'

'Oh, darling, I'm so sorry. I'll get you some bicarbonate.'

'Oh, it's all right now. What was the matter with you this evening?'

'With me?'

'Yes, you were quite different.'

'I suppose I was excited. Different in what way?'

'Well, you're usually so sensible. Tonight you

were talking and laughing and quite unlike yourself.'

'Didn't you like it? I thought I was getting on so well.'

A queer, cold feeling began to form in Celia's inside.

'Well, I thought it sounded rather silly — that's all.'

'Yes,' said Celia slowly. 'I suppose I was being silly . . . But people seemed to like it — they laughed.'

'Oh, people!'

'And, Dermot — I enjoyed it myself . . . It's awful, but I believe I like being silly sometimes.'

'Oh, well, that's all right, then.'

'But I won't be again. Not if you don't like it.'

'Well, I do rather hate it when you sound silly. I don't like silly women.'

It hurt — oh, yes, it hurt . . .

A fool — she was a fool. Of course she was a fool, she'd always known it. But she'd hoped, somehow — that Dermot wouldn't mind. That he'd be — what did she mean exactly? — tender to her over it. If you loved a person, their faults and failings endeared them more to you — not less. You said, 'Now, isn't that *like* so and so?' But you said it, not with exasperation but with tenderness.

But then men didn't deal much in tenderness . . .

A queer little pang of fright swept over Celia.

No, men weren't tender . . .

They weren't like mothers . . .

A sudden misgiving assailed her. She didn't

really know anything about men. She didn't really know anything about Dermot . . .

'The men!' Grannie's phrase came back to her. Grannie had seemed perfectly confident of knowing exactly what men liked and didn't like.

But Grannie, of course, wasn't silly . . . She had often laughed at Grannie, but Grannie wasn't silly.

And she, Celia, was . . . She'd always known it really, deep down. But she had thought, with Dermot, it wouldn't matter. Well, it *did* matter.

In the darkness the tears ran down her cheeks unchecked . . .

She'd have her cry over — there, in the night, under the shelter of the darkness. And in the morning, she'd be different. She would never be silly in public again.

She'd been spoilt, that's what it was. Everyone had always been so kind to her — encouraged her . . .

But she didn't want Dermot to look as just for one moment he had looked . . .

It reminded her of something — something long ago.

No, she couldn't remember.

But she'd be very careful not to be silly any more.

13

Companionship

1

There were several things, Celia found, that Dermot didn't like about her.

Any sign of helplessness annoyed him.

'Why do you want me to do things for you when you can perfectly well do them for yourself?'

'Oh, Dermot, but it's so nice having you do them for me.'

'Nonsense, you'd get worse and worse if I'd let you.'

'I expect I should,' said Celia sadly.

'It isn't as though you can't do all these things perfectly. You're perfectly sensible and intelligent and capable.'

'I expect,' said Celia, 'that it goes with slightly sloping Victorian shoulders. You want, automatically, to cling — like ivy.'

'Well,' said Dermot good-humouredly, 'you can't cling to me. I'm not going to let you.'

'Do you mind very much, Dermot, my being dreamy and fancying things and imagining things that might happen and what I should do if they did?'

'Of course I don't mind, if it amuses you.'

Dermot was always fair. He was independent

himself, and he respected independence in other people. He had, presumably, his own ideas about things, but he never put them into words or wanted to share them with anyone else.

The trouble was that Celia wanted to share everything. When the almond tree in the court below came into flower it gave her a queer ecstatic feeling just under her heart, and she longed to put her hand into Dermot's and drag him to the window and make him feel the same. But Dermot hated having his hand taken. He hated being touched at all unless he was in a recognizably amorous mood.

When Celia burnt her hand on the stove and immediately after pinched a finger in the kitchen window she longed to go and put her head on Dermot's shoulder and be comforted. But felt that that sort of thing would annoy Dermot — and she was perfectly right. He disliked being touched, or leaned on for comfort, or asked to enter into other people's emotion.

So Celia fought heroically against her passion for sharing, her weakness for caresses, her longing for reassurance.

She told herself that she was babyish and foolish. She loved Dermot, and Dermot loved her. He loved her, probably, more deeply than she loved him since he needed less expression of love to satisfy him.

She had passion and comradeship from him. It was unreasonable to expect affection as well. Grannie would have known better. 'The men' were not like that.

2

At week-ends Dermot and Celia went into the country together. They took sandwiches with them and then went by rail or bus to a chosen spot and then walked across country and came home by another train or bus.

All the week Celia looked forward to the week-ends. Dermot came back from the City every day thoroughly tired, sometimes with a headache — sometimes with indigestion. After dinner he liked to sit and read. Sometimes he told Celia of incidents that had happened during the day, but on the whole he preferred not to talk. He usually had some technical book that he wanted to read uninterrupted.

But at week-ends Celia got her comrade back. They walked through woods and made ridiculous jokes, and sometimes, going up hill, Celia would say, 'I'm very fond of you, Dermot,' and put her hand through his arm. This was because Dermot raced up hills and Celia got out of breath. Dermot didn't mind his arm being held if it was only a joke and really to help her up the hill.

One day Dermot suggested that they should play golf. He was very bad, he said, but he could play a little. Celia got out her clubs and cleaned the rust off them — and she thought of Peter Maitland. Dear Peter — dear, *dear* Peter. That warm affection she felt for Peter would stay with her to the end of her life. Peter was part of things . . .

They found an obscure golf links where the

263

green fees were not too high. It was fun to play golf again. She was frightfully rusty, but then Dermot wasn't much good either. He hit terrific long shots but they were pulled or sliced wildly.

It was great fun playing together.

It didn't just remain fun, though. Dermot, in games as in work, was efficient and painstaking. He bought a book and studied it deeply. He practised swings at home and bought some cork balls to practise with.

The next week-end they didn't play a round. Dermot did nothing but practise shots. He made Celia do the same.

Dermot began to live for golf. Celia tried to live for golf too, but not with much success.

Dermot's game improved by leaps and bounds. Celia's stayed much the same. She wished, passionately, that Dermot was a little more like Peter Maitland . . .

Yet she had fallen in love with Dermot, attracted by precisely those qualities which differentiated him from Peter.

3

One day Dermot came in and said:

'Look here, I'm going down to Dalton Heath with Andrews next Sunday. Is that all right?'

Celia said of course it was all right.

Dermot came back enthusiastic.

Golf was wonderful; played on a first-rate course. Celia must come down next week and see Dalton Heath. Women couldn't play at the week-ends, but she could walk round with him.

They went once or twice more to their little cheap course, but Dermot took no further pleasure in it. He said that that sort of place was no good to him.

A month later he told Celia that he was going to join Dalton Heath.

'I know it's expensive. But, after all, I can economize in other ways. Golf is the only recreation I've got, and it's going to make all the difference to me. Both Andrews and Weston belong there.'

Celia said slowly:

'What about me?'

'It wouldn't be any good your belonging. Women can't play at week-ends and I don't suppose you'd care to go down by yourself in the week.'

'I mean, what am I going to do at the week-ends? You'll be playing with Andrews and people.'

'Well, it would be rather silly to join a golf club and not use it.'

'Yes, but we've always spent the week-ends together, you and I.'

'Oh, I see. Well, you can get someone to go about with, can't you? I mean, you've got lots of friends of your own.'

'No, I haven't. Not now. The few friends I had who lived in London have all married and gone away.'

'Well, there's Doris Andrews, and Mrs Weston, and people.'

'Those aren't exactly my friends. They're your

friends' wives. It isn't quite the same thing. Besides, that isn't it at all. You don't understand. I like being with *you*. I like doing things with you. I liked our walks and our sandwiches, and playing golf together, and all the fun. You're tired all the week, and I don't worry you or bother you to do things in the evening, but I looked forward to the week-ends. I loved them. Oh, Dermot, I like being with you, and now we shall never do anything together any more.'

She wished her voice wouldn't tremble. She wished she could keep the tears back from her eyes. Was she being dreadfully unreasonable? Would Dermot be cross? Was she being selfish? She was clinging — yes, undoubtedly she was clinging. Ivy again!

Dermot was trying hard to be patient and reasonable.

'You know, Celia, I don't think that's quite fair. I never interfere with what you want to do.'

'But I don't want to do things.'

'Well, I shouldn't mind if you did. If any week-end you'd said that you wanted to go off with Doris Andrews or some old friend of yours, I should have been quite happy. I'd have hunted up somebody and gone off somewhere else. After all, when we married we did agree that each side should be free and do just what they wanted to do.'

'We didn't agree or talk about anything of the kind,' said Celia. 'We just loved each other and wanted to marry each other and thought it would be perfectly heavenly always to be together.'

'Well, so it is. It isn't that I don't love you. I love you just as much as ever. But a man likes doing things with other men. And he needs exercise. If I was wanting to go off with other women, well, then you might have something to complain about. But I never want to be bothered with any other woman but you. I hate women. I just want to play a decent game of golf with another man. I do think you're rather unreasonable about it.'

Yes, probably she was being unreasonable . . .

What Dermot wanted to do was so innocent — so natural . . .

She felt ashamed . . .

But he didn't realize how terribly she was going to miss those week-ends together . . . She didn't only want Dermot in her bed at night. She loved Dermot as play-fellow even better than Dermot as lover . . .

Was it true what she had so often heard women say that men only wanted women as bedfellows and housekeepers? . . .

Was that the whole tragedy of marriage — that women wanted to be companions, and that men were bored by it?

She said something of the kind. Dermot, as always, was honest.

'I think, Celia, that that *is* true. Women always want to do things with men — and a man would always rather have another man.'

Well, she had got it flat. Dermot was right, and she was wrong. She *had* been unreasonable. She said so, and his face cleared.

'You are so sweet, Celia. And I expect you'll

really enjoy it better in the end. I mean you'll find people to go about with who enjoy talking about things and feelings. I know I'm rather bad at all that kind of thing. And we'll be just as happy. In fact, I shall probably only play golf either Saturday or Sunday. The other day we'll go out together as we did before.'

The next Saturday he went off, radiant. On Sunday he suggested of his own accord that he and she should go for a ramble.

They did, but it was not the same. Dermot was perfectly sweet, but she knew that his heart was at Dalton Heath. Weston had asked him to play but he had refused.

He was full of conscious pride in his sacrifice.

The next week-end Celia urged him to play golf both days, and he went off happily.

Celia thought: 'I must learn to play by myself again. Or else — I must find some friends.'

She had scorned 'domestic women'. She had been proud of her companionship with Dermot. Those domestic women — absorbed in their children, their servants, their house running — relieved when Tom or Dick or Fred went off to play golf at the week-end because there was no mess about the house — 'It makes it so much easier for the servants, my dear — ' Men were necessary as breadwinners, but they were an inconvenience in the house . . .

Perhaps, after all, domesticity paid best.

It looked like it.

14

Ivy

1

How lovely to be at home. Celia lay full length on the green grass — it felt deliciously warm and alive . . .

The beech tree rustled overhead . . .

Green — green — all the world was green . . .

Trailing a wooden horse behind her, Judy came toiling up the slope of the lawn . . .

Judy was adorable with her firm legs, her rosy cheeks and blue eyes, her thickly curling chestnut brown hair. Judy was her own little girl, just as she had been her mother's little girl.

Only, of course, Judy was quite different . . .

Judy didn't want to have stories told to her — which was a pity, because Celia could think of heaps of stories without any effort at all. And, anyway, Judy didn't like fairy stories.

Judy wasn't any good at make-believe. When Celia told Judy how she herself had pretended that the lawn was a sea and her hoop a river horse, Judy had merely stared and said: 'But it's grass. And you bowl a hoop. You can't ride it.'

It was so obvious that she thought Celia must have been a rather silly little girl that Celia felt quite dashed.

First Dermot had found out that she was silly, and now Judy!

Although only four years old Judy was full of common sense. And common sense, Celia found, can be often very depressing.

Moreover, Judy's common sense had a bad effect upon Celia. She made efforts to appear sensible in Judy's eyes — clear blue appraising eyes — with the result that she often made herself out sillier than she was.

Judy was a complete puzzle to her mother. All the things that Celia had loved doing as a child bored Judy. Judy could not play for three minutes in the garden by herself. She would come marching into the house declaring that there was 'nothing to do'.

Judy liked doing real things. She was never bored in the flat at home. She polished tables with a duster, assisted in bed making, and helped her father to clean his golf clubs.

Dermot and Judy had suddenly become friends. A thoroughly satisfying communion had grown up between them. Though still deploring Judy's well-covered frame, Dermot could not but be charmed by her evident delight in his company. They talked to each other seriously, like grown-up people. When Dermot gave Judy a club to clean, he expected her to do it properly. When Judy said, 'Isn't that nice?' about anything — a house she had built of bricks — or a ball she had made of wool, or a spoon she had cleaned — Dermot never said it was unless he thought so. He would point out errors or faulty construction.

'You'll discourage her,' Celia would say.

But Judy was not in the least discouraged, and her feelings were never hurt. She liked her father better than her mother because her father was more difficult to please. She liked doing things that were difficult.

Dermot was rough. When he and Judy romped together, Judy nearly always got damaged — games with Dermot always ended in a bump or a scratch or a pinched finger. Judy didn't care. Celia's gentler games seemed to her tame.

Only when she was ill did she prefer her mother to her father.

'Don't go away, Mummy. Don't go away. Stay with me. Don't let Daddy come. I don't want Daddy.'

Dermot was quite satisfied for his presence not to be desired. He didn't like ill people. Anybody ill or unhappy embarrassed him.

Judy was like Dermot about being touched. She hated to be kissed or picked up. One good-night kiss from her mother she bore, but nothing more. Her father never kissed her. When they said good night they grinned at each other.

Judy and her grandmother got on very well together. Miriam was delighted with the child's spirit and intelligence.

'She's extraordinarily quick, Celia. She takes a thing in at once.'

Miriam's old love of teaching revived. She taught Judy her letters and small words. Both grandmother and grandchild enjoyed the lessons.

Sometimes Miriam would say to Celia:

'But she's not you, my precious . . .'

It was as though she were excusing herself for her interest in youth. Miriam loved youth. She had the teacher's joy in an awakening mind. Judy was an abiding excitement and interest to her.

But her heart was all Celia's. The love between them was stronger than ever. When Celia arrived she would find her mother looking a tiny old woman — grey — faded. But in a day or two she would revive, the colour would come back to her cheeks, the sparkle to her eyes.

'I've got my girl back,' she would say happily.

She always asked Dermot down too, but she was always delighted when he didn't come. She wanted Celia to herself.

And Celia loved the feeling of stepping back into her old life. To feel that happy tide of reassurance sweeping over her — the feeling of being loved — of being *adequate* . . .

For her mother, she was perfect . . . Her mother didn't want her to be different . . . She could just be herself.

It was so restful to be yourself . . .

And then she could let herself go — in tenderness — in *saying* things . . .

She could say, 'I am so happy,' without having to catch back the words at Dermot's frown. Dermot hated you to say what you were feeling. He felt it, somehow, to be indecent . . .

At home Celia could be as indecent as she liked . . .

She could realize better at home how happy

272

she was with Dermot and how much she loved him and Judy . . .

And after an orgy of loving and saying all the things that came into her head, she could go back and be a sensible, independent person such as was approved of by Dermot.

Oh, dear home — and the beech tree — and the grass — growing — growing — against her cheek.

She thought dreamily: 'It's alive — it's a Great Green Beast — the whole earth is a Great Green Beast . . . it's kind and warm and alive . . . I'm so happy — I'm so happy . . . I've got everything I want in the world . . .'

Dermot drifted happily in and out of her thoughts. He was a kind of motif in her melody of life. Sometimes she missed him terribly.

She said to Judy one day:

'Do you miss Daddy?'

'No,' said Judy.

'But you'd like him to be here?'

'Yes, I suppose so.'

'Aren't you sure? You're so fond of Daddy.'

'Of course I am, but he's in London.'

That settled it for Judy.

When Celia got back, Dermot was very pleased to see her. They had a happy, lover-like evening. Celia murmured:

'I've missed you a lot. Have you missed me?'

'Well, I haven't thought about it.'

'You mean you haven't thought about me?'

'No. What would be the good? Thinking of you wouldn't bring you here.'

That, of course, was quite true and very sensible.

'But you're pleased now that I am here?'

His answer satisfied her.

But later, when he was asleep, and she lay awake, dreamily happy, she thought:

'It's awful, but I believe I wish that Dermot could sometimes be a tiny bit *dishonest* . . .

'If he could have said, 'I missed you terribly, darling,' how comforting and warming it would have been, and it really wouldn't have mattered if it had been true or not.'

No, Dermot was Dermot. Her funny, devastatingly truthful Dermot. Judy was just like him . . .

It was wiser, perhaps, not to ask them questions if you didn't fancy the truth for an answer.

She thought drowsily:

'I wonder if I shall get jealous of Judy some day . . . She and Dermot understand each other so much better than he and I do.'

Judy, she had fancied, was sometimes jealous of her. She liked her father's attention to be entirely focused on herself.

Celia thought: 'How queer. Dermot was so jealous of her before she was born — and even when she was a tiny baby. It's funny the way things turn out the opposite way from what you expect . . . '

Darling Judy . . . darling Dermot . . . so alike — so funny — and so sweet . . . and *hers*. No — not hers. *She* was *theirs*. One liked it better that way. It felt warmer — more comfortable. She belonged to them.

Celia invented a new game. It was really, she thought, a new phase of 'the girls'. 'The girls' themselves were moribund. Celia tried to resurrect them, gave them babies and stately homes in parks and interesting careers — but it was all no good. 'The girls' refused to come to life again.

Celia invented a new person. Her name was Hazel. Celia followed her career from childhood upwards with great interest. Hazel was an unhappy child — a poor relation. She acquired a sinister reputation with nursemaids by a habit of chanting, 'Something's going to happen — something's going to happen'; and as something usually did happen — even if it was only a nurserymaid's pricked finger — Hazel found herself established as a kind of witch's familiar. She grew up with the knowledge of how easy it was to impose on the credulous . . .

Celia followed her with great interest into a world of spiritualism, fortune-telling, séances, and so on. Hazel ended up at a fortune-telling establishment in Bond Street, where she acquired a great reputation, aided by a little coterie of impoverished society 'spies'.

Then she fell in love with a young Welsh naval officer and there were scenes on Welsh villages, and slowly it began to be apparent (to everyone but Hazel herself) that side by side with her fraudulent practices went a genuine gift.

At last Hazel herself found it out and was terrified. But the more she tried to cheat the more her uncanny guesses came right . . . The power had got hold of her and wouldn't let her go.

Owen, the young man, was more nebulous, but in the end he proved himself to be a plausible rotter.

Whenever Celia had a little leisure, or when she was wheeling Judy to the Park, the story went on in her mind.

It occurred to her one day that she might write it down . . .

She might, in fact, make a book of it . . .

She bought six penny exercise books and a lot of pencils, because she was careless about pencils, and started . . .

It wasn't quite so easy when it came to writing down. Her mind had always gone on about six paragraphs farther than the one she was writing down — and then by the time she got to that, the exact wording had gone out of her head.

But still she made progress. It wasn't quite the story she had had in her head, but it was something that read recognizably like a book. It had chapters and all that. She bought six more exercise books.

She didn't tell Dermot about it for some time, not, in fact, till she had successfully wrestled with an account of a Welsh Revivalist meeting at which Hazel had 'testified'.

That particular chapter had gone much better than Celia hoped. She felt so flushed by victory that she wanted to tell somebody.

'Dermot,' she said, 'do you think I could write a book?'

Dermot said cheerfully:

'I think that's an excellent idea. I should, if I were you.'

'Well, as a matter of fact, I have — that is, I've begun. I'm halfway through.'

'Good,' said Dermot.

He had put down a book on economics when Celia spoke. Now he picked it up again.

'It's about a girl who's a medium — but doesn't know she is. And she gets tangled up in a bogus fortune-telling place, and she cheats at séances. And then she falls in love with a young man in Wales and she goes to Wales and queer things happen.'

'I suppose there's some kind of story?'

'Of course there is. I'm saying it badly — that's all.'

'Do you know anything about mediums or séances or things?'

'No,' said Celia rather stricken.

'Well, isn't it a bit risky to write about them, then? And you've never been to Wales, have you?'

'No.'

'Well, hadn't you better write about something you do know about? London or your part of the country. It seems to me you're simply making difficulties for yourself.'

Celia felt abashed. As usual, Dermot was right. She had behaved like a simpleton. Why on earth choose subjects she knew nothing about? That revivalist meeting, too. She had never been to a revivalist meeting. Why on earth try to describe one?

All the same, she couldn't give up Hazel and

Owen now . . . They were *there* . . . No, but something must be done about them.

For the next month Celia read every conceivable work she could find on spiritualism, séances, mediumistic powers, and fraudulent practices. Then, slowly and laboriously, she rewrote all the first part of the book. She did not enjoy her task. All the sentences seemed to run haltingly, and she even got into the most amazingly complicated grammatical tangles for no apparent reason.

That summer Dermot very obligingly agreed to go to Wales for his fortnight's holiday. Celia could then look about for 'local colour'. They duly carried out the project, but Celia found local colour extremely elusive. She took round a little notebook with her, so as to be able to put down anything that struck her. But she was by nature remarkably unobservant, and days passed when it seemed quite impossible to put down anything at all.

She had an awful temptation to abandon Wales and to turn Owen into a Scotsman called Hector who lived in the Highlands.

But then Dermot pointed out to her that the same difficulty would arise. She knew nothing about the Highlands either.

In despair Celia abandoned the whole thing. It just wouldn't go any more. Besides, she was already playing in her mind with a family of fishing folk on the Cornish coast . . .

Amos Polridge was already quite well known to her . . .

She didn't tell Dermot, because she felt guilty,

realizing perfectly well that she knew nothing about fishermen or the sea. It would be useless writing it down, but it was fun to think about. There would be an old grandmother too — very toothless and rather sinister . . .

And some time or other she would finish the Hazel book. Owen could perfectly well be a rotten young stockbroker in London.

Only, or so it seemed to her, Owen didn't want to be that . . .

He sulked and became so vague that he really didn't exist at all.

3

Celia had become quite used to being poor and living carefully.

Dermot expected to make money some day. In fact, he was quite sure of it. Celia never expected to be rich. She was quite content to remain as they were but hoped it wouldn't be too much of a disappointment to Dermot.

What neither of them expected was a real financial calamity. But the boom after the war was over. It was followed by the slump.

Dermot's firm went into liquidation, and he was out of a job.

They had fifty pounds a year of Dermot's and a hundred pounds a year of Celia's, they had two hundred pounds saved in War Loan and there was the shelter of Miriam's house for Celia and Judy.

It was a bad time. It affected Celia principally

through Dermot. Dermot took misfortune — especially undeserved misfortune (for he had worked well) such as this, hard. It made him bitter and bad tempered. Celia dismissed Kate and Denman and proposed to run the flat by herself until such times as Dermot got another job. Denman, however, refused to be dismissed.

Fiercely and angrily she said: 'I'm stopping. It's no good arguing. I'll wait for my wages. I'm not going to leave my little love now.'

So Denman remained. She and Celia did turn and turn about with housework, cooking, and Judy. One morning Celia took Judy to the Park and Denman cooked and cleaned. The next morning Denman went and Celia remained.

Celia found a queer enjoyment in this. She liked to be busy. In the evenings she found time to go on with Hazel. She finished the book painstakingly, consulting her Welsh notes, and sent it to a publisher. It might bring in something.

It was, however, promptly returned, and Celia tossed it into a drawer and did not try again.

Celia's chief difficulty in life was Dermot. Dermot was utterly unreasonable. He was so sensitive to failure that he was quite unbearable to live with. If Celia was cheerful, he told her she might show a little more appreciation of his difficulties. If she was silent, he said she might try to brighten him up.

Celia felt desperately that if only Dermot would help they might make a kind of picnic of it all. Surely to laugh at trouble was the best way of meeting it.

But Dermot couldn't laugh. His pride was involved.

However unkind and unreasonable he was, Celia did not feel hurt as she had done over the party episode. She understood that he was suffering, and suffering on her account more than his own.

Sometimes he came near to expressing himself.

'Why don't you go away — you and Judy? Take her to your mother's. I'm no good just now. I know I'm not fit to live with. I told you once before — I'm no good in trouble. I can't stand trouble.'

But Celia would not leave him. She wished she could make it easier for him, but there seemed nothing she could do.

And as day followed day and Dermot was unsuccessful in finding a job, his mood grew blacker and blacker.

Then, at last, when Celia felt her courage failing her entirely, and she had almost decided to go to Miriam as Dermot so constantly suggested she should, the tide turned.

Dermot came into the flat one afternoon a changed man. He looked his young boyish self again. His dark blue eyes danced and sparkled.

'Celia — it's splendid. You remember Tommy Forbes? I looked him up — just on chance — and he jumped at me. Was just looking for a man like me. Eight hundred a year to start with, and in a year or two I may be making anything up to fifteen hundred or two thousand. Let's go out somewhere and celebrate.'

What a happy evening! Dermot so different
— so childlike in his zest and excitement. He
insisted on buying Celia a new frock.

'You look lovely in that hyacinth blue. I — I
still love you frightfully, Celia.'

Lovers — yes, they were still lovers.

That night, lying awake, Celia thought: 'I hope
— I hope things will always go well for Dermot.
He minds so much when they don't.'

'Mummy,' said Judy suddenly the next
morning, 'what's a fair-weather friend? Nurse
says her friend in Peckham is one.'

'It means somebody who is nice to you when
everything is all right but doesn't stand by you in
trouble.'

'Oh,' said Judy. 'I see. Like Daddy.'

'No, Judy, of course not. Daddy is unhappy
and not very gay when he is worried, but if you
or I were ill or unhappy, Daddy would do
anything for us. He's the most loyal person in the
world.'

Judy looked thoughtfully at her mother and
said:

'I don't like people who are ill. They go to bed
and can't play. Margaret got something in her
eye yesterday in the Park. She had to stop
running and sit down. She wanted me to sit with
her, but I wouldn't.'

'Judy, that was very unkind.'

'No, it wasn't. I don't like sitting down. I like
running about.'

'But if you had something in your eye you
would like someone to sit and talk to you — not
go off and leave you.'

'I wouldn't mind . . . And, anyway, I hadn't got something in my eye. It was Margaret.'

15

Prosperity

1

Dermot was prosperous. He was making nearly two thousand a year. Celia and he had a lovely time. They both agreed that they ought to save, but they also agreed that they wouldn't start just yet.

The first thing they bought was a second-hand car.

Then Celia longed to live in the country. It would be so much nicer for Judy, and she herself hated London. Always before, Dermot had negatived the idea on the score of expense — railway fares for him, food being cheaper in town, etc.

But now he admitted that he liked the idea. They would find a cottage not too far from Dalton Heath.

They eventually settled in the lodge of a big estate that was being cut up for building. Dalton Heath golf course was ten miles away. They also bought a dog — an adorable Sealyham called Aubrey.

Denman refused to accompany them to the country. Having been angelic all through the bad times, she became a positive fiend with the advent of prosperity. She was rude to Celia, went about tossing her head in the air, and finally gave notice saying that as some she knew were getting stuck up it was time she made a change.

They moved in spring, and the most exciting thing to Celia was the lilacs. There were hundreds of lilacs, all shades of mauve and purple. Wandering out into the garden in the early morning with Aubrey at her heels, Celia felt that life had become almost perfect. No more dirt and dust and fog. This was Home . . .

Celia adored the country life and the long rambling walks with Aubrey. There was a small school near by where Judy went in the mornings. Judy took to school as a duck takes to water. She was very shy with individuals, but completely unabashed by large numbers.

'Can I go to a really big school one day, Mummy? Where there are hundreds and hundreds and hundreds of girls? What's the biggest school in England?'

Celia had one passage of arms with Dermot over their little home. One of the front top rooms was to be their bedroom. Dermot wanted the other for his dressing-room. Celia insisted that it should be Judy's nursery.

Dermot was annoyed.

'I suppose you'll have it your own way. I shall be the only person in the house who is never to have a bit of sun in his room.'

'Judy ought to have a sunny room.'

'Nonsense, she's out all day. That room at the back is quite large — plenty of room for her to run about in.'

'There's no sun in it.'

'I don't see why sun for Judy is more important than sun for me.'

But Celia, for once, stood firm. She wanted badly to give Dermot his sunny room, but she didn't.

In the end Dermot was perfectly good-natured about his defeat. He adopted it as a grievance — but quite good-temperedly — and pretended to be a downtrodden husband and father.

2

They had a good many neighbours near them — most of them with children. Everyone was friendly. The only thing that made a difficulty was Dermot's refusal to go out to dinner.

'Look here, Celia, I come down from London tired out, and you want me to dress up and go out and not get home and to bed till past midnight. I simply can't do it.'

'Not every night, of course. But I don't see that one night a week would matter.'

'Well, I don't want to. You go, if you like.'

'I can't go alone. People don't ask you to dinner except in pairs. And it sounds so odd for me to say that you never go out at night — because, after all, you're quite young.'

'I'm sure you could manage to go without me.'

But that wasn't so easy. In the country, as Celia said, people were asked in couples or not at all. Still, she saw the justice of what Dermot said. He was earning the money he ought to have the say in their joint life. So she refused the

286

invitations, and they sat at home, Dermot reading books on financial subjects, and Celia sometimes sewing, sometimes sitting with her hands clasped, thinking about her family of Cornish fishermen.

3

Celia wanted to have another child.

Dermot didn't.

'You always said there was no room in London,' said Celia. 'And of course we were very poor. But we've got enough now, and there's heaps of room and two wouldn't be any more trouble than one.'

'Well, we don't want one just now. All the fuss and bother and crying and bottles all over again.'

'I believe you'll always say that.'

'No, I shan't. I'd like to have two more children. But not now. There's heaps of time. We're quite young still. It will be a sort of adventure for when we're getting bored with things. Let's just enjoy ourselves now. You don't want to begin being sick again.' He paused. 'I tell you what I did look at today.'

'Oh, Dermot!'

'A car. This second-hand little beast is pretty rotten. Davis put me on to this. It's a sports model — only done eight thousand miles.'

Celia thought:

'How I love him! He's such a boy. So eager . . . And he's worked so hard. Why shouldn't he have the things he likes? . . . We'll have another baby some day. In the meantime let him have his car . . . After all, I care more for him than for any baby in the world . . . '

4

It puzzled Celia that Dermot never wanted any of his old friends to stay.

'But you used to be so fond of Andrews.'

'Yes — but we've grown out of touch with each other. We never meet nowadays. One changes . . . '

'And Jim Lucas — you and he used to be inseparable when we were engaged.'

'Oh, I can't be bothered with any of the old army crowd.'

One day Celia had a letter from Ellie Maitland — Ellie Peterson, as she now was.

'Dermot, my old friend Ellie Peterson is home from India. I was her bridesmaid. Shall I ask her and her husband down for the week-end?'

'Yes, of course, if you like. Does he play golf?'

'I don't know.'

'Rather a bore if he doesn't. However, it won't really matter, you won't want me to stay at home and entertain them will you?'

'Couldn't we play tennis?'

There were a number of courts for the use of residents on the estate.

'Ellie used to be awfully keen on tennis, and Tom plays, I know. He used to be good.'

'Look here, Celia, I simply can't play tennis. It absolutely ruins my game. And there's the

288

Dalton Heath Cup in three weeks' time.'

'Does nothing matter but golf? It makes it so difficult.'

'Don't you think, Celia, that it's ever so much better if everyone does as they like? I like golf you like tennis. You have your friends down and do as you like with them. You know I never interfere with anything you want to do.'

That was true. It all sounded perfectly all right. But somehow it made things difficult in practice. When you were married, Celia reflected, you were somehow so tied up with your husband. Nobody considered you as a separate unity. It would be all right if it were only Ellie coming down, but surely Dermot ought to do something about Ellie's husband.

After all, when Davis (with whom Dermot played nearly every week-end) and his wife came to stay, she, Celia, had to entertain Mrs Davis all day. Mrs Davis was nice but dull. She just sat about and had to be talked to.

But she didn't say these things to Dermot because she knew he hated to be argued with. She asked the Petersons down and hoped for the best.

Ellie had changed very little. She and Celia enjoyed talking over old times. Tom was a little quiet. He had gone a little grey. He seemed a nice little man, Celia thought. He had always seemed a little absent-minded but very pleasant.

Dermot behaved angelically. He explained that he was obliged to play golf on Saturday (Ellie's husband didn't play), but he devoted Sunday to entertaining his guests and took them on the river, a form of spending an afternoon which Celia knew he hated.

When they had gone he said to her: 'Now then, have I been noble or have I not?'

Noble was one of Dermot's words. It always made Celia laugh.

'You have. You've been an angel.'

'Well, don't make me do it again for a long time, will you?'

Celia didn't. She rather wanted to invite another friend and her husband down two weeks later, but she knew the man wasn't a golfer, and she didn't want Dermot to have to make a sacrifice a second time . . .

It was so difficult, thought Celia, living with a person who was sacrificing himself. Dermot was rather trying as a martyr. He was much better to live with when he was enjoying himself . . .

And, anyway, he was unsympathetic about old friends. Old friends, in Dermot's opinion, were usually a bore.

Judy was obviously in sympathy with her father over this, for a few days later when Celia mentioned her friend Margaret, Judy merely stared.

'Who's Margaret?'

'Don't you remember Margaret? You used to play with her in the Park in London?'

'No, I didn't. I never played with a Margaret anywhere.'

'Judy, you must remember. It's only a year ago.'

But Judy couldn't remember any Margaret at all. She couldn't remember anyone she had played with in London.

'I only know the girls at school,' said Judy comfortably.

5

Something rather exciting happened. It began by Celia being rung up and asked to take someone's place at a dinner party at the last minute.

'I know you won't mind, dear . . . '

Celia didn't mind. She was delighted.

She enjoyed the evening frightfully.

She wasn't shy. She found it easy to talk. There was no need to watch whether she were being 'silly' or not. Dermot's critical eyes were not upon her.

She felt as though she had been suddenly wafted back to girlhood.

The man on her right had travelled a lot in the East. Above everything in the world Celia longed to travel.

She felt sometimes that if the chance were to be given her she would leave Dermot and Judy and Aubrey and everything and dash off into the blue . . . To wander . . .

The man at her side spoke of Baghdad, of Kashmir, of Ispahan and Teheran and Shiraz (such lovely words — nice to say them even without any meaning attached). He told her, too, of wandering in Baluchistan where few travellers had been.

The man on her left was an elderly, kindly person. He liked the bright young creature at his

291

side who turned to him at last with a rapturous face still full of the glamour of far lands.

He had something to do with books, she gathered, and she told him, laughing a good deal, about her one unlucky venture. He said he'd like to see her manuscript. Celia told him that it was very bad.

'All the same, I'd like to see it. Will you show it to me?'

'Yes, if you like, but you'll be disappointed.'

He thought that probably he would. She didn't look like a writer — this young creature with her Scandinavian fairness. But, just because she attracted him, it would interest him to see what she had written.

Celia came home at one A.M. to find Dermot happily asleep. She was so excited that she woke him up.

'Dermot — I've had such a lovely evening. Oh! I have enjoyed myself! There was a man there who told me all about Persia and Baluchistan, and there was a nice publisher man — and they made me sing after dinner. I sang awfully badly, but they didn't seem to mind. And then we went out in the garden, and I went with the travelling man to see the lily pond — and he tried to kiss me — but quite nicely — and it was all so lovely — with the moon and the lilies and everything that I would have liked him to — but I didn't because I knew you wouldn't have liked it.'

'Quite right,' said Dermot.

'But you don't mind, do you?'

'Of course not,' said Dermot kindly. 'I'm glad

you enjoyed yourself. But I don't know why you've got to wake me up to tell me about it.'

'Because I have enjoyed myself so much.' She added apologetically, 'I know you don't like me to say so.'

'I don't mind. It just seems to me rather silly. I mean, one can enjoy one's self without having to say so.'

'I can't,' said Celia honestly. 'I have to say so a great deal, otherwise I'd burst.'

'Well,' said Dermot, turning over, 'you've told me now.'

And he went to sleep again.

Dermot was like that, thought Celia, a little sobered as she undressed, rather damping but quite kind . . .

6

Celia had forgotten all about her promise to show the publisher man her book. To her great surprise he walked in upon her the following afternoon and reminded her of her promise.

She hunted out a bundle of dusty manuscripts from a cupboard in the attic, reiterating her statement that it was very stupid.

A fortnight later she had a letter asking her to come up to town to see him.

From behind a very untidy table strewn with bundles of manuscript he twinkled at her from behind his glasses.

'Look here,' he said, 'I understood this was a book. There's only a little more than half of it here. Where's the rest? Have you lost it?'

Puzzled, Celia took the manuscript from him. Her mouth fell open with dismay.

'I've given you the wrong one. This is the old one I never finished.'

Then she explained. He listened attentively, then told her to send him the revised version. He would keep the unfinished one for the moment.

A week later she was summoned again. This time her friend's eyes were twinkling more than ever.

'The second edition's no good,' he said. 'You won't find a publisher to look at it — quite right too. But your original story is not bad at all — do you think you could finish it?'

'But it's all wrong. It's full of mistakes.'

'Now look here, my dear child, I'm going to talk to you quite plainly. You're not a heaven-sent genius. I don't think you'll ever write a masterpiece. But what you certainly *are* is a born storyteller. You think of spiritualism and mediums and Welsh Revivalist meetings in a kind of romantic haze. You may be all wrong about them, but you see them as ninety-nine per cent of the reading public (who know nothing about them either) see them. That ninety-nine per cent won't enjoy reading about carefully acquired facts — they want fiction — which is plausible untruth. It must be plausible, mind. You'll find it will be the same with your Cornish fisher folk that you told me about. Write your book about them, but, for heaven's sake, don't go near Cornwall or fishermen until you've finished. Then you'll write the kind of grimly realistic stuff that people expect when they read about Cornish fisher folk. You don't want to go there and find out that Cornish fishermen are not a breed by themselves but something quite closely allied to a Walworth plumber. You'll never write well about anything you really know about, because you've got an honest mind. You can be imaginatively dishonest but not practically dishonest. You can't write lies about something you know, but you'll be able to tell the most splendid lies about something you don't know. You've got to write about the fabulous (fabulous to you) and not about the real. Now, go away and do it.'

A year later Celia's first novel was published. It was called *Lonely Harbour*. The publishers corrected any glaring inaccuracies.

Miriam thought it splendid, and Dermot thought it rather awful.

Celia knew that Dermot was right, but she was grateful to her mother.

'Now,' thought Celia, 'I'm pretending to be a writer. I think it's almost queerer than pretending to be a wife or a mother.'

16

Loss

1

Miriam was ailing. Every time that Celia saw
her mother, her heart had a sudden squeezed
feeling.

Her mother looked so small and pathetic.

And she was so lonely in that big house.

Celia wanted her mother to come and live
with them, but Miriam refused energetically.

'It never works. It wouldn't be fair to Dermot.'

'I've asked Dermot. He's quite willing.'

'That is nice of him. But I shouldn't dream of
doing it. Young people *must* be left alone.'

She spoke vehemently. Celia did not protest.

Presently Miriam said:

'I've wanted to tell you — for some time. I
was wrong about Dermot. When you married
him, I didn't trust him. I didn't think he was
honest or loyal . . . I thought there would be
other women.'

'Oh, Mother, Dermot never looks at anything
but a golf ball.'

Miriam smiled.

'I was wrong . . . I'm glad . . . I feel now that
when I go I'm leaving you with someone who
will look after you and take care of you.'

'He will. He does.'

296

'Yes — I'm satisfied . . . He's very attractive — he is attractive to women, Celia, remember that . . . '

'He's a frightfully stay-at-home person, Mummy.'

'Yes, that's lucky. And I think he really loves Judy. She is exactly like him. She's not like you. She's Dermot's child.'

'I know.'

'So long as I feel that he will be kind to you . . . I didn't think so at first. I thought he was cruel — ruthless — '

'He isn't. He's frightfully kind. He was sweet before Judy was born. He's just one of those people who hate to say things. It's all there underneath. He's like a rock.'

Miriam sighed.

'I've been jealous. I haven't been willing to recognize his good qualities. I want you so much to be happy, my darling.'

'I am, Mother dear, I am.'

'Yes, I think you are . . . '

Celia said after a minute or two:

'There's really nothing I want in the world — except another baby, perhaps. I'd like a boy as well as a girl.'

She had expected her mother to be in sympathy with her wish, but a slight frown crossed Miriam's forehead.

'I don't know that you will be wise. You care for Dermot so much — and children take you away from a man. They are supposed to bring you together, but it isn't so . . . no, it isn't so.'

'But you and Father — '

Miriam sighed.

'It was difficult. Pulling — always pulling both ways. It's difficult.'

'But you and Father were perfectly happy . . . '

'Yes — but I minded . . . There were heaps of things I minded. Giving up things for the sake of the children annoyed him sometimes. He loved you all, but we were happiest when he and I went away together for a little holiday . . . Don't ever leave your husband too long alone, Celia. Remember, a man forgets . . . '

'Father would never have looked at anyone but you.'

Her mother answered musingly.

'No, perhaps he wouldn't. But I was always on the look out. There was a parlourmaid — a big handsome girl — the type I had often heard your father admire. She was handing him the hammer and some nails. As she did it she put her hand over his. I saw her. Your father hardly noticed — he just looked surprised. I don't suppose he thought anything of it — probably imagined it was just an accident — men are very simple . . . But I sent that girl away — at once. Just gave her a good reference and said she didn't suit me.'

Celia was shocked.

'But Father would never — '

'Probably not. *But I wasn't taking any risks.* I've seen so many things. A wife who's in bad health and a governess or companion takes charge — some young, bright girl. Celia, promise me you'll be very careful what kind of governesses you have for Judy.'

Celia laughed and kissed her mother.

'I won't have any fine big girls,' she promised. 'They shall be thin and old and wear glasses.'

2

Miriam died when Judy was eight years old. Celia was abroad at the time. Dermot had got ten days' leave at Easter, and he had wanted Celia to go to Italy with him. Celia had been a little unwilling to leave England. The doctor had told her that her mother's health was bad. She had a companion who looked after her, and Celia went down to see her every few weeks.

Miriam, however, would not hear of Celia's remaining behind and letting Dermot go alone. She came up to London and stayed with Cousin Lottie (a widow now), and Judy and her governess came to stay there also.

At Como, Celia got a telegram advising her return. She took the first train available. Dermot wanted to go too, but Celia persuaded him to stay behind and finish his holiday. He needed a change of air and scene.

It was as she was sitting in the dining car on her way through France that a curious cold certainty seemed to invade her body.

She thought:

'Of course, I shall never see her again. She's dead . . . '

She found on arrival that Miriam had died just about that hour.

Her mother . . . her little gallant mother . . .

Lying there so still and strange with flowers and whiteness and a cold, peaceful face . . .

Her mother, with her fits of gaiety and depression — her enchanting changeableness of outlook — her steadfast love and protection . . .

Celia thought: 'I'm alone now . . .'

Dermot and Judy were strangers . . .

She thought: 'There's no one to go to any more . . .'

Panic swept over her . . . and then remorse . . .

How full her mind had been of Dermot and Judy all these last years . . . She had thought so little of her mother . . . her mother had just been *there* . . . always *there* . . . at the back of everything . . .

She knew her mother through and through, and her mother knew her . . .

As a tiny child she had found her mother wonderful and satisfying . . .

And wonderful and satisfying her mother had always remained . . .

And now her mother had gone . . .

The bottom had fallen out of Celia's world . . .

Her little mother . . .

17

Disaster

1

Dermot meant to be kind. He hated trouble and unhappiness, but he wanted to be kind. He wrote from Paris suggesting Celia should come over and have a day or two to cheer her up.

Perhaps it was kindness, perhaps it was because he funked going home to a house of mourning . . .

That, however, was what he had to do . . .

He arrived at the Lodge just before dinner. Celia was lying on her bed. She was awaiting his coming with passionate intensity. The strain of the funeral was over, and she had been anxious not to upset Judy by an atmosphere of grief. Little Judy, so young and cheerful and important over her own affairs. Judy had cried about Grandmamma but had soon forgotten. Children ought to forget.

Soon Dermot would be here, and then she could let go.

She thought passionately: 'How wonderful that I've got Dermot. If it weren't for Dermot I should want to die too . . .'

Dermot was nervous. It was sheer nervousness that made him come into the room and say:

'Well, how's everybody, bright and jolly?'

At another time Celia would have recognized the cause that made him speak flippantly. Just at the moment it was as though he had hit her in the face.

She shrank back and burst into tears.

Dermot apologized and tried to explain.

In the end Celia went to sleep holding his hand, which he withdrew with relief when he saw she was really asleep.

He wandered off and joined Judy in the nursery. She waved a cheerful spoon at him. She was drinking a cup of milk.

'Hullo, Daddy. What shall we play?'

Judy wasted no time.

'It mustn't be noisy,' said Dermot. 'Your mother's asleep.'

Judy nodded comprehendingly.

'Let's play Old Maid.'

They played Old Maid.

2

Life went on as usual. At least, not quite as usual.

Celia went about as usual. She displayed no outward signs of grief. But all the spring had gone out of her for the time being. She was like a run-down clock. Both Dermot and Judy felt the change, and they didn't like it.

Dermot wanted some people to stay a fortnight later, and Celia cried out before she could stop herself.

'Oh, not just now. I just can't bear to have to

talk to a strange woman all day.'

But immediately afterwards she repented and went to Dermot, telling him that she didn't mean to be silly. Of course he must have his friends. So they came, but the visit wasn't a great success.

A few days later Celia had a letter from Ellie. Its contents surprised and grieved her very much.

My Dear Celia [wrote Ellie]: I feel I should like to tell you myself (since you'll probably hear a garbled version otherwise) that Tom has gone off with a girl we met on the boat coming home. It has been a terrible grief and shock to me. We were so happy together, and Tom loved the children. It seems like some terrible dream. I feel absolutely broken-hearted, I don't know what to do. Tom has been such a perfect husband — we never even quarrelled.

Celia was very upset over her friend's trouble.

'What a lot of sad things there are in the world,' she said to Dermot.

'That husband of hers must be rather a rotter,' said Dermot. 'You know, Celia, you sometimes seem to think that I'm selfish — but you might have much worse things to put up with. At any rate, I am a good, straight, undeceiving husband, aren't I?'

There was something comic in his tone. Celia kissed him and laughed.

Three weeks later she went home, taking Judy

with her. The house had got to be turned out and gone through. It was a task she dreaded. But no one else could do it.

Home without her mother's welcoming smile was unthinkable. If only Dermot could have come with her.

Dermot himself tried in his own fashion to cheer her up. 'You'll enjoy it really, Celia. You'll find lots of old things you've forgotten all about. And it will be lovely down there this time of year. It will do you good to have a change. Here am I having to grind along in an office every day.'

Dermot was so inadequate! He persistently ignored the significance of emotional stress. He shied away from it like a frightened horse.

Celia cried out — angry for once:

'You talk as though it was a holiday!'

He looked away from her.

'Well,' he said, 'so it will be in a way . . . '

Celia thought: 'He's *not* kind . . . he's *not* . . . '

A great wave of loneliness passed over her. She felt afraid . . .

How cold the world was — without her mother . . .

3

Celia went through a bad time in the next few months. She had lawyers to see, all kinds of business questions to settle.

Her mother had, of course, left hardly any

money. There was the question of the house to consider — whether to keep it or sell it. It was in a very bad state — there had been no money for repairs. A fairly large sum would have to be spent on it almost immediately if the whole place were not to go to rack and ruin. In any case, it was doubtful if a purchaser would consider it in its present condition.

Celia was torn by indecision.

She could not bear to part with it — yet common sense whispered that it was the best thing to do. It was too far from London for her and Dermot to live in it — even if the idea had appealed to Dermot (and Celia was sure it would not appeal to him). The country, to Dermot, meant a first-class golf course.

Was it not, then, mere sentiment on her part to insist on clinging to the place?

Yet she could not bear to give it up. Miriam had made such valiant struggles to keep it for her. It was she herself who had dissuaded her mother from selling it long ago . . . Miriam had kept it for her — for her and her children.

Did Judy care for it as she had done? She thought not. Judy was so aloof — so unattached — she was like Dermot. People like Dermot and Judy lived in places because they were convenient. In the end Celia asked her daughter. Celia often felt that Judy, at eight years old, was far more sensible and practical than herself.

'Will you get a lot of money for it if you sell it, Mummy?'

'No, I'm afraid not. You see, it's an

305

old-fashioned house — and it's right in the country — not near a town.'

'Well, then, perhaps you'd better keep it,' said Judy. 'We can come here in the summer.'

'Are you fond of being here, Judy? Or do you like the Lodge best?'

'The Lodge is very small,' said Judy. 'I'd like to live in the Dormy House. I like big — big — houses.'

Celia laughed.

It was true what Judy had said — she would get very little for the house if she sold it now. Surely even as a business proposition it would be better to wait until country houses were less of a drug in the market. She went into the question of the minimum repairs that were absolutely necessary. Perhaps, when they were completed, she could find a tenant for the house furnished.

The business side of things had been worrying, but it had kept her mind away from sad thoughts.

Now there came the part she had dreaded — the turning out. If the house was to be let, it must first be cleared. Some of the rooms had been locked up for years — there were old trunks, drawers, and cupboards, all crammed with memories of the past.

4

Memories . . .

It was so lonely — so strange in the house.

No Miriam . . .

Only trunks full of old clothes — drawers full of letters and photographs . . .

It hurt — it hurt horribly.

A japanned box with a stork on it that she had loved as a child. Inside it folded letters. One from Mummy. 'My own precious lamb pigeony pumpkin . . . ' The scalding tears fell down Celia's cheeks . . .

A pink silk evening dress with little rosebuds — shoved into a trunk — in case it might be 'renovated' — and forgotten. One of her first evening dresses . . . She remembered the last time she had worn it . . . Such a gauche, eager, idiotic creature . . .

Letters belonging to Grannie — a whole trunk full. She must have brought them with her when she came. Photograph of an old gentleman in a Bath chair, 'Always your devoted admirer,' and some initials scrawled on it. Grannie and 'the men'. Always 'the men' even when they were reduced to Bath chairs on the sea front . . .

A mug with a picture of two cats on it that Susan had once given her for a birthday present . . .

Back — back into the past . . .

Why did it hurt so?

Why did it hurt so abominably?

If only she wasn't alone in the house . . . If only Dermot could be with her!

But Dermot would say: 'Why not burn the lot without looking through them?'

So sensible, but somehow she couldn't . . .

She opened more locked drawers.

Poems. Sheets of poems in flowing faded handwriting. Her mother's handwriting as a girl . . . Celia looked through them.

Sentimental — stilted — very much of the period. Yes, but something — some quick turn of thought, some sudden originality of phrase — that made them essentially her mother's. Miriam's mind — that quick, darting, bird-like mind . . .

'*Poem to John on his birthday* . . . '

Her father — her bearded, jolly father . . .

Here was a daguerreotype of him as a solemn cleanshaven boy.

Being young — growing old — how mysterious — how frightening it all was. Was there any particular moment at which you were more you than at any other moment?

The future . . . Where was she, Celia, going in the future? . . .

Well, it was clear enough. Dermot growing a little richer . . . a large house . . . another child . . . two, perhaps. Illnesses — childish ailments — Dermot growing a little more difficult, a little more impatient still of anything interfering with what he wanted to do . . . Judy growing up — vivid, decided, intensely alive . . . Dermot and Judy together . . . Herself, rather fatter — faded — treated with just a touch of amused contempt by those two . . . 'Mother, you *are* rather silly, you know . . . ' Yes, more difficult to disguise that you were silly as your looks left you. (A sudden flash of memory: 'Don't ever grow less beautiful, will you, Celia?') Yes, but that was all over now.

They'd lived together long enough for such things as the beauty of a face to have lost its meaning. Dermot was in her blood and she in his. They *belonged* — essentially strangers, they belonged. She loved him because he was so different — because though she knew by now exactly how he reacted to things, she did not know and never would know *why* he reacted as he did. Probably he felt the same about her. No, Dermot accepted things as they were. He never thought about them. It seemed to him a waste of time. Celia thought: 'It's right — it's absolutely right to marry the person you love. Money and outside things don't count. I should always have been happy with Dermot even if we'd had to live in a tiny cottage and I'd had to do all the cooking and everything.' But Dermot wasn't going to be poor. He was a success. He would go on succeeding. He was that kind of person. His digestion, of course, *that* would get worse. He would continue to play golf . . . And they'd go on and on and on — probably at Dalton Heath or somewhere like it . . . She'd never see things — far-away things — India, China, Japan — the wilds of Baluchistan — Persia, where the names were like music: Ispahan, Teheran, Shiraz . . .

Little shivers ran over her . . . If one could be free — quite free — nothing, no belongings, no houses, or husband or children, nothing to hold you, and tie you, and pull at your heart . . .

Celia thought: 'I want to run away . . . '

Miriam had felt like that.

For all her love of her husband and children

she had wanted, sometimes, to get out . . .

Celia opened another drawer. Letters. Letters from her father to her mother. She picked up the top one. It was dated the year before his death.

Dearest Miriam: I hope you will soon be able to join me. Mother seems very well and is in good spirits. Her eyesight is failing, but she knits just as many bedsocks for her beaux!

I had a long talk with Armour about Cyril. He says the boy is *not* stupid. He is just indifferent. I talked to Cyril too, and, I hope, made some impression.

Try and be with me by Friday, my dearest — our twenty-second anniversary. I find it hard to put into words all that you have meant to me — the dearest, most devoted wife any man could have. I am humbly grateful to God for you, my darling.

Love to our little Poppet.

Your devoted husband, John.

Tears came again to Celia's eyes.

Some day she and Dermot would have been married twenty-two years. Dermot wouldn't write a letter like that, but, deep down, he would perhaps feel the same.

Poor Dermot. It had been sad for him having her so broken and battered this last month. He didn't like unhappiness. Well, once she had got through with this task she would put grief behind her. Miriam, alive, had never come between her and Dermot. Miriam, dead, must not do so . . .

She and Dermot would go forward together — happy and enjoying things.

That was what would please her mother best.

She took all her father's letters out of the drawer, and making a pile of them on the hearth, she set a match to them. They belonged to the dead. The one she had read she kept.

At the bottom of the drawer was a faded old pocketbook embroidered in gold thread. Inside it was a folded sheet of paper, very old and worn. On it was written: 'Poem sent me by Miriam on my birthday.'

Sentiment . . .

The world despised sentiment nowadays . . .

But to Celia, at that moment, it was somehow unbearably sweet . . .

5

Celia felt ill. The loneliness of the house was getting on her nerves. She wished she had someone to speak to. There were Judy and Miss Hood, but they belonged to such an alien world that being with them brought more strain than relief. Celia was anxious that no shadow should cloud Judy's life. Judy was so vivid — so full of enjoyment of everything. When she was with Judy, Celia made a point of being gay. They had strenuous games together with balls, and battledores, and shuttlecocks.

It was after Judy had gone to bed that the silence of the house wrapped itself round Celia like a pall. It seemed so empty — so empty . . .

It brought back so vividly those happy, cosy evenings spent talking to her mother — about Dermot, about Judy, about books and people and ideas.

Now, there was no one to talk to . . .

Dermot's letters were infrequent and brief. He had gone round in seventy-two — he had played with Andrews — Rossiter had come down with his niece. He had got Marjorie Connell to make a fourth. They'd played at Hillborough — a rotten course. Women were a nuisance in golf. He hoped Celia was enjoying herself. Would she thank Judy for her letter?

Celia began to sleep badly. Scenes came up out of the past and kept her awake. Sometimes she awoke frightened — not knowing what it was that had frightened her. She looked at herself in the glass and knew she looked ill.

She wrote to Dermot and begged him to come down for the week-end.

He wrote back:

Dear Celia: I've looked up the train service and it really isn't worth it. I'd either have to go back Sunday morning or else land in town about two in the morning. The car's not running very well now, and I'm having her overhauled. I know you'll realize that I feel it a bit of a strain working all the week. I feel dog-tired by the week-end — and don't want to embark on train journeys.

312

In another three weeks I shall get off for my holiday. I think your idea of Dinard is quite a good one. I'll write about rooms. Don't do too much and overtire yourself. Get out a good deal.

You remember Marjorie Connell, rather nice dark girl, niece of the Barretts? She's just lost her job. I may be able to get her one here. She's quite efficient. I took her to a theatre one night as she was down on her luck.

Take care of yourself and go easy. I think you're right not to sell the house now. Things may improve and you might get a better price later. I don't see that it's ever going to be much use to us, but if you feel sentimental about it I don't suppose it would cost much to shut it up with a caretaker — and you might let it furnished. The money you get in from the books would pay the rates and a gardener, and I'll help towards it, if you like. I'm working frightfully hard and come home with a headache most nights.

It will be good to get right away.

Love to Judy.

Your loving,

Dermot.

The last week Celia went to the doctor and asked him to give her something to make her sleep. He had known her all her life. He asked her questions, examined her, then he said:

'Can't you get someone to be with you?'

'My husband is coming in a week's time. We are going abroad together.'

'Ah, excellent! You know, my dear, you're heading for a breakdown. You're very run down — you've had a shock, and you've been fretting. Very natural. I know how attached you were to your mother. Once you get away with your husband into fresh surroundings you'll be as right as rain.'

He patted her on the shoulder, gave her a prescription, and dismissed her.

Celia counted the days one by one. When Dermot came, everything would be all right. He was to arrive the day before Judy's birthday. They were to celebrate that, and then they were to start for Dinard.

A new life . . . Grief and memories left behind . . . She and Dermot going forward into the future.

In four days Dermot would be here . . .

In three days . . .

In two days . . .

Today!

6

Something was wrong . . . Dermot had come, but it wasn't Dermot. It was a stranger who looked at her — quick sideways glances — and looked away again . . .

Something was the matter . . .

He was ill . . .

314

In trouble . . .

No, it was different from that.

He was — a stranger . . .

7

'Dermot, is anything the matter?'

'What should be the matter?'

They were alone together in Celia's bedroom. Celia was doing up Judy's birthday presents with tissue paper and ribbon.

Why was she so frightened? Why this sick feeling of terror?

His eyes — his queer shifty eyes — that looked away from her and back again . . .

This wasn't Dermot — upright, handsome, laughing Dermot . . .

This was a furtive, shrinking person . . . he looked — almost — like a criminal . . .

She said suddenly:

'Dermot, there isn't anything — with money — I mean, you haven't done anything — ?'

How put it into words? Dermot, who was the soul of honour, an embezzler? Fantastic — fantastic!

But that shifty evasive glance . . .

As though she would care what he had done!

He looked surprised.

'Money? Oh, no, money's all right. I'm — I'm doing very well.'

She was relieved.

'I thought — it was absurd of me . . .'

He said:

'There is something ... I expect you can guess.'

But she couldn't. If it wasn't money (she had had a fleeting fear the firm might have failed) she couldn't imagine what it could be.

She said: 'Tell me.'

It wasn't — it couldn't be *cancer* ...

Cancer attacked strong people, young people, sometimes.

Dermot stood up. His voice sounded strange and stiff.

'It's — well, it's Marjorie Connell. I've seen a lot of her, I'm very fond of her.'

Oh, the relief! *Not* cancer ... But Marjorie Connell — why on earth Marjorie Connell? Had Dermot — Dermot who never looked at a girl —

She said gently:

'It doesn't matter, Dermot, if you've been rather silly ... '

A flirtation. Dermot wasn't used to flirting. All the same, she was surprised. Surprised and hurt. While she had been so miserable — so longing for Dermot's comfort and presence — he had been flirting with Marjorie Connell. Marjorie was quite a nice girl and rather good-looking. Celia thought: 'Grannie wouldn't have been surprised.' And the idea flashed through her mind that perhaps Grannie *had* known men rather well, after all.

Dermot said violently:

'You don't understand. It's not at all as you think. There has been nothing — nothing — '

Celia flushed.

'Of course. I didn't think there had . . . '

He went on:

'I don't know how to make you see. It isn't her fault . . . She's very distressed about it — about you . . . Oh, God!'

He sat down and buried his face in his hands . . .

Celia said wonderingly:

'You really care for her — I see. Oh, Dermot, I am so sorry . . . '

Poor Dermot, overtaken by this passion. He was going to be so unhappy. She mustn't — she simply mustn't be beastly about it. She must help him to get over it — not reproach him. It hadn't been his fault. She hadn't been there — he'd been lonely — it was quite natural . . .

She said again:

'I'm so dreadfully sorry for you.'

He got up again.

'You don't understand. You needn't be sorry for *me* . . . I'm a rotter. I feel a cur. I couldn't be decent to you. I shall be no more use to you and Judy . . . You'd better cut me right out . . . '

She stared . . .

'You mean,' she said, 'you don't love me any longer? Not at all? But we've been so happy . . . Always so happy together.'

'Yes, in a way — a quiet way . . . This is quite different.'

'I think to be quietly happy is the best thing in the world.'

Dermot made a gesture.

She said wonderingly:

'You want to go away from us? Not to see me and Judy any more? But you're Judy's father . . . She loves you.'

'I know . . . I mind terribly about her. But it's no good. I'm never any use doing anything I don't want to do . . . I can't behave decently when I'm unhappy . . . I should be a brute.'

Celia said slowly:

'You're going away — with *her?*'

'Of course not. She's not that kind of a girl. I would never suggest such a thing to her.'

He sounded hurt and offended.

'I don't understand — you just want to leave *us?*'

'Because I can't be any good to you . . . I should be simply foul.'

'But we've been so happy — so happy . . . '

Dermot said impatiently:

'Yes, of course, we have — in the past. But we've been married eleven years. After eleven years one needs a change.'

She winced.

He went on, his voice persuasive, more like himself:

'I'm making quite a good income, I'd allow you plenty for Judy — and you're making money yourself now. You could go abroad — travel — do all sorts of things you've always wanted to do . . . '

She put up her hand as though he had struck her.

'I'm sure you'd enjoy it. You'd really be much happier than you would be with me . . . '

'Stop!'

After a minute or two she said quietly:

'It was on this night, nine years ago, that Judy began to be born. Do you remember? Doesn't it mean anything to you? Isn't there any difference between me and — a mistress you would try to pension off?'

He said sulkily:

'I've said I was sorry about Judy . . . But, after all, we both agreed that the other should be perfectly free . . . '

'Did we? When?'

'I'm sure we did. It's the only decent way to regard marriage.'

Celia said:

'I think, when you've brought a child into the world — it would be more decent to stick to it.'

Dermot said:

'All my friends think that the ideal of marriage should be freedom . . . '

She laughed. His friends. How extraordinary Dermot was — only he would have dragged in his friends.

She said:

'You are free . . . You can leave us if you choose . . . if you really choose . . . but won't you wait a little — won't you be sure? There's eleven years' happiness to remember — against a month's infatuation. Wait a year — make sure of things — before bursting up everything . . . '

'I don't want to wait. I don't want the strain of waiting . . . '

Suddenly Celia stretched out and caught at the door handle.

All this wasn't real — couldn't be real . . . She called out: 'Dermot!'

The room went black and whirled round her.

She found herself lying on the bed. Dermot was standing beside her with a glass of water. He said:

'I didn't mean to upset you.'

She stopped herself laughing hysterically . . . took the water and drank it . . .

'I'm all right,' she said. 'It's all right . . . You must do as you please . . . You can go away now. I'm all right . . . You do as you like. But let Judy have her birthday tomorrow.'

'Of course . . . '

He said: 'If you're sure you're all right . . . '

He went slowly through the open door into his room and shut it behind him.

Judy's birthday tomorrow . . .

Nine years ago she and Dermot had wandered in the garden — had been parted — she had gone down into pain and fear — and Dermot had suffered . . .

Surely — surely — no one in the world could be so cruel as to choose this day to tell her . . .

Yes, Dermot could . . .

Cruel . . . cruel . . . cruel . . .

Her heart cried out passionately:

'How could he — how could he — be so cruel to me? . . . '

8

Judy must have her birthday.

Presents — special breakfast — picnic — sitting up to dinner — games.

Celia thought: 'There's never been a day so long — so long — I shall go mad. If only Dermot would play up a little more.'

And Judy noticed nothing. She noticed her presents, her fun, the readiness of everyone to do what she wanted.

She was so happy — so unconscious — it tore at Celia's heart.

9

The next day Dermot left.

'I'll write from London, shall I? You'll stay here for the present?'

'Not here — no, not here.'

Here, in the emptiness, the loneliness, without Miriam to comfort her?

Oh, Mother, Mother, come back to me, Mother . . .

Oh, Mother, if you were here . . .

Stay here alone? In this house so full of happy memories — memories of Dermot?

She said: 'I'd rather come home. We'll come home tomorrow.'

'As you please. I'll stay in London. I thought you were so fond of it down here.'

She didn't answer. Sometimes you couldn't. People either saw or they didn't see.

When Dermot had left, she played with Judy. She told her they were not going to France after all. Judy accepted the pronouncement calmly, without interest.

Celia felt terribly ill. Her legs ached, her head swam. She felt like an old, old woman.

The pain in her head increased till she could have screamed. She took aspirin, but it was no use. She felt sick, and the thought of food repelled her.

10

Celia was afraid of two things: she was afraid of going mad, and she was afraid of Judy noticing anything . . .

She didn't know whether Miss Hood noticed anything. Miss Hood was so quiet. It was a comfort to have Miss Hood — so calm and incurious.

Miss Hood managed the going home. She seemed to think it quite natural that Celia and Dermot weren't going to France after all.

Celia was glad to get back to the Lodge. She thought: 'This is better. I mayn't go mad after all.'

Her head felt better but her body worse — as though she had been battered all over. Her legs felt too weak to walk . . . That and the deathly sickness made her limp and unresisting . . .

She thought: 'I'm going to be ill. Why does your mind affect your body so?'

Dermot came down two days after her return.

It was still not Dermot . . . Queer — and frightening — to find a stranger in the body of your husband . . .

It frightened Celia so much that she wanted to scream . . .

Dermot talked stiffly about outside matters. 'Like someone who's come to call,' thought Celia.

Then he said:

'Don't you agree that it is the best thing to do — to part, I mean?'

'The best thing — for whom?'

'Well, for all of us.'

'I don't think it's the best thing for Judy or me. You know I don't.'

Dermot said: 'Everybody can't be happy.'

'You mean it's you who are going to be happy and Judy and I who aren't . . . I don't see really why it should be you and not us. Oh, Dermot, can't you go and do what you want to do, and not insist on talking about it. You've got to choose between Marjorie and me — no, that's not it — you're tired of me and perhaps that's my fault — I ought to have seen it coming — I ought to have tried more, but I was so sure you loved me — I believed in you as I believed in God. That was stupid — Grannie would have told me so. No, what you have to choose between is Marjorie and Judy. You *do love* Judy — she's your own flesh and blood — and I can never be to her what you can be. There's a tie between you two that there isn't between her and me. I love her, but I don't understand her. I don't want you to abandon Judy — I don't want

323

her life maimed. I wouldn't fight for myself, but I will fight for Judy. It's a mean thing to do, to abandon your own child. I believe — if you do it — you won't be happy. Dermot, dear Dermot, won't you *try*? Won't you give a year out of your life? If, at the end of a year, you can't do it, you feel you must go to Marjorie — well, then, you must go. But I'd feel then that you'd tried.'

Dermot said: 'I don't want to wait . . . A year is a long time . . . '

Celia gave a discouraged gesture.

(If only she didn't feel so deathly sick.)

She said: 'Very well — you've chosen . . . But if ever you want to come back — you'll find us waiting, and I won't reproach you . . . Go, and be — be happy, and perhaps you'll come back to us some day . . . I think you will . . . I think that underneath everything it's really me and Judy you love . . . And I think, too, that underneath you're straight and loyal . . . '

Dermot cleared his throat. He looked embarrassed.

Celia wished he would go away. All this *talking* . . . She loved him so — it was agony to look at him — if only he would go away and do what he wanted to do — not ram the agony of it home to her . . .

'The real point is,' said Dermot, 'how soon can I get my freedom?'

'You are free. You can go now.'

'I don't think you understand what I am talking about. All my friends think there should be a divorce as soon as possible.'

Celia stared.

'I thought you told me there wasn't — there wasn't — well, any grounds for divorce.'

'Of course there aren't. Marjorie is as straight as a die.'

A wild desire to laugh passed over Celia. She repressed it.

'Well, then?' she said.

'I'd never suggest anything of that kind to her,' said Dermot in a shocked voice. 'But I believe that, if I were free, she would marry me.'

'But you're married to me,' said Celia, puzzled.

'That's why there must be a divorce. It can all be put through quite easily and quickly. It will be no bother to you. And all the expense will fall on me.'

'You mean that you and Marjorie *are* going away together after all?'

'Do you think I'd drag a girl like that through the divorce court? No, the whole thing can be managed quite easily. Her name need never appear.'

Celia got up. Her eyes blazed.

'You mean — you mean — oh, I think that's disgusting! If I loved a man I'd go away with him even if it was wrong. I might take a man from his wife — I don't think I would take a man from his child — still, one never knows. But I'd do it *honestly*. I'd not skulk in the shadow and let someone else do the dirty work and play safe myself. I think both you and Marjorie are disgusting — disgusting. If you really loved each other and couldn't live without each other I would at least respect you. I'd divorce you if you wanted me to — although I think divorce is wrong. But I won't have anything to do with lying and pretending and making a put-up job of it.'

'Nonsense, everybody does.'

'I don't care.'

Dermot came up to her.

'Look here, Celia, I'm going to have a divorce. I won't wait for it, and I won't have Marjorie dragged into it. And you've got to agree to it.'

Celia looked him full in the face.

'I won't,' she said.

18

Fear

1

It was here, of course, that Dermot made his mistake.

If he had appealed to Celia, if he had thrown himself on her mercy, if he had told her that he loved Marjorie and wanted her and couldn't live without her, Celia would have melted and agreed to anything he wanted — no matter how repugnant to her own feelings. Dermot unhappy she could not have resisted. She had always given him anything he wanted, and she would not have been able to keep from doing so again.

She was on the side of Judy against Dermot, but if he had taken her the right way, she would have sacrificed Judy to him, although she would have hated herself for doing so.

But Dermot took an entirely different line. He claimed what he wanted as a right and tried to bully her into consenting.

She had always been so soft, so malleable, that he was astonished at her resistance. She ate practically nothing, she did not sleep, her legs felt so weak she would hardly walk, she suffered tortures from neuralgia and earache, but she stood firm. And Dermot tried to bully her into giving her consent.

He told her that she was behaving disgracefully, that she was a vulgar, clutching woman, that she ought to be ashamed of herself, that he was ashamed of her. It had no effect.

Outwardly, that is. Inwardly his words cut her like wounds. That Dermot — Dermot — could think she was like that.

She grew worried about her physical condition. Sometimes she lost the thread of what she was saying — her thoughts, even became confused . . .

She would wake up in the night in a condition of utter terror. She would feel sure that Dermot was poisoning her — to get her out of the way. In the daytime she knew these for the wildest night fancies, but, all the same, she locked up the packet of weed killer that stood in the potting shed. As she did so, she thought: 'That isn't quite sane — I mustn't go mad — I simply mustn't go mad . . . '

She would wake up in the night and wander about the house looking for something. One night she knew what it was. She was looking for her mother . . .

She must find her mother. She dressed and put on a coat and hat. She took her mother's photograph. She would go to the police station and ask them to trace her mother. Her mother had disappeared, but the police would find her . . . And once she had found her mother everything would be all right . . .

She walked for a long time — it was raining and wet . . . She couldn't remember what she was walking for. Oh, yes, the police station

— where was the police station? Surely in a town, not out in the open country.

She turned and walked in the other direction . . .

The police would be kind and helpful. She would give them her mother's name — what was her mother's name? . . . Odd, she couldn't remember . . . What was her own name?

How frightening — she couldn't remember . . .

Sybil, wasn't it? Or Yvonne — how awful not to be able to remember . . .

She *must* remember her own name . . .

She stumbled over a ditch . . .

The ditch was full of water . . .

You could drown yourself in water . . .

It would be better to drown yourself than to hang yourself. If you lay down in the water . . .

Oh, how cold it was! — she couldn't — no, she couldn't . . .

She would find her mother . . . Her mother would put everything right.

She would say, 'I nearly drowned myself in a ditch,' and her mother would say, 'That would have been very silly, darling.'

Silly — yes, silly. Dermot had thought her silly — long ago. He had said so and his face had reminded her of something.

Of course! Of the Gun Man!

That was the horror of the Gun Man. All the time Dermot had really been the Gun Man . . .

She felt sick with fear . . .

She must get home . . . she must hide . . . The Gun Man was looking for her . . . Dermot was stalking her down . . .

She got home at last. It was two o'clock. The house was asleep . . .

She crept up the stairs . . .

Horror, the Gun Man was there — behind that door — she could hear him breathing . . . Dermot, the Gun Man . . .

She daren't go back to her room. Dermot wanted to be rid of her. He might come creeping in . . .

She ran wildly up one flight of stairs. Miss Hood, Judy's governess, was there. She burst in.

'Don't let him find me — don't let him . . . '

Miss Hood was wonderfully kind and reassuring.

She took her down to her room and stayed with her.

Just as Celia was falling asleep she said suddenly:

'How stupid, I couldn't have found my mother. I remember — *she's dead . . .* '

2

Miss Hood got the doctor in. He was kind and emphatic. Celia was to put herself in Miss Hood's charge.

He himself had an interview with Dermot. He told him plainly that Celia was in a very grave condition. He warned him of what might happen unless she was to be left entirely free from worry.

Miss Hood played her part very efficiently. As far as possible, she never left Celia and Dermot alone. Celia clung to her. With Miss Hood she felt safe . . . She was *kind* . . .

One day Dermot came in and stood by the bed.

He said: 'I'm sorry you're ill . . . '

It was Dermot who spoke to her — not the stranger.

A lump came in her throat . . .

The next day Miss Hood came in with rather a worried face.

Celia said quietly: 'He's gone, hasn't he?'

Miss Hood nodded. She was relieved that Celia took it so quietly.

Celia lay there motionless. She felt no grief — no pang . . . She was just numb and peaceful . . .

He had gone . . .

Some day she must get up and start life again — with Judy . . .

It was all over . . .

Poor Dermot . . .

She slept — she slept almost continuously for two days.

3

And then he came back.

It was Dermot who came back — not the stranger.

He said he was sorry — that as soon as he had gone he had been miserable. He said he thought that Celia was right — that he ought to stick to her and Judy. At any rate, he would try . . . He

said: 'But you must get well. I can't bear illness
. . . or unhappiness. It was partly because you
were unhappy this spring that I got to be friends
with Marjorie. I wanted someone to play
with . . . '

'I know. I ought to have 'stayed beautiful', as
you always told me.'

Celia hesitated, then she said: 'You — you do
really mean to give it a chance? I mean, I can't
stand any more . . . If you'll honestly try — for
three months. At the end of it, if you can't, then
that's that. But — but — I'm afraid to go queer
again . . . '

He said that he'd try for three months. He
wouldn't even see Marjorie. He said he was
sorry.

4

But it didn't stay like that.

Miss Hood, Celia knew, was sorry that
Dermot had come back.

Later, Celia admitted that Miss Hood had
been right.

It began gradually.

Dermot became moody.

Celia was sorry for him, but she didn't dare to
say anything.

Slowly things went worse and worse.

If Celia came into a room, Dermot went out of
it.

If she spoke to him, he wouldn't answer. He
talked only to Miss Hood and Judy.

332

Dermot never spoke to her or looked at her. He took Judy out in the car sometimes.

'Is Mummy coming?' Judy would ask.

'Yes, if she likes.'

When Celia was ready, Dermot would say:

'Mummy had better drive you. I believe I'm busy.'

Sometimes Celia would say *No*, she was busy, and then Dermot and Judy would go off.

Incredibly, Judy noticed nothing — or so Celia thought.

But occasionally Judy said things that surprised her.

They had been talking about being kind to Aubrey, who was the adored dog of the house by now, and Judy said suddenly:

'You're kind — you're very kind. Daddy's not kind, but he's very, very jolly . . . '

And once she said reflectively:

'Daddy doesn't like you much . . . ' Adding with great satisfaction, 'But he likes *me*.'

One day Celia spoke to her.

'Judy, your father wants to leave us. He thinks he would be happier living with somebody else. Do you think it would be kinder to let him go?'

'I don't want him to go,' said Judy quickly. 'Please, please, Mummy, don't let him go. He's very happy playing with me — and besides — besides, he's my father.'

'He's my father!' Such pride, such certainty in those words!

Celia thought: 'Judy or Dermot? I've got to be on one side or the other . . . And Judy's only a child, I *must* be on her side . . . '

But she thought: 'I can't stand Dermot's unkindness much longer. I'm losing grip again . . . I'm getting frightened . . . '

Dermot had disappeared again — the stranger was here in Dermot's place. He looked at her with hard, hostile eyes . . .

Horrible when the person you loved most in the world looked at you like that. Celia could have understood infidelity, she couldn't understand the affection of eleven years turning suddenly — overnight as it were — to dislike . . .

Passion might fade and die, but had there never been anything else? She had loved him and lived with him and borne his child, and gone through poverty with him — and he was quite calmly prepared never to see her again . . . Oh, frightening — horribly frightening . . .

She was the Obstacle . . . If she were dead . . .

He wished her dead . . .

He must wish her dead; otherwise she wouldn't be so afraid.

5

Celia looked in at the nursery door. Judy was sleeping soundly. Celia shut the door noiselessly and came down to the hall and went to the front door.

Aubrey hurried out of the drawing-room.

'Hallo,' said Aubrey: 'A walk? At this time of night? Well, I don't mind if I do . . . '

But his mistress thought otherwise. She took

Aubrey's face between her hands and kissed him on the nose.

'Stay at home. Good dog. Can't come with missus.'

Can't come with missus — no, indeed! No one must come where missus was going . . .

She knew now that she couldn't bear any more . . . She'd got to escape . . .

She felt exhausted after that long scene with Dermot . . . But she also felt desperate . . . She must escape . . .

Miss Hood had gone to London to see a sister come home from abroad. Dermot had seized the opportunity to 'have things out'.

He admitted at once he'd been seeing Marjorie. He'd promised — but he hadn't been able to keep the promise . . .

None of that mattered, Celia felt, if only he wouldn't begin again battering at her . . . But he had . . .

She couldn't remember much now . . . Cruel, hurting words — those hostile stranger's eyes . . . Dermot, whom she loved, hated her . . .

And she couldn't bear it . . .

So this was the easiest way out . . .

She had said when he had explained that he was going away but would come back two days later: 'You won't find me here.' By the flicker in his eyelids she had felt sure that he knew what she meant . . .

He had said quickly: 'Well, of course, if you like to go away.'

She hadn't answered . . . Afterwards, when it was all over, he would be able to tell everybody (and convince himself) that he hadn't under-stood her meaning . . . It would be easier for him like that . . .

He had known . . . and she had seen just that momentary flicker — of hope. He hadn't, perhaps, known that himself. He would be shocked to admit such a thing . . . *but it had been there* . . .

He did not, of course, prefer that solution. What he would have liked was for her to say that, like him, she would welcome 'a change'. He wanted her to want her freedom too. He wanted, that is, to do what he wanted, and at the same time to feel comfortable about it. He would like her to be happy and contented travelling about abroad so that he could feel, 'Well, it's really been an excellent solution for both of us.'

He wanted to be happy, and he wanted to feel his conscience quite at ease. He wouldn't accept facts as they were — he wanted things to be as he would like them to be.

But death *was* a solution . . . It wasn't as though he'd feel himself to blame for it. He would soon persuade himself that Celia had been in a bad way ever since the death of her mother. Dermot was so clever at persuading himself . . .

She played for a minute with the idea that he would be sorry — that he would feel a terrible remorse . . . She thought for a moment, like a child: 'When I'm dead he'll be sorry . . . '

But she knew that wasn't so . . . Once admit to himself that he was in any way responsible for her death, and he would go to pieces . . . His very salvation would depend on his deceiving himself . . . And he would deceive himself . . .

No, she was going away — out of it all.

She couldn't bear any more.

It hurt too much . . .

She no longer thought of Judy — she had got past that . . . Nothing mattered to her now but her own agony and her longing for escape . . .

The river . . .

Long ago there had been a river through a valley — and primroses . . . long ago before anything happened . . .

She had walked rapidly. She came now to the point where the road crossed over the bridge.

The river, running swiftly, ran beneath it . . .

There was no one about . . .

She wondered where Peter Maitland was. He was married — he'd married after the war. Peter would have been kind. She would have been happy with Peter . . . happy and safe . . .

But she would never have loved him as she loved Dermot . . .

Dermot — Dermot . . .

So cruel . . .

The whole world was cruel, really — cruel and treacherous . . .

The river was better . . .

She climbed up on the parapet and jumped . . .

Book Three

The Island

1

Surrender

That, to Celia, was the end of the story.

Everything that happened afterwards seemed to her not to count. There were proceedings in a police court — there was the cockney young man who pulled her out of the river — there was the magistrate's censure — the paragraphs in the Press — Dermot's annoyance — Miss Hood's loyalty — all that seemed unimportant and dreamlike to Celia as she sat up in bed telling me about it.

She didn't think of committing suicide again.

She admitted that it had been very wicked of her to try. She was doing exactly what she blamed Dermot for doing — abandoning Judy.

'I felt,' she said, 'that the only thing I could do to make up was to live only for Judy and never think of myself again . . . I felt ashamed . . . '

She and Miss Hood and Judy had gone abroad to Switzerland.

There Dermot had written to her, enclosing the necessary evidence for divorce.

She hadn't done anything about it for some time.

'You see,' she said, 'I felt too bewildered. I just wanted to do anything he asked, so that I should be left in peace . . . I was afraid — of more things happening to me. I've been afraid ever since . . .

'So I didn't know what to do about it . . . Dermot thought I didn't do anything because I was vindictive . . . It wasn't that. I'd promised Judy not to let her father go . . . And here I was ready to give in just through sheer disgusting cowardice . . . I wished — oh, how I wished — that he and Marjorie would go away together — then I could have divorced them . . . I could have said to Judy afterwards: 'I had no choice . . . ' Dermot wrote to me saying all his friends thought I was behaving disgracefully . . . all his friends . . . that same phrase!

'I waited . . . I wanted just to rest — somewhere safe — where Dermot couldn't get at me. I was terrified of his coming and storming at me again . . . You can't give in to a thing because you're terrified. It isn't decent. I know I'm a coward — I've always been a coward — I hate noise or scenes — I'll do anything — *anything* to be left in peace . . . But I *didn't* give in out of fear. I stuck it out . . .

'I got strong again in Switzerland . . . I can't tell you how wonderful it was. Not to want to cry every time you walked up a hill. Not to feel sick whenever you looked at food.

And that awful neuralgia in my head went away. Mental misery and physical misery is too much to have together . . . You can bear one *or* the other — not both . . .

'In the end, when I felt really strong and well again, I went back to England. I wrote to Dermot. I said I didn't believe in divorce . . . I believed (though it might be old-fashioned and wrong in his eyes) in staying together and bearing things for the sake of the children. I said that people often told you that it was better for children if parents who didn't get on together parted. I said that I didn't think that was true. Children needed their parents — both parents — because they were their own flesh and blood — quarrels or bickering didn't matter half so much to children as grown-up people imagine — perhaps even it's a good thing. It teaches them what life is like . . . My home was *too* happy. It made me grow up a fool . . . I said too, that he and I never had quarrelled. We had always got on well together . . .

'I said I didn't think love affairs with other people ought to matter very much . . . He could be quite free — so long as he was kind to Judy and a good father to her. And I told him again that I knew he meant more to Judy than I could ever mean. She only wanted me physically — like a little animal when she was ill, but it was he and she who belonged together in mind.

'I said if he came back I wouldn't reproach him — or ever throw things in his face. I asked if we couldn't just be kind to each other because we'd both suffered.

'I said the choice lay with him, but he must remember that I didn't want or believe in divorce, and that if he chose that, the responsibility rested with him only.

'He wrote back and sent me fresh evidence . . .

'I divorced him . . .

'It was all rather beastly . . . divorce is . . .

'Standing up before a lot of people . . . answering questions . . . intimate questions . . . chambermaids . . .

'I hated it all. It made me sick.

'It must be easier to be divorced. You don't have to be *there* . . .

'So, you see, I gave in, after all. Dermot got his way. I might as well have given way at the beginning and saved myself a lot of pain and horror . . .

'I don't know whether I'm glad I didn't give in earlier or not . . .

'I don't even know why I did give in — because I was tired and wanted peace — or because I became convinced it was the only thing to be done, or because, after all, I wanted to give in to Dermot . . .

'I think, sometimes, it was the last . . .

'That's why, ever since, I've felt guilty when Judy looked at me . . .

'In the end, you see, I betrayed Judy for Dermot.'

2

Reflection

Dermot had married Marjorie Connell a few days after the decree was made absolute.

I was curious about Celia's attitude to the other woman. She had touched on it so little in her story — almost as though the other woman hadn't existed. She never once took up the attitude that a weak Dermot had been led astray, although that is the most common attitude for a betrayed wife.

Celia answered my question at once and honestly.

'I don't think he was — led astray, I mean. Marjorie? What did I think about her? I can't remember . . . It didn't seem to matter. It was Dermot and me that mattered — not Marjorie. It was his being cruel to me that I couldn't get over . . .'

And there, I think, I see what Celia will never be able to see. Celia was essentially tender in her attitude towards suffering. A butterfly pinned in his hat would never have upset Dermot as a child. He would have assumed firmly that the butterfly liked it!

That is the line he took with Celia. He was fond of Celia, but he wanted Marjorie. He was an essentially moral young man. To enable Dermot to marry Marjorie, Celia had to be got rid of. Since he was fond of Celia, he wanted her to like the idea too. When she didn't, he was angry with her. Because he felt badly about hurting her, he hurt her all the more and was unnecessarily brutal about it . . . I can understand — I can almost sympathize . . .

If he had let himself believe he was being cruel to Celia he couldn't have done it . . . He was, like many brutally honest men, dishonest about himself. He thought himself a finer fellow than he really was . . .

He wanted Marjorie, and he had to get her. He'd always got everything that he wanted — and life with Celia hadn't improved him.

He loved Celia, I think, for her beauty and her beauty only . . .

She loved him enduringly and for life. He was, as she once put it, in her blood . . .

And, also, she clung. And Dermot was the type of man who cannot endure being clung to. Celia had very little devil in her, and a woman with very little devil in her has a poor chance with men.

Miriam had devil. For all her love for her John, I don't believe he always had an easy life with her. She adored him, but she tried him too. There's a brute in man that likes being stood up to . . .

Miriam had something that Celia lacked. What is vulgarly called guts, perhaps.

When Celia stood up to Dermot it was too late . . .

She admitted that she had come to think differently about Dermot now that she was no longer bewildered by his sudden apparent inhumanity.

'At first,' she said, 'it seemed as though I had always loved him and done anything he wanted, and then — the first time that I *really* needed him and was in trouble, he turned round and stabbed me in the back. That's rather journalese, but it expresses what I felt.

'There are words in the Bible that say it exactly.' She paused, then quoted:

'*For it is not an open enemy that hath done me this dishonour: for then I could have borne it; . . . But it was even thou, my companion: my guide, and mine own familiar friend.*

'It was that, you see, that hurt. 'Mine own familiar friend.'

'If *Dermot* could be treacherous, then anyone could be treacherous. The world itself became unsure. I couldn't trust anyone or anything any more . . .

'That's horribly frightening. You don't know how frightening that is. Nothing anywhere is safe.

'You see — well, you see the Gun Man everywhere . . .

'But, of course, it was my fault really, for trusting Dermot too much. You shouldn't trust anyone as much as that. It's unfair.

'All these years, while Judy has been growing up, I've had time to think . . . I've thought a great deal . . . And I've seen that the real trouble was that *I* was stupid . . . Stupid and arrogant!

'I loved Dermot — and I didn't keep him. I ought to have seen what he liked and wanted, and been that . . . I ought to have realized (as he himself said) that he would 'want a change' . . . Mother told me not to go away and leave him alone . . . I did leave him alone. I was so arrogant I never thought of such a possibility as happened. I was so sure that I was the person he loved and always would love. As I said, it's unfair to trust people too much, to try them too high, to put them on pedestals just because you like them there. I never saw Dermot clearly . . . I could have . . . if I hadn't been so arrogant — thinking that nothing that happened to other women could ever happen to me . . . I was stupid.

'So I don't blame Dermot now — he was just made that way. I ought to have known and been on my guard and not been so cocksure and pleased with myself. If a thing matters to you more than anything in life, you've got to be clever about it . . . I wasn't clever about it . . .

'It's a very common story. I know that now. You've only got to read the papers — especially the Sunday ones that go in for that sort of thing. Women who put their heads in gas ovens — or take overdoses of sleeping draughts. The world is like that — full of cruelty and pain — because people are stupid.

'I was stupid. I lived in a world of my own. Yes, I was stupid.'

3

Flight

1

'And since?' I asked Celia. 'What have you done since? That's some time ago.'

'Yes, ten years. Well, I've travelled. I've seen the places I've wanted to see. I've made a lot of friends. I've had adventures. I think, really, I've enjoyed myself quite a lot.'

She seemed rather hazy about it all.

'There were Judy's holidays, of course. I always felt guilty with Judy . . . I think she knew I did. She never said anything, but I thought that, secretly, she blamed me for the loss of her father . . . And there, of course, she was right. She said once: 'It was *you* Daddy didn't like. He was fond of *me*.' I failed her. A mother ought to keep a child's father fond of her. That's part of a mother's job. I hadn't. Judy was unconsciously cruel sometimes, but she did me good. She was so uncompromisingly honest.

'I don't know whether I've failed with Judy or succeeded. I don't know whether she loves me or doesn't love me. I've given her material things. I haven't been able to give her the other things — the things that matter to me — because she doesn't want them. I've done the only other thing I could. Because I love her, I've let her

349

alone. I haven't tried to force my views and my beliefs upon her. I've tried to make her feel I'm there if she wants me. But, you see, she didn't want me. The kind of person I am is no good to the kind of person she is — except, as I said before, for material things . . . I love her, just as I loved Dermot, but I don't understand her. I've tried to leave her free, but at the same time not to give in to her out of cowardice . . . Whether I've been any use to her I shall never know. I hope I have — oh, how I hope I have . . . I love her so . . . '

'Where is she now?'

'She's married. That's why I came here. I mean, I wasn't free before. I had to look after Judy. She was married at eighteen. He's a very nice man — older than she is — straight, kind, well off, everything I could wish. I wanted her to wait, to be sure, but she wouldn't wait. You can't fight people like her and Dermot. They have to have their own way. Besides, how can you judge for someone else? You might ruin their lives when you thought you were helping them. One mustn't interfere . . .

'She's out in East Africa. She writes me occasionally, short happy letters. They're like Dermot's, they tell you nothing except facts, but you can feel it's all right.'

2

'And then,' I said, 'you came here. Why?'

She said slowly:

'I don't know whether I can make you understand . . . Something a man said to me once made an impression on me. I'd told him a little of what had happened. He was an understanding person. He said: 'What are you going to do with your life? You're still young.' I said that there was Judy and travelling and seeing things and places.

'He said: 'That won't be enough. You'll have either to take a lover or lovers. You will have to decide which it's to be.'

'And, you know, that frightened me, because I knew he was right . . .

'People, ordinary unthinking people, have said, 'Oh, my dear, some day you'll marry again — some nice man who'll make it all up to you.'

'Marry? I'd be terrified to marry. Nobody can hurt you except a husband — nobody's near enough . . .

'I didn't mean ever to have anything more to do with men . . .

'But that young man frightened me . . . I wasn't old . . . not old enough . . .

'There might be a — a lover? A lover wouldn't be so terrifying as a husband — you'd never get to depend so on a lover — it's all the little shared intimacies of life that hold you so with a husband and tear you to pieces when you part . . . A lover you just have occasional meetings with — your daily life is your own . . .

'Lover — or lovers . . .

'Lovers would be best. You'd be — almost safe — with lovers!

'But I hoped it wouldn't come to that. I hoped

351

I'd learn to live alone. I tried.'

She didn't speak for some moments. 'I tried,' she had said. Those two words covered a good deal.

'Yes?' I said at last.

She said slowly:

'It was when Judy was fifteen that I met someone . . . He was rather like Peter Maitland . . . Kind, not very clever. He loved me . . .

'He told me that what I needed was gentleness. He was — very good to me. His wife had died when their first baby was born. The baby died too. So, you see, he'd been unhappy too. He understood what it was like.

'We enjoyed things together . . . we seemed to be able to share things. And he didn't mind if I was myself. I mean, I could say I was enjoying myself and be enthusiastic without his thinking me silly . . . He was — it's an odd thing to say, but he really was — like a *mother* to me. A mother, not a father! He was so gentle . . . '

Celia's voice had grown gentle. Her face was a child's — happy, confident . . .

'Yes?'

'He wanted to marry me. I said I could never marry anyone . . . I said I'd lost my nerve. He understood that too . . .

'That was three years ago. He's been a friend — a wonderful friend . . . He's always been there when I wanted him. I've felt *loved* . . . It's a happy feeling . . .

'After Judy's wedding he asked me again to marry him. He said that he thought I could trust him now. He wanted to take care of me. He said we'd go back home — to *my* home. It's been shut up with a caretaker all these years — I couldn't bear to go there, but I've always felt it's there waiting for me . . . Just waiting for me . . . He said we'd go there and live, and that all this misery would seem like a bad dream . . .

'And I — I felt I wanted to . . .

'But, somehow, I couldn't. I said we'd be lovers if he liked. It didn't matter now that Judy was married. Then, if he wanted to be free, he could leave me any minute. I could never be an obstacle, and so he'd never have to hate me because I stood in the way of his wanting to marry someone else . . .

'He wouldn't do that. He was very gentle but firm. He had been a doctor, you know, a surgeon, rather a celebrated one. He said I'd got to get over this nervous terror. He said once I was actually married to him it would be all right . . .

'At last — I said I would . . . '

3

I didn't speak and in a minute or two Celia went on:

'I felt happy — really happy . . .

'At peace again and as though I were safe . . .

'And then *it* happened. It was the day before we were to be married.

'We'd driven out of town to dinner. It was a hot night . . . We were sitting in a garden by the river. He kissed me and said I was beautiful

. . . I'm thirty-nine, and worn and tired, but he said I was beautiful.

'*And then he said the thing that frightened me — that broke up the dream.*'

'What did he say?'

'He said: 'Don't ever be less beautiful . . . '

'He said it just in the same voice that Dermot had said it . . . '

4

'I expect you don't understand — nobody could . . .

'*It was the Gun Man all over again . . .*

'Everything happy and at peace, and then you feel *He*'s there . . .

'It all came back again — the terror . . .

'I couldn't face it — not going through it all again . . . being happy for years — and then, perhaps, being ill or something . . . and the whole misery coming over again . . .

'*I couldn't risk going through it again.*

'I think what I really mean is that I couldn't face being frightened of going through it again . . . Being terrified that the same experience would come nearer and nearer — every day of happiness would make it more frightening . . . I couldn't face the suspense . . .

'And so I ran away . . .

'Just like that . . .

'I left Michael — I don't think he knew why I went — I just made some excuse — I went through the little inn and asked for the station. It was about ten minutes' walk. I just jumped on a train.

'When I got to London I went home and fetched my passport and went and sat in the ladies' waiting-room at Victoria till morning. I was afraid Michael might find me and persuade me . . . I might have been persuaded, because, you see, I did love him . . . He was so sweet to me always.

'But I can't face going through everything again . . .

'*I can't* . . .

'It's too ghastly to live in fear . . .

'And it's awful to have no trust left . . .

'I simply couldn't trust *anyone* . . . not even Michael.

'It would be Hell for them as well as for me . . . '

5

'That's a year ago . . .

'I never wrote to Michael . . .

'I never gave him any explanation . . .

'I've treated him disgracefully . . .

'I don't mind. Ever since Dermot, I've been hard . . . I haven't cared whether I've hurt people or not. When you've been hurt too much yourself you don't care . . .

'I travelled about, trying to be interested in things and make my own life . . .

'Well, I've failed . . .

'I can't live alone . . . I can't make up stories

about people any more — it doesn't seem to come . . .

'So it means being alone all the time even if you're in the middle of a crowd . . .

'And I can't live with someone . . . I'm too miserably afraid . . .

'I'm beaten . . .

'I can't face the prospect of living, perhaps, another thirty years. I'm not, you see, sufficiently brave . . . '

Celia sighed . . . Her lids drooped . . .

'I remembered this place, and I came here on purpose . . . It's a very nice place . . . '

She added:

'This is a very long stupid story . . . I seem to have been talking a lot . . . it must be morning . . . '

Celia fell asleep . . .

4

Beginning

1

Well, you see, that's where we are — except for the one incident I referred to at the beginning of the story.

The whole point is, is that significant, or isn't it?

If I'm right, the whole of Celia's life led up to and came to its climax in that one minute.

It happened when I was saying goodbye to her on the boat.

She was dead sleepy. I'd wakened her up and made her dress. I wanted to get her away from the island quickly.

She was like a tired child — obedient and very sweet and completely bemused.

I thought — I may be wrong — but I thought that the danger was over . . .

And then, suddenly, as I was saying goodbye, she seemed to wake up. She, as it were, *saw* me for the first time.

She said: 'I don't know your name even . . . '

I said: 'It doesn't matter — you wouldn't know it. I used to be a fairly well-known portrait painter.'

'Aren't you now?'

'No,' I said, 'something happened to me in the war.'

'What?'

'This . . . '

And I pushed forward my stump where the hand ought to have been.

2

The bell rang and I had to run . . .

So I've only got my impression . . .

But that impression is very clear.

Horror — and then *relief* . . .

Relief's a poor word — it was more than that — *Deliverance* expresses it better.

It was the Gun Man again, you see — her symbol for fear . . .

The Gun Man had pursued her all these years . . .

And now, at last, she had met him face to face . . .

And he was just an ordinary human being.

Me . . .

3

That's how I see it.

It is my fixed belief that Celia went back into the world to begin a new life . . .

She went back at thirty-nine — to grow up . . .

And she left her story and her fear — with me . . .

I don't know where she went. I don't even know her name. I've called her Celia because that name seems to suit her. I could find out, I suppose, by questioning hotels. But I can't do that . . . I suppose I shall never see her again . . .

GIANT'S BREAD

Agatha Christie

Vernon Deyre spends his childhood in fear of the grand piano, which seems to him a great and terrible Beast with ivory teeth. In consequence, he grows up regarding music with distaste and distrust. Then, years later, he attends an orchestral concert as a favour to a friend, and is enraptured by the performance. Vernon becomes a sensitive and brilliant composer — quite possibly a genius. But there is a high price to be paid for his talent, especially by his family and the two women in his life . . .

ABSENT IN THE SPRING

Agatha Christie

If you'd nothing to think about but yourself for days and days I wonder what you'd find out about yourself . . . Returning from a visit to her daughter in Iraq, Joan Scudamore finds herself unexpectedly stranded in an isolated rest house, thanks to the railway line flooding. As she waits for the next train out, the days of enforced solitude weigh stiflingly upon her, with nowhere to escape to but the recesses of her own mind. Looking back over the years, Joan ruminates on her attitudes, relationships, and actions — and becomes increasingly uneasy about the person who is revealed to her.

THE ROSE AND THE YEW TREE

Agatha Christie

Everyone expected Isabella Charteris, sheltered and aristocratic, to marry Rupert St Loo when he came back from the war. She had known Rupert since childhood. He was handsome, strong, and deeply in love with her. It would have been such a suitable marriage: they were a perfect match. How strange, then, that war hero and politician John Gabriel should appear in her life. Nobody expected Isabelle to fall for him. John was Rupert's opposite — a man of ruthless ambition and overwhelming appetites. From the moment they met, Isabella knew John would gladly destroy her - yet she could not resist him . . .

A DAUGHTER'S A DAUGHTER

Agatha Christie

Ann Prentice is a quiet woman, a widow devoted to Sarah, her only child. She likes the simple things in life — soft firelight and evenings at home. After nineteen-year-old Sarah goes off to Switzerland with her friends for three weeks, Ann attends a dinner party with an old friend. There she meets Richard Cauldfield, also widowed. As the two fall in love, she hopes for new happiness. But Sarah cannot contemplate the idea of her mother marrying him. Resentment and jealousy corrode their relationship, and it seems that mother and daughter are destined to be enemies for life . . .